I0659338

REQUIEM BELL

TOMMY CONLON
BOOK 1

DAVID MICHAEL NOLAN

ROUGH
EDGES
PRESS

Requiem Bell
Paperback Edition
Copyright © 2023 (As Revised) David Michael Nolan

Rough Edges Press
An Imprint of Wolfpack Publishing
9850 S. Maryland Parkway, Suite A-5 #323
Las Vegas, Nevada 89183

roughedgespress.com

This book is a work of fiction. Any references to historical events, real people or real places are used fictitiously. Other names, characters, places and events are products of the author's imagination, and any resemblance to actual events, places or persons, living or dead, is entirely coincidental.

All rights reserved. No part of this book may be reproduced by any means without the prior written consent of the publisher, other than brief quotes for reviews.

Paperback ISBN 978-1-68549-251-9
eBook ISBN 978-1-68549-250-2

REQUIEM BELL

DUBLIN, 1917

EVEN IN THE MURKY LIGHT THROWN BY THE GAS LAMPS, Conlon could see the men waiting to hurt him as soon as he turned the corner.

There were three of them, one on the far side of the street, two on the near side. He saw one recognize him —an actual expression of surprise at his appearance— and nod to the others across the road as he rounded the bend. Two of the attackers threw down cigarettes. All of them moved forward, slowly, the big one crossing the street until they took up much of the pavement across his path, waiting for him.

At least somebody wants to welcome me home, Conlon thought grimly.

They wore caps and dark coats, all three of them, white shirts with no ties—the usual uniform of young men across the city. One was tall and broad-shouldered, and he walked with a cocky strut, slightly ahead of his smaller friends. Conlon assumed he was the leader and the one who would do the talking if there was to be any talking. He was the one to put down first. One of the others was wiry and had something about him, something coiled and alert. Conlon said to himself: Watch him. The third would be easy if he didn't run. His eyes looked wide and frightened just at the prospect of the violence that was coming.

The big one spoke when Conlon was still fifteen feet away. "Grand night for a walk, wha?"

"It is, yeah," Conlon said and made to walk around them, stepping into the street. They moved sideways, blocking that course for him.

He stopped and looked at them. "Can I help yis with something, lads?"

"You don't remember me, no?" the big one said. "Sure, why would ye?" His gestures were exaggerated for the benefit of his mates.

"Sorry, no."

"You fought my brother Harry in 1914. Gave him a real beating."

"Harry Enright, that'd be? He had some right on him."

"He had yeah. He's dead now. The Somme."

"Sorry to hear that. He was a good lad. That'd make you Aidan, then."

"It would."

Conlon was scanning the street as they talked. No people or traffic. There were lights on in the windows of the houses, this last street of Georgian townhouses before the two-up two-down terraces and cottages which ran from Smithfield to the Broadstone. He didn't want this and would try to talk his way around it if he could. But something about these young men told him that he couldn't. He could almost smell the violence on them, like animals. A pack embarked upon the hunt. It was a familiar smell, too familiar to him.

"Well, it's been nice to see you, Aidan. You look like you could be handy in the ring, too, now. But I've somebody to see."

"You were told, Conlon. You're not to be coming around here. You should've stayed out of Dublin. You were told."

So there it was. At least now he knew what this was and where he stood. But how had they known he was back and where he was? And then he realized: Farrell, from Podge's shop. A flame of anger lit within him.

"Well, now. I never actually was told. They thought I was dead. But nobody ever really told me anything. So, you know, you can't really blame me for thinking it might be all right to come home."

"We're telling you."

"Yeah, I hear you. Now, as I said, I have somebody to see."

He was calculating and planning as he spoke, as he had been all along, remembering his training. Take down Enright first, quickly, then the one by the railings. Two he could handle. Three at once was too many. He had to cut them down in an instant.

Enright stepped forward and put his hand on Conlon's chest. "This is as far as you go tonight, Conlon."

Conlon took a step backwards, forced a smile, and said, "You should've just jumped me from behind like they did in Donegal. Unless you've got guns, this was only going to end badly for you."

Enright raised his eyebrows. "You weren't that good in the ring, Conlon."

"That's true. But this isn't a ring, is it? Last chance, Aidan. I'd rather not do this tonight."

Enright started to laugh, a big, fake boom of a laugh, and turned his head to look at his friends as he did so.

Conlon hit him then, a body blow swung hard into his belly, and Enright exploded like a burst football. Air erupted from his mouth in a stunned cry as he doubled up.

Conlon was already moving around him on feet quick from years of ring-training and, from behind, he kicked him full force between the legs. Enright screamed and collapsed, moaning.

Conlon had already turned to face the other two. One of them had a hand tightly grasping the railings, his mouth slightly open. The other's eyes had narrowed, and he had a short, thin blade in his hand. It glinted under the lights as he waved it between them. He took a cautious step in Conlon's direction.

Conlon raised his fists and the man lunged at him, his hand a flitting bird in the air. Conlon stepped away and leaned in and planted a right cross on the man's eye. The man staggered, slashing blindly up with the knife. Moving again already, Conlon hit him with a left to the chin. Teeth cracked together.

The last one took a tentative half-step away from his spot against the railings and Conlon grabbed the back of his head and swung him hard over an outstretched leg, using his own unbalanced weight against him. He sprawled into the one with the knife and they both went down in a heap of limbs and grunts. The knife skittered away into the gutter. Conlon grasped the hair of the one who had dropped it and dragged him moaning across the pavement, then smashed his head into the railing. It tolled like a bell. Conlon let the young man fall, prone, onto his side by the fencing.

The other one was limping away, and Enright still lay whimpering, clutching at himself.

Conlon grabbed him by the ear and pulled him close. "Now. You tell him that I'm here to see my ma. You tell him that if he wants to see me, then he should come himself. No more errand boys. All right? You able to remember all that?"

The man stammered a yes.

"Good lad. Now piss off."

Enright staggered away into the night.

Conlon had not planned that. He had almost hoped he would be able to slip back into Dublin as if nothing had happened. He turned. The one by the fence was still down, groaning.

It had been easy. Violence had always been easy for him, a simple matter of seeing what he needed to do and the capacity to do it. He felt fear beforehand, yes, but never during. During fights—even in France, with the world exploding around him and his friends' blood caking his face—he was clear and cool and, he felt, at his best. The Major had seen that in him. That was why he had been chosen.

He allowed his breathing to settle once again, adjusted his clothes quickly. And then he walked on.

———

Nobody was there at the docks to meet him.

He had expected that, but still it hurt somewhere deep down, in a sentimental part of himself he rarely even admitted to these days. Over the years, in his barracks and sleeping against the bone-deep cold of the mud in France, he had imagined this homecoming, and his fantasies had always been well-populated with familiar, smiling old faces. Music played in the background along with a lilting female voice, singing just for him.

Life so often fell short of his imaginings—for good and bad.

The ferry arrived late and he stood with a few strangers at the prow as it cut through the darkness of the rolling Irish Sea. Most of them smoked but there was no chatting, and their eyes were all fixed straight ahead. It was a grim little group, hungry for the comfort of Ireland, returning from the horrors of the front or the camps or the bruising anonymity of life in London or Birmingham or Manchester with all the boarding houses and intense loneliness. All were dressed in dark suits and jackets, and most wore hats. They didn't speak, he thought, out of some shared sense of embarrassment, the unpleasant recognition of the same feeling behind the eyes of another; like looking in a warped mirror and hating what you saw there.

It was a warm night and a pleasant breeze swept over them from the sea, salt on its breath. Dublin was dark, lights twinkling in its depths, a muted glow gray above its sprawl. As his eyes took it in, he realized that he wanted to hear it, to be walking its streets alive to the music of the city, its streetcars and horse-drawn carts, washerwomen and night watchmen, the burble of humanity muted from inside pubs.

He felt an unexpected surge of emotion, tears springing suddenly to his eyes. That had not happened in all his time away. With everything he had been through, he had never cried. And yet here he was. The mere sight of his city. Everything it meant to him, all that had occurred here. He bit down on that emotion. Later, he thought.

TOMMY CONLON WATCHED THE SHOP FOR A GOOD HOUR before making his decision.

At first, he did it from the street with a copy of the *Irish Times* held open before him. He read not a word of the paper. Leaning there against a lamppost, he turned the pages in big arcs, rattled it straight, and used it to hide his face as he focused intently on the shop.

He was patient. If there was one thing the last few years had given him it was the ability to wait, to turn off his natural desire to force things to happen. He would wait. At least, here, he was warm and comfortable. Nobody was trying to kill him. Nobody was going to order him to do anything dangerous or force him to do anything he didn't want to do. His clothes contained no mites, that he knew of. He had some money—just a few bob—in his pocket.

Here was absolutely fine. He would wait.

Podge wasn't there. Conlon didn't know the man he saw behind the counter; he had never seen him before. He was middle-aged and had a big mottled ruddy face topped with a square patch of heavily-oiled hair. The whole hour Conlon watched him from across Gardner Street, he worked busily, dusting, restocking cigarettes on the shelves behind him and tidying the newspapers piled upon his counter. A steady stream of customers filed through the small shop. The man chatted to each of them, laughing with wobbling jowls at jokes Conlon couldn't hear. So many of them paused as soon as they were outside the shop to light cigarettes that it became almost funny to Conlon. The same pose: head down, hands cupped to shield the flame, a little twitch to put out the match, and then they were away, trailing plumes of smoke.

Conlon didn't smoke—even after everything—due to the bad lungs he had suffered with as a child, but watching them almost made him wish he did. The repeated, habitual gestures looked so satisfying, so simple and comforting.

The streetcar stopped just up the road at the corner, and this was the first tobacconist the passengers would encounter after they got off, making it ideal for anybody needing a cigarette. That was partly why Podge had bought in, five years before. Business was steady, the hours were fine, and he'd wanted to own his own place. Their unexpected windfall had provided him with the opportunity to buy himself a new life, a way out of the struggle he had assumed would be his existence, and he had greedily accepted it. Who could blame him? Conlon remembered his excitement the day he'd first gone to see it, the way he'd beamed and talked and talked about it. What he would change, how he could make it work when they were in the pub.

And then, when he did own it, if Conlon wanted to

see him, he'd just show up. Podge was always here. If it was open, he was here. If it wasn't, he was still there, in the flat upstairs. He had a girl—a maid out in Blackrock, Conlon remembered, from Waterford or somewhere culchie—and, if she was there with him, he would stick his head out of the window to tell Conlon to go away.

And then everything had happened, and Conlon had been forced to leave.

He had been away in the War for a few years, and now, when he was back and he went to see his old friend, Podge was gone. So he stood and watched and waited, unsure of what to think. Life had made him suspicious. Suspicious of Dublin, anyway. Too much had happened here for it to be any other way. He had enemies here now. Did that make them Podge's enemies, too?

He hoped nothing had happened to him.

He changed vantage point a few times, moving around the street just in case the man looked out and saw him. He even discarded the newspaper. He tried to blend in, to look bored and casual. He wasn't sure if he could anymore. Dublin still felt like home, like his city, but he felt different. He *was* different. He wondered if he looked different. He wondered if anybody would look at him and then again, with more precise scrutiny, wondering what that strange man was doing.

He was still a young man, handsome and healthy, with a thick head of black hair under his hat. Yet there were a couple of things he was aware of: his short hair suggested a recent period in the military while there was something in his eyes, a wary, hardened hurt, that anyone who had been through war would instantly recognize.

The street was busy. The streetcar, buses, horses, and carts—reminding him of the front, the mud, casualties bouncing and grimacing in the back—and lots of bicycles passed in a blur. Pedestrians moved around him. He tried not to look at any of them, never to make eye contact. The newspaper was as much to hide his face from them as from the man. Dublin was a small city. He fully expected he might run into an old friend or acquaintance at any minute. He had been back less than a day and was amazed he had run into so few familiar faces so far.

He waited until near closing time—around half five, according to his da's old pocket watch—before crossing the road, letting a trap go noisily by before he made his way across.

The bell over the door chimed when he walked in and the man looked up. "What can I get ye?" he said.

"I'm looking for the owner," Conlon said, smiling, reaching for his hat and sliding it from his head as he did so.

"Well, that'd be me, so it would. How can I help?" He had a Cork accent, Conlon thought, soft but unmistakable.

"Ah, sorry, there must be a mistake. I'm looking for Podge. Podge O'Riordan."

"Ah." The man nodded and busied himself clearing his counter, only glancing up at Conlon as he spoke. "He sold the place to me six months ago. You're a friend of his, hah?"

"That I am. I'd be correct to assume then that he no longer lives upstairs, then, would I?"

"I haven't seen him since the day I took over. He was

moving his possessions onto a cart that day but I wasn't privy to where he was going."

"No forwarding address?"

"None. Sure if you're his friend you'll be knowing where he's likely to be, hah?"

"Well, you'd think I would, wouldn't you? But it's been a while. If you could, I'd be in your debt if you do see him, or hear where he is, that you tell him Tommy was in looking for him."

"Tommy."

"Yeah. He'll know who you mean."

"But, just in case he doesn't, it'd do to have a surname also..."

Conlon laughed drily but he didn't like something in this man's manner. There was something calculated in every word. His eyes were too watchful but trying to pretend otherwise.

"Conlon. Tommy Conlon."

"Nice to meet you, Mr. Conlon or can I call you Tommy?"

"What's your name?"

"I'm Francis Farrell. Pleased to meet you, Tommy." He offered his hand and Tommy gave it a curt shake.

"Can I interest you in a paper? Maybe some smokes or tobacco?"

"No thanks. Can I ask if you have any idea why Podge sold the shop?"

"I wouldn't know at all. Didn't speak much to the man."

Conlon nodded and took a few steps sideways, looking around the shop. It appeared identical, just as he remembered it when Podge had been here.

"How's it going for you? Business healthy?" he asked Farrell over his shoulder.

"Ah I can't complain. Hard work, mind you. What line of work would you be in yourself, Tommy?"

"I'm between jobs at the moment. Something will turn up soon, I'm sure."

"Well, good luck with it. I hear the brewery are looking for men."

"That's good to know. Thanks."

Farrell was out from behind the counter now, closing off the shop to Conlon the way a boxer tries to close off the ring. Conlon registered this, just as he had everything else that felt a bit off, and put it away.

"You're very welcome," Farrell said. "I'll be sure to tell him you were here if I do see him."

Conlon looked at him, not moving—long enough for Farrell to understand that he would not move unless he wanted, then he nodded, thanked the man, and left.

———

CONLON HAD SPENT the night before on a Ferry from Liverpool and the day before that on a train from London. Since he had been discharged five days ago, apart from two days in a gloomy Kilburn boarding house full of Irish soldiers on leave from the Army, he felt as if he had been traveling continually.

And here he was, home, yet he felt as if he had nowhere to go. He put his head down and made toward Sackville Street, rather than stand outside the shop with Farrell watching him through the window.

Podge was his best friend, and he would have put Conlon up without hesitation. Tommy had never considered that Podge would be gone. He had no alternative plan. But then hadn't he been taught to always have an alternative plan? Had he become so dulled already by being back among civilians that he had forgotten everything he had learned? Focus, think, come up with a plan.

He would have to go home sometime, he knew. Might as well be now.

The electric lamps were flickering on as he made his way, a chill wind cutting down through the streets off the Liffey. Men—office workers, he thought, watching them in their suits and hats and coats, newspapers under their arms, briefcases in their fists—flicked up their collars against the cold coming on with the night.

In France, when he had thought of home, which had been often, all his memories were of summer. Summer out in Malahide with his ma and da when he was a boy. Summer evenings in the park with Orla. He could see some of the dresses she had worn, feel the soft cheap fabric of them, even now. Trying to sleep in that close, crowded bedroom on summer nights with the heat pressing like a blanket of wool, the windows open but not a breath of wind coming through, just the distant wails and constant hum of the city's life. The smell of summer.

So it was something of a surprise to find himself home just as winter took hold, its cruel little teeth testing the soft flesh of Dublin before the true onslaught. He wasn't dressed for winter. He had left his trench coat in Kilburn along with some of his bad memories and his suit was not up to an Irish winter. He was sure they would have sold his clothes at home. For the money. He would have to do something.

Coming off the side street, he'd know he was at Sackville Street even if he had been blindfolded. The noise was unique: a deafening clatter of streetcars and horse hooves on cobbles, bells ringing as customers signaled trams should stop, the odd motorcar puttering along. And the smell: horseshit, oil, so many people. It had always felt like the literal center of the city to him, it's heart. No wonder the fighting had climaxed here.

He crossed the street, dodging carriages, eying the General Post Office from across the road as he went.

In the trenches, the stories had circulated that it had been destroyed in 1916, in the "rising", as they were calling it, yet here it stood, somehow. As he approached it, he could see that it had the look of a ruined skull. Its roof was gone, there were chunks of its side walls missing but still it stood, proud and defiant. A lot of rubbish had been spoken in the trenches.

But then further along, Sackville Street and Henry Street proved that some of the rubbish was in fact true. Whole buildings had vanished, leaving the street looking like a smile with some teeth missing. Shop-keepers were out as he passed, closing up for the evening, dragging in crates and rails, chatting to one another on the pavements. The usual crowds thinned and now composed of clerks and foreman returning home from work rather than shoppers. He eyed them with distant curiosity in their smart suits and hats, some in tweed, with shining shoes clapping along the cobbles. Passing Moore Street, he picked up its unmis-takable odor—that mix of flowers and rotting fish—as the market dismantled itself. That smell made him feel more at home than anything else had up to this point, as if that smell was Dublin.

He pressed on and walked the length of the street until Henry Street became Mary Street. He crossed Capel Street, too, and, passing a few of his old haunts, he felt a heightened nervousness about spotting an old friend. Then, he really was home, in his area, these streets where he had ranged and roamed in shorts as a boy.

Finally, he turned a corner, and there were three young men waiting to hurt him.

———

COLON HAD FOUND his ma the house about six months before he left. She had lived, then, in a crowded tenement on the edge of the Monto, sharing a humid bedroom with four others. He remembered well how lost she had felt in her first weeks in the new house with all those empty rooms for her to fill. But he also remembered how awful that tenement had been; the smell, the filth in the hallways.

To her, the little house was akin to a palace, and it had given him more pride than anything else he had done in his life to see how much pleasure she took from it. He had sent her most of his wage home every month from France, hopeful that she would use the money to pay her rent. But since he was supposed to be dead, he never contacted her directly so that she had no idea where the money was coming from. In doing so, he had never heard back from her. So, really, he did not know if she still lived there, even.

These streets were tight and orderly, filled with ranks of identical redbricks with tiny yards behind, separated by little alleyways. Streetlights were arrayed along each pavement, casting out a sickly orange halo onto the ground below. Conlon cut through a patch of light, watching his shadow move under his feet. Trees on the corners, a row of shops out near the turn to Church Street, a bunker of a pub which was loud and light as he passed by.

There weren't many people out now. It was teatime, he knew. Families were eating behind these doors, listening to wirelesses maybe, if they were lucky enough.

He hoped his ma was so lucky.

He was walking slowly, nervous of what was to come. He shook that off and made for the house. There was a light on in the back, he could see its glow through the marbled glass windows set in the front door, which was still painted that bright blue his ma had loved so much. Lace curtains hung in the window next to it and he knocked, then idly rubbed his shoe along the edge of the foot-scraper beside the step as he waited. His heart was pounding.

With some dread, he had been expecting her to have aged, withered, shrunk somehow, but she had not changed. She blinked as she opened the door, and then tears were in her eyes. Her arms were open and he stepped toward her and she hugged him, saying his name and kissing his head, his hair, his cheek.

She had him inside, talking in a stream of choked sentences, and he couldn't really take in the house as she pulled him through the hall toward the sitting room and the kitchen. Molly was there, she was saying, and he thought of course she is, Molly was always there, why hadn't he expected that?

That meant another hug but unlike his ma, Molly

had changed. She had lost enough weight that her skin hung from her face like sliced and folded meat, and she looked a sickly shade of yellow. Small in his arms.

His ma had a cup of tea in front of him before he had even sat down and then the two women were off, a whirl of talk, questions and information, far too much for him to process. But above all of that, there was laughter. They jiggled with it. It bounced off the walls and disappeared up the fireplace, the two women setting each other off as they had always done, a contagious grin becoming a giggle then a chuckle and then they were both hooting and screaming with it.

He thought about how long it had been since he had been in the presence of anything so pure and uncomplicated. And it felt good.

It was good to be home.

———

HE SLEPT on the floor in the sitting room that night. His ma made it as comfortable as she could with cushions and blankets. As he lay there, thinking over the day and its events, he could smell her perfume—the tiny bottle she had owned since he was a child and only took out for the most special of occasions—above the faint mustiness.

Her happiness at his presence had provided a warmth he had not expected. After so long away, he had beaten his homesickness, defeated any need to see his mother, but it had only taken a few seconds in her presence for it all to come rushing back.

As expected, though she had been receiving his pay, she had not stopped working herself. She had always had a demonic energy, unable to sit still, always fussing and fidgeting, barely able to let somebody finish a cup of tea before she had swept the cup away to rinse it out, dry it with the tea-towel seemingly always clutched in her left hand, and set it in the small Delph cupboard in the kitchen.

So she and Molly were still charwomen in Ranelagh, a job she claimed to enjoy, though Molly's declining health suggested that her feelings might well be different. They asked him little about the war, little about his disappearance. His ma said that she had always known he was fine and left it at that. She said it with the kind of stubborn certainty she usually reserved for any discussion of the Church and our lord Jesus Christ and he nodded, just glad that she was happy, and grateful not to have to explain anything to her. Molly had mentioned Arthur Callaghan, who'd joined up after him but come back after Gallipoli. He had been called a traitor to his face as he walked the streets in his uniform. Nothing like that had motivated Conlon to change into civvies after his discharge in London but, hearing it, he was glad that he had.

The politics in the city now seemed baffling, but then he had always stayed clear of politics, even when his pals were preaching Socialism, some of them joining the Irish Citizen Army. He was more concerned with getting by, earning a steady wage in whatever way he could, helping his ma out after his da was gone. He had been the man of the house from a young age and never thought beyond making money to buy them food, to pay off the landlord, to try and get them out of the one room in a tenement where he had grown up. For a while, he'd done all right and then, for a very short time, much more than all right. But that had obviously gone wrong and now he idly wondered where he would be if he had joined up with the Citizen Army or the Brotherhood or the Volunteers. Dead in the GPO or on Moore Street?

But then...he had survived the Great War. He had thrived, even, if the Major was to be believed. He lay there a few moments, eyes open in the darkness, and all he could see was France and the faces of the dead. He had to clear his mind of memories, of the emotions they carried with them.

He could do that. One thing he had come to know about himself was that he could handle what other people struggled with. Violence, horror, fear, death: he was at his best in the face of such implacable forces and, afterward, he washed them away like so much mud from his hands.

For the most part, at any rate. But sometimes, in the night, in the dark, sometimes they came back to him. And he had to wash his hands all over again.

Instead, he thought of Orla as he so often did at night. The pain was still there when he remembered her but he focused upon the warmth of it all, the glory of the way she had made him feel.

Sleep eventually came.

———

HIS MOTHER HAD BEEN OUT EARLY and there were rashers for breakfast. The smell woke him. There was nothing more likely to make him immediately hungry than the smell of bacon frying. He rose and passed her in the tiny kitchen on his way out to their lavatory in the even tinier back yard, feeling the familiar sting of a chilly Dublin morning. He washed quickly in the sink when he came back in to the kitchen's warmth. The rashers spat and sizzled in the pan. She had boiled an egg or two for him and there was already toast and butter on the table. Molly came downstairs just as he sat to eat.

"What are you doing today?" his ma asked him after he had finished eating.

"See some of the lads, I think, find Podge if I can."

"George Byrne is living above his mother," Molly said through a wet mouthful.

"On his own? Where's he working?"

"He's on the boats, in the kitchens."

His mother volunteered, "Molly ran into his mother at Mass on Sunday, didn't you?"

"She looks awful shook."

"George is not long after getting married. Nice country lassie."

"George? Have you seen Sean at all?"

"Sean?"

The women shared a look.

"Sean Murray? You remember him, Ma."

"No, I haven't seen him since you left, love."

———

HIS MA HAD KEPT some of his clothes, it turned out. His old suit, his good one, was hanging on a bedroom door, waiting for him when she told him to climb the stairs. His best shoes, too. One of his hats. He changed quickly and the suit felt tighter now. The muscle he had acquired in the war, the added bulk, moved against the fabric. But it was fine, it would do. It made him feel strong, powerful.

He came back downstairs and the women told him he looked handsome, his mother getting teary again and saying he looked just like his father. She asked if he was all right for money and he said he was. Conlon told them he'd be back for tea and then he went out. Into his city.

SEAN LIVED CLOSER, JUST OFF CHURCH STREET, SO THAT was where Conlon headed first. He had missed the morning rush and the inner city was quiet now, the sky bright. Seagulls pinwheeled overhead against the blue. There were people out shopping, and a worker was unloading vegetables outside a green grocer.

He said hello and tipped his hat to the people he passed.

Sean's room was in a redbrick that had seen better days, a handsome old hound whose fur was now mangy. Paint peeled on the door, and the windows were dirty and smeared and weeds clambered from cracks in the crooked steps. Conlon knocked and waited, trying to remember the last time he had seen Sean. That meeting in O'Flaherty's, when they had divided up the last of the money, he thought. Sean had been jolly that night, talkative and full of laughter, high on the success of their discovery. The last Conlon had seen of him, he had been bound for Harcourt Street to pick up a floozie.

He waited and, after a minute or so, knocked once more.

A voice said, "Can I help you?"

He looked around, unable to locate the origin.

"Down here."

Looking over the railings, he saw an old lady standing in the doorway of the basement, squinting up at him.

"Hello, Ma'am. I'm looking for Sean Murray."

Her face creased. "Mr. Murray? He disappeared. Owes me a month's rent, so he does."

"I'm sorry to hear that. And it doesn't sound like Sean, to be honest with you. He was an honest man."

"Oh, I agree with you; it was a fierce shock. I think he came to some kind of harm. He went out one day and he never came back."

Conlon thought about that for a moment. The sense in him that something was not right grew more certain. And with that came fear, fear and anger.

"Did he leave anything?"

"He didn't have much to leave. I put his things in a box if you'd like to see those. I'm thinking you'd be a friend of his."

"I am. Thomas Conlon."

"Nice to meet you. Come on down, then, and I'll get that box for you. I closed the house last year. Mr. Murray was my last tenant."

———

SHE GAVE him a cup of tea and some fried bread, and he pulled out Sean's clothes, checked the pockets, glanced through the few papers wrapped in a scarf, and finally found a little notebook, which he pocketed. He finished his tea, then he said goodbye to the old lady, who had spent ten minutes nattering to him about last year's hurling final, and her recent trip to the Picture show on Sackville Street, and the shameful price of coal.

He opened the notebook on the corner of the street. Most of the pages were blank but for odd little doodles of what looked like nude women. But there was a page with a list of four addresses scattered all across the city, written in pencil, and another with what Conlon rapidly decided was a telephone number, this in fountain pen, blue blotches filling the page like flowers crowding a window box.

None of the addresses meant anything to Conlon. One was in Glasnevin, one the East Wall, one in Monkstown, the last Crumlin. He frowned at the words and felt the anxiety build in him again. Something was off here. He could feel that. And it felt like it had been waiting for him to return. As if only he could address it correctly. And that could only be bad.

———

GEORGE BYRNE WAS at work but Conlon met his young wife. She was tiny, a doll-like figure peeking out at him through the gap she allowed in the door.

He smiled ingratiatingly. "You must be Mrs. Byrne. I'm an old friend of George's."

She had shockingly black hair, crow-black, and her skin was so pale it almost appeared white. That made her lips sting with red, her eyes bright and shining above them.

"George doesn't have any friends," she said in a quiet, even voice.

He laughed. "He used to. He might've mentioned me? Tommy Conlon?"

He saw the recognition in her eyes.

"His ma knows me, too, but she's not in or else I would've had her bring me up to you. I'm sorry for just knocking. But I've been away and I'd like to see him. We're good friends."

She opened the door and nodded. "He has mentioned you a few times. You were off in the War, weren't you?"

"I was."

They regarded one another for an instant and he felt something he had not felt for a long time at the frank way she appraised him, something he had been unsure he could even feel. She was beautiful, tiny and perfectly formed. He liked the way she had no fear and, instead, a sort of fierceness in her steely blue eyes.

"Well, sure are you coming in then?" she said. He could hear the humor in it and laughed again.

"I was waiting for an invitation but if that's the way things work around here, I'll just make myself at home."

She offered him tea and, again, he accepted and they sat at the little dining table and drank tea, which she poured from a delicate china set.

"A wedding present," she said, tracing his eyes. "From my Auntie in London."

"It's very nice."

"A man who appreciates china! You are not what I expected at all, Mr. Conlon."

"Tommy, please, Mrs. Byrne. And I'm no expert on china. But I like to be polite."

"I am teasing you, Mr. Conlon."

"Tommy. And I know, Mrs. Byrne."

"If I'm calling you Tommy, then you are calling me Theresa."

He nodded. "Theresa. So what were you expecting, then? What has George said about me?"

She raised an eyebrow. "You were the fighter, weren't you? Boxer? George always said you weren't afraid of anything."

Conlon was quiet. "I was good at giving that impression, maybe."

"So what are you afraid of, Tommy?"

He looked at her and took a drink of tea before answering. "Clever women. Questions like that."

She laughed. "I'm sorry, I'm stuck in the house most days. It is lovely to have company."

"What do you do with yourself?"

"I try to be creative with George's wages. How can I make three potatoes last five days? How much coal is enough coal? Coal is the real problem for the poor in Dublin now, Tommy."

He remembered the old woman's gripes and nodded. "Not enough of it?"

"Not cheap enough for us to afford, no."

"Some things never change then. Where are you from? I've never been great with country accents."

"Westport."

"D'you miss it?"

"I do. I missed it when I was working up here and I miss it more now. The work was boring but sitting around waiting for my husband is even worse."

"Where did you work?"

"In the big munitions factory on the North Wall. Making the bombs you were firing at the Germans."

"You had your own money, then. A decent job."

"But no husband. And then I met George."

Conlon was trying to work out how George had snagged a woman like this—so complex and challenging.

"Are you hungry?" she asked.

"I'm grand, thanks."

"What was the food like over there? I've often wondered."

"Why would you wonder about that?"

"Well, isn't French food only the poshest?"

He laughed. "We didn't get much posh French food in the trenches. Bully beef and Maconochie most days until we were sick of it. Biscuits to dip in it that were so hard they'd break your teeth if you bit one dry."

He looked at her and could see she was fascinated, so he continued. "Sometimes one of the lads would get something nice from home and share it around—cake or even chocolate, if we were really lucky. The officers went into Amiens to the fine restaurants or so we heard, anyway. Some of the lads were obsessed with food because all we ever got were the same things. Something like condensed milk; you'd only dream about. It made life here—even with the rationing—seem lovely and spoiled. You'd dream of variety. It was better when we were behind the lines, when I was in my second unit. Some of the French turned their houses into cafes and would sell us chips and ham and loads of plonk. Bread and cheese were easy enough to get if you had money. Some of the lads hated French cheese because it smells awful. But I thought it tasted delicious."

"At least you saw some of the world, then, eh?" she said with a raised eyebrow.

He laughed. "I did that, yeah."

"George complains that all he gets to see is Hollyhead. But I'd take that every once in a while."

"He couldn't get you on a boat?"

"We can't afford it. We can't afford jam!"

"He couldn't sneak you on?"

"Ah he's not like Tommy Conlon, afraid of nothing. My George is a fearful man. It's not worth his job, he'd say."

He wanted to tell her that if she were his, he would make it happen, take any risk, get her on a boat and hold her hand as the coast of Britain rose over the waves. He wanted to say that he had been in love with a girl once and been willing to take such risks then. Even if she had been taken from him, he did not regret any of that and would do it all again in a heartbeat. He wanted to say that a woman like her reminded him of that, even sitting here now in this little flat, with the way her beauty rose above her life, the way her spirit shone in her eyes, the way she filled this room with herself.

He wanted to but he just nodded, his face intensely serious. He felt exhilarated just to feel something. Since the War, feelings had seemed muted and distant. This felt real. It reminded him of his old self. He felt almost as if he should thank her.

"So what time does he get back at?" is what he said instead, breaking the spell they had conjured just by talking.

"Tonight, he should be here by seven. Will you be coming back?"

"Probably not today but I'll see how I feel."

"Will you be bringing him out drinking and carousing with loose women?"

"I won't let him do any carousing; don't you worry now Theresa."

"Oh I'm sure you'd take care of him, Tommy."

"How is he? Is he all right?"

"You know George. He's quiet. He doesn't talk about how he's feeling a lot."

She looked at him coolly. "You ask an awful lot of questions. It's like being in bloody confession."

He laughed. "I'm sorry. I was trained to always find out as much as possible. Allows you more control of any situation if you understand the stakes and the players. That's what the man who trained me said to me."

"But why would you want to control this situation? Just chatting to me?"

"Yeah, you're right. But it's like a reflex; I can't help it. My mind just starts up, and the questions come."

She said, "It's not that bad, Tommy. Avoids the awkward silences I always hate. That doesn't sound like normal training to me though: left, right, left, right and all that. Were you some kind of spy or something?"

"Nah. I was a good soldier, Theresa, I was efficient."

"At what? Killing people?"

"Yeah, killing people. So, they put me with people where I could do what I was good at all the time." He shrugged as if to lessen the meaning of his words.

She was looking at him with those piercing eyes and he looked back at her and she nodded.

"But now you're home," she said quietly.

"I am. At last."

"Has it changed much?" The way she weighed down every word with thick irony was impressive and he laughed. "Apart from half of town being rubble, you mean? No, it's exactly the same."

He took a last mouthful of tea and said, "Right."

Smiling then, he stood and they had a moment of awkwardness as she walked him out and they made polite comments.

"Well, it was nice to meet you," he said. "I'm sure we'll see each other again."

"I hope so," she said as he stepped out. "Goodbye, Mr. Conlon. I'll tell George you were looking for him."

"Goodbye, Mrs. Byrne. I'd appreciate that."

And she nodded and so did he and she shut the door with a rattle and click.

———

O'FLAHERTY'S SMELLED JUST the same—that warm pub smell of oats and smoke and people. It was quiet with perhaps a half dozen men scattered around the small room, cigarettes and glasses in their hands. Ronnie, behind the bar, laughed at the sight of him.

"Jaysus Christ, if it isn't Tommy Conlon. What the fuck are you doing here?"

"I was hoping to get a drink or two."

"How long have you been back? Where are the lads?"

"I was hoping you could tell me that, too..."

He shook his head. "Haven't seen them in many a month. Not since I've seen you, I'd say."

"None of them?"

"Well yis were always a unit, weren't yis?"

"You haven't seen any of them? Who was the last one that was in?"

Ronnie grinned, eyes narrowing in mockery." You'll be wanting that drink while I tell you, won't you?"

"Pint please, Ronnie," Conlon said. He slowed himself down. No point being angry now or worried. He had to be alert. Notice everything, the way he had been taught. It would be important later, he knew.

Ronnie placed a pint before him. Conlon handed him some coins; Ronnie opened the drawer and dropped them in and then the barman leaned in front of him.

"So, I imagine you have some fine stories since last I saw you?"

"None that I really want to share though."

"I understand that. Good to be back?"

"I don't know. Strange to be back, that's for sure."

Ronnie nodded. "Aye, some changes here, too."

"How was it?"

"A bloody awful mess, son."

"Well. I know a bit about those."

"That you do."

Conlon took a long, slow mouthful and Ronnie watched him.

"First one?"

"In Dublin, yeah. Good as ever, Ronnie."

"Somebody was in asking about you and your friends a few months back," he said, his voice lower, no humor now.

"Somebody?"

"I didn't know the men. Strangers."

"Where were they from? I never met a man with as good an ear for an accent as you."

Ronnie smiled at the flattery. "One of them never said a word. Big lad with a scar on his face, under his eye right down to his neck, like somebody pushed his face into a fire and held him there, he just stared at me."

"The other one?"

"Galway maybe, Mayo. He liked the sound of his own voice. Knew all your names."

"What did he look like?"

"Handsome fella. Nice suit on him. They talked to Nelligan, I think."

"Harry Nelligan?"

"Yeah. Sat at his table for a good while."

Conlon thought for a moment. "Harry still a regular?"

"He is. He'll be in later if you have time to waste."

"Where's he working nowadays?"

"I believe he's a gardener out in Dalkey. Some big house. Ask Ivan there, he'll tell you." Conlon looked around but Ronnie wasn't patient enough. "Ivan!" he shouted. "Where does Nelligan work these days?"

"The Shelbourne," came the lazy reply.

Ronnie shrugged at Conlon, "Don't listen to me, then."

Conlon finished his pint slowly. When he rose and placed his hat back on his head, he tugged the brim down in Ronnie's direction. Then he was off.

———

CONLON USED the employee entrance at the back of the Shelbourne. The front was all glamour and bustle. The squat, imposing building occupied one corner of Stephens Green with its endless parade of Dublin humanity, traffic constantly heading up Baggot Street and coming from Merrion Square. As he walked up the

Green from Grafton Street, he remembered that the Rebels had dug trenches in the park and been forced to retreat by English snipers and machine guns. Stupid tactics, he thought now, obvious to anybody with any proper military training.

But his main thought was of how odd it must have been. He had arrived in Turkey to find the battle already joined, the battlefield a place defined by that status. The same in France, in each place he found himself sent. What must it have been like to come under fire in Stephens Green? He and Orla had come here together once. He could not imagine dodging bullets and crouching in trenches there.

It was late afternoon by now, but still it was busy around the hotel entrance.

In contrast, the staff entered via an alleyway at the back, past bins and greasy puddles. A trio of barefoot boys were playing with a stick halfway along, jumping around each other and shouting. Conlon had been one of those boys once, he thought.

There was no security here and no sooner had Conlon passed through a pair of heavy doors than he was in a corridor. There were cloakrooms for men and women and he could hear the ring and clatter of the kitchens from the far end.

He kept his hat down and, as he walked with brisk confidence, nobody challenged him. Near the doors leading out to the bar, he pulled aside a lounge boy he found carrying a tray with some cocktails.

"Where's Harry Nelligan work, son?"

The boy barely looked at him. "Kitchen porter," he said.

Conlon saw him as soon as he entered the kitchen.

Gaunt and dark-eyed, slightly stooping, Harry loved cards and his eyes had a way of flitting about as if he was always in a poker game, sizing up, evaluating odds. He was washing dishes in the far corner of the big room, away from the shouting and clattering pans of the chefs.

Conlon went and stood near him, saying nothing.

Nelligan looked at him after a few seconds, his face dropping when he recognized Conlon.

"You know who I am?"

Nelligan nodded, eyes wide.

"Let's go and have a chat." Conlon gestured to the doors nearby.

Nelligan nodded again and was drying his hands on his apron as he warily led Conlon to the doors. They opened straight out onto the alley and this area was virtually carpeted in cigarette butts. Still, the boys played further down the alley, their cries and hoots echoing off the walls.

Nelligan reached for his own smokes, his hands shaking. Then he looked to Conlon for permission. Conlon nodded and watched him light and inhale.

"The men who were looking for me. Who were they?"

"I only know one of them. His name is McPhail; he's a gambler."

"McPhail. Where do you know him from?"

"Just the card circuit. He's around. We're not friends or anythin'."

"What does he do?"

"I don't know, I swear. In O'Flaherty's was the first time he's ever said more than two words to me. I've heard he's involved with the Rebels. And I think he's a money lender. That's all I know. He dresses real well but he's good with the cards. He might be making enough from that to pay for the suits and shoes and that."

Conlon nodded. "What did he say about me?"

"He mentioned that he was looking for you and your friends. I said you were regulars but hadn't been in for a while. That was it, Tommy, I swear."

"Why are you scared?"

"What?"

"Why are you scared? I'm not here to hurt you."

"I don't know. They were scary, too. They didn't threaten me but it felt like they did."

"So you think it was bad? Whatever they wanted."

"It felt like they were after a debt. That's why he felt like a money lender. I've had dealings with money lenders and the way they talk to you...there's nothing else like it. Makes you feel like a rat in a bucket. That's how he was. Always use a Jewman if you need money. But yeah, it felt like they were after a debt. Was it that?"

"I don't know. Not my debt, anyway." Tommy looked at the older man's tense body language, his wide, alarmed eyes, and said: "I'm not going to hurt you, Harry, for God's sake. Is my reputation that bad?"

"You used to work for Xavier, didn't you?"

Conlon rolled his eyes. "Not really."

"Well, there are stories..."

"I'm sure there are."

"People still talk about you beating the lives out of the Kearns boys at a ruggy-up."

Conlon laughed abruptly. A memory he had not entertained for a long time. That violence—so serious and important then—now seemed facile and silly, after the War. But in that mass brawl—with half the street watching in a baying, delighted mob, and dozens hanging from tenement windows for a better view—he had cut a swath through the Kearns brothers that had made him a legend.

"That was a long time ago," he said now.

"I just—I haven't done anythin'", Mr. Conlon. I don't want this coming back on me at all."

"Why would it? You telling me the truth?"

"I swear I am."

"Well then. But if I find you're lying to me..."

"I'm not, I'm not."

"Ok. This McPhail. Where'd I be likely to find him if he likes his cards so much? Where are the main games these days?"

"The same old pubs. You know."

"Anywhere else?"

The older man took a long drag and shrugged. "He has money. One time, when I had a few bob, I was put onto a game out in Sandymount. Big house, loads of high rollers and a few Brits. McPhail was there that night."

"What house?"

"I can't remember, can I? BOD put me onto it, ask him."

"O' Doherty?"

"Yeah. He's got interests in every game from here to Kenmare. He'll know. He might even know where McPhail lives."

Conlon nodded. "Well. Thanks, Harry. You've been most helpful."

"Ah, you're all right. As long as nothin' comes back to me."

"It won't."

Nelligan nodded and took another long drag, then

venomously threw the cigarette at the ground, stamping on it with great vigor. As he turned to go, Conlon asked, "Did you win?"

"When?"

"At the big house in Sandymount. Did you win?"

Nelligan laughed with genuine delight. "Lost every penny. Never play with men who don't care about money. See ya, Mr. Conlon."

"See ya."

3

BOD. Brendan O'Doherty was his given name but
everybody called him BOD. And that "everybody" was
no exaggeration. Conlon had known who he was even as
a child. His name was known by everyone Conlon knew,
it seemed. His name came up. He was generous, classy,
dressed well, and always had a kind word for everyone.

Conlon had walked up Grafton Street with his
mother, ogling the rich people and the smart shops. But
BOD existed both in that world and in theirs. He had
somehow managed to bridge that divide. Even as a boy
of the streets, Conlon had been impressed by this,
impressed by the grace, and seeming ease of it.

BOD did everything as if it were easy. Always
smiling.

When Conlon first started fighting, BOD was there
from his earliest fights. At first, he was just another face
in the crowd. But after Conlon's first win, he appeared in
the dressing rooms as Conlon and the other fighters
were washing off and dressing.

Just a bunch of boys—mostly from the tenements—dribbling off blood and sweat into dented pails of cold water, dressing tenderly in a big, echoey room with an October chill in its corners. And in comes this son of Limerick, wearing a sharp suit and shiny shoes, walking with a cocky but slightly feminine little jiggle, and literally throwing money to the boys he liked.

Everybody else seemed to know him and so Conlon felt at a disadvantage from the start. But BOD obviously favored him. He wanted a proper introduction. He shook Conlon's hand with enthusiasm, and smiled, and smiled.

He was there every fight after that. Conlon figured out quickly that he had interests with some of the bookies that he was some sort of boss. But his interest seemed more personal, somehow. And he knew boxing. His comments were always astute and to the point. He noticed when Conlon had protected his ribs through three punishing rounds against Mick McCardle. He appreciated how Conlon had worked out inside a minute that Dickie Brody lowered his guard for an instant after every straight right and devastatingly exploited that. He told Conlon to work on his feet, to move, and to dance a bit. And he was right. He knew boxing.

When Conlon started to drift away, BOD had drifted away, too. Xavier was on another level and BOD was too shrewd to get mixed up with him over small fry like Conlon. So those last months in Dublin, he had not seen the older man. He had heard some of Xavier's men talk about him—joking about his liking for a certain kind of boy—but he was involved with Orla and the fights had begun to dry up as his reputation grew. And of course: the money.

But they had been friendly, once. Conlon was counting on that. His office was wherever he happened to be but Tommy knew he kept rooms—almost a suite —upstairs at Wynn's. He didn't have security. He had never needed it, Conlon supposed. Everybody liked him. Which meant that Conlon could just go up and knock on the door. He hoped the rooms were still the same.

But it turned out that the hotel had been damaged in the Rising and whole sections were undergoing repair and reconstruction. Conlon had to ask about BOD at the front desk, unsure if there were any guests still here.

He had only been here once, years before, that day he had seen Orla. It would have been early—had they even spoken yet? Maybe once, or twice. But she had been in his mind, blotting out every other thought and feeling, as if he had stared too long at the sun and now its burn prevented him from seeing anything else. He had felt that way for months. People talking to him and laughing as they repeated themselves because he was so distant. BOD looking at him with what he now saw had been concern.

He had sat in a chair waiting for BOD to do something, he could not remember what now. Change his hat? Replace scuffed shoes? Those were the kind of extravagances BOD was capable of. Conlon had not cared because he had been thinking of her. It was a suite without a decent view. The Liffey was out those windows but hidden behind the backs of the houses visible over the alley and yards. Brickwork was painted black by smoke from the kitchens below; the windows were greasy and fogged.

Now, he was told that yes, Mr. O' Doherty was still a resident, and given the room number.

Conlon knocked twice and waited. He heard movement inside. BOD opened the door, dressed in an ostentatious suit as ever, only lacking his hat. His gray hair was wild without it. The suit was black with a hint of purple. His face registered instant surprise and then he controlled it and smeared a smile onto his lips.

"Thomas. I didn't know you were back!"

Conlon had forgotten that BOD always addressed him as Thomas.

"Surprise. I'm back."

"Wonderful! Wonderful! Come in, son, come in."

He ushered Conlon inside with a flourish. The room was exactly as Conlon remembered it. A hotel room; bland, efficiently hospitable. BOD offered Conlon a chair and a drink then excused himself and moved into his bedroom. When he returned, he was wearing his hat. He seemed more vital and more confident with it on.

Conlon studied him as he moved around the room, collecting possessions from tables and shelves and donning them: a pocket watch, a claddagh ring, a small purse of some sort. He talked incessantly, a stream of words with no end in sight or discernable point. He talked just to talk. Conlon had known many soldiers just like that. The War had knocked it out of all but the strongest of them. Those who remained that way did it as if in direct defiance of death itself.

BOD had always done it, Conlon remembered. It was a way of ingratiating, a way of making people underestimate him, a way of encouraging others to speak when perhaps they didn't want to. BOD was a master of such things.

He looked old, his face bearing the signs of a strain which had not been there when Conlon had first known him.

Finally, satisfied, he stopped and looked Conlon right in the eye. "So, Thomas. Did you just come to have a gawk at your old friend or is there something I can do for you? Tell me you'll be making a comeback. You in the ring was a glorious thing, son."

"I think I've done enough fighting."

BOD nodded at that with a comically exaggerated solemnity. "What then, son? Its lovely to see you, so it is, but there must be something I can do for ye."

"I'm looking for somebody. You remember my friends: Podge and Murray, Sean Murray?"

"I never really knew them, Thomas. I remember you had a load of lads you palled around with. I wouldn't know where to start."

"It's not them, BOD. There was a man asking around after me. A gambler, apparently. You must know him."

"What is this poor unfortunate's name?"

"McPhail."

BOD didn't hide the grimace that moved over his face. "What are you going to do, Thomas, with any information I give you?"

"Just go and have a chat with him."

"I would advise you not to."

"Why not?"

"Did you not learn a solitary thing from your...your experience with Mr. Xavier? Did you not? You don't want to be coming home and getting involved with people like that again."

"You're involved with people like that."

"Not in that way. I broker deals. We do business." He shrugged. "It's different, Thomas."

Conlon nodded. "Who is he?"

"He's dangerous. His...friends are dangerous."

"Who is he?"

"He's a gambler. Fine gambler. Clever. Knows when to stop which is rare enough. And a money lender. Cruel if anybody can't pay. Does the kinds of things will get a man a bad reputation. But he's involved with the rebels, too. Gun running, I hear."

"Who are his friends?"

"I don't really know them. Couldn't even name any. But people fear them and that should be enough for you."

"Why would they be looking for me, BOD?"

BOD sat down, slumped, tired, defeated. "There was some money, wasn't there? You and your friends found yourselves some money, somehow. I believe that McPhail and his gang of savages think it was their money."

Conlon nodded but knew it wasn't that; it couldn't have been. He fixed BOD with a cold, dead-eyed look. "When I said I was looking for somebody, you assumed it was my friends. How did you know they were missing?"

"For Jaysus sake, it's my job to know things like that, Thomas. Don't be giving me that hard eye."

"So where can I find him?"

There was a knock on the door. They looked at one

another and BOD shrugged theatrically. He did everything theatrically.

"Who is it?" he said, standing.

"It's me." A thick country accent, obvious even from two syllables.

BOD opened the door. "McPhail," he said, "I have company."

"Not another one of your fuckin' boys, is it?" McPhail said moving past the older man and into the room without invitation.

"Not quite," Conlon said.

He and McPhail regarded one another while BOD closed the door. "McPhail, this is Thomas; Thomas, McPhail."

"Howya," McPhail said. Conlon just nodded.

"How do you know O'Doherty?" McPhail asked. He had a slow drawl, the vowel sounds rounded and chewed on, but he said it with a degree of insolence that surprised Conlon. This was a man who was always ready to fight, it seemed, aggression bubbling constantly near the surface.

"We're old friends," Conlon said. "What about you?"

"Business." He seemed nervous, jumpy. Conlon wondered if he was always this way.

Conlon nodded and they eyed one another for a few seconds more.

McPhail turned to BOD and, almost whispering, he said, "In private, O'Doherty."

BOD gestured toward the bedroom and they moved there together, McPhail looking back at Conlon over his shoulder as he went.

He was a dangerous man; McPhail. Conlon had a nose for such things now and it was obviously the case here. He moved quickly, smoothly, his dark little eyes active and mobile. He was handsome and knew it, vanity like a scar on his face.

Conlon was wondering if he should take him now or wait. He was alone now; it would be easy. He was probably armed. A gun or a small knife. Conlon could handle that. Would he have somebody waiting for him outside? Possibly. Best then to wait, observe, act when he had more information. His training kicked in without him even thinking about it. All he wanted was a few answers but he knew that there would be violence. Already he could feel his adrenaline surging.

They were in the bedroom for perhaps three minutes. When they emerged, McPhail carried a case in one hand. He seemed a little less tense and he attempted a smile at Conlon.

"So, Thomas. What's your line of work, hah?"

"At the moment, I find people."

"You find them? Jobs, you mean? You a foreman or somethin'?"

"No. I find missing people."

"That's not a fuckin' job. Nobody does that."

"You callin' me a liar?"

At that, McPhail's eyes gleamed. His right hand twitched. He sized up Conlon who was still slouched in the chair, legs crossed. BOD was almost vibrating with anxiety.

McPhail said, "We could go into that if we were somewhere else, couldn't we. But I'm a guest here, like yourself. I'll take your word for it."

"Fair enough. And what do you do?"

"This and that."

"Enough to get by?"

"More than enough."

"That's good. You're a lucky man in a city with so many with so little."

"It's not luck, Thomas. Hard work and brains. That's what gets you anywhere in this world. Hard work and brains."

"I've never been much for hard work."

BOD sensed his opportunity and interrupted, "Sure I can vouch for that, ha?"

McPhail turned to look at the older man and the spell was broken.

"I'll be off, then, gentlemen. Good day to you, Thomas." He gave the brim of his hat a gentle pull and Conlon nodded in reply.

Then he was gone, BOD shutting the door behind him. Conlon was already out of his seat. BOD put his hands out to placate him, his eyes wide, and whispered, "No, no Thomas. He's a dangerous man, that one. What're you thinking?"

Conlon stood still, perfectly calm, and looked BOD straight into the eyes. "I need to find where he lives. It's all right, BOD. I've done worse and faced a lot worse. I'll be all right."

BOD's eyes flickered, wavering, but still he stood between Conlon and the door.

"BOD, I need to go now or else I'll lose him."

BOD nodded. Conlon put a hand on his shoulder—a gesture of gratitude but also a calming touch. "Thank you. I'll see you soon."

And then he, too, was gone, into the corridor, bounding down the stairwell, across the lobby, and then out into the street. He knew McPhail had taken the elevator and he beat it to the lobby so that he was already outside when McPhail emerged. He watched him from across Abbey Street, staring at his reflection as it was joined by two other men, both in long coats and hats, smoking cigarettes.

They set off together, turning onto Sackville Street and turning south, toward the Liffey. Conlon, feeling a strange excitement—the kind he had not experienced since before he went to war—build in him. He gave the men a few seconds to build some distance and then he followed.

4

CONLON'S LIFE HAD CHANGED DURING HIS THIRD FIGHT. The first two had barely been fights at all.

First, he had been matched up against Jacob McEvoy. They knew each other slightly, knew to say hello around the gym and the streets, because their mothers would gossip after mass on a Sunday and because they were both friendly with Paul Lamb. But they didn't *really* know one another.

Conlon knew him as dopey-looking, with a manner that suggested it took him a long time to tie his shoelaces each morning. He knew that he always wore a dark suit and a hat that seemed too small for his outsized watermelon of a head. He knew he had won his first fight against Alan O'Callaghan. But nobody had been too impressed, which is probably why Conlon found himself up against him for his first time out, and thus the world turned.

They were low down on the undercard and neither of them really knew what he was doing. The reality of a real fight dawned on both halfway through the first round when the soul-deep weariness began to make limbs droop and sag, and movement seemed impossibly slow. But it dragged on for two clumsy, awkward rounds until Conlon landed a lucky uppercut plum on McEvoy's prominent chin and he went up and over like a salmon swimming upstream. When he hit the canvas, he just lay there for what felt to Conlon like a half an hour.

So he had his first knockout and his first win. But Conlon knew that it was not true, that he had been lucky. That it was a fluke. He knew these things.

Second, he had fought John Byrne, out of Belfast. Byrne had a reputation. He was fearsome. He won fights in the first round with terrifyingly powerful shots. That may have been true for Byrne ten or even five years before he fought Conlon, but now he was older. He was slower. His shots weren't as powerful.

That didn't even matter. Byrne could barely hit Conlon.

When he had eyed his opponent across the ring before the fight, Conlon had been afraid. He had never seen a body like the other man's—muscles that looked like he had packed something beneath his skin. But within twenty seconds, he knew he would win this fight. Byrne moved like a cow; slowly and with a blinking and stupefied air. Conlon could anticipate most of his punches and, those he could not, he could avoid. Though this would come to be second nature, at that point, it was a supernatural ability he knew some other boxers had found bestowed upon them—not one Conlon himself possessed. But it did not matter. Byrne drew himself back to throw each punch, taking a slight step, leaning away, then triggering and delivering.

At first, Conlon just allowed the fists to cut through the air on either side of his head. But before the end of the round, he began to cut in and jab at Byrne whenever he wound up a shot. By the bell, the big Northern Irishman had cuts over both eyes. Midway through the second round, he couldn't see at all and, a minute into the third, his corner threw in the towel.

For his third fight, Conlon fought James Sheers. Sheers had been making a name for himself. He was viper-fast, brutally strong, and moved around the ring constantly, his feet a blur. He was also a loudmouth, talking to Conlon from the second he entered the ring, slagging off his Northside origins, telling him he would have to be carried out of the ring, asking him if he liked hospital food. Conlon felt different this time. A stillness had descended upon him. He felt no fear. He knew what he had to do.

He did it inside a minute of the bell.

It seemed simple now, somehow. He had felt something similar when he had taken on both of the Kearns brothers in a street battle, months before. It was as if time slowed to a crawl and he could choose how to live each second. For all his speed, Sheers seemed slow and predictable as he approached and threw his first few tentative jabs. Conlon circled him, waiting, and then, when Sheers stepped in and swung a straight right, Conlon dodged it and hit him with two successive lefts. Sheers took two steps away but Conlon was already following up with a hooked right. Sheers guard came down and Conlon hit him with a five-punch combination which put him down.

It had been easy. He knew how hard to punch. He could see exactly where, could feel when. The application of force made perfect sense to him. What it felt like, once the first blows had landed, was like chopping down a tree. It would put up no fight; all he had to do was find the right spots to hit and hit them hard enough and down it would come. And so it had proved.

Standing in the ring as the referee counted down for Sheers was the first time Conlon had known he could be a fighter. A good one.

And so he was. After that, his attitude had changed. He understood now what he needed to do to improve. He understood the things he could force his body to withstand in the pursuit of his own physical development. He understood why, too. He would be stronger. He would be faster.

He saw what to do in the fights, and it started to happen in sparring sessions, too. But he had to make his body harder and faster and deadlier so that he could make the things he saw reality. He worked hard. He willed his punches to match what he wanted them to be: pulverizing explosions of force. He wanted to be able to choose when to put somebody down if he saw a gap just by modulating the power he applied.

He began thinking about fighting differently. He started to dream about it. He thought about it in the moments that lie outside conscious experiences of thought—the idle seconds when individuals stare at nothing, lost to the world and their surroundings and themselves. In those moments he was visualizing, thinking about his feet and how he moved on them, remembering the way his arms moved when he threw different combinations. He was at the gym all of the time, training, sparring, watching, listening. His fights became short exercises in precision and brutality. He ended them inside a round or two.

When the quality of his opponents improved, the results were the same. It was just a matter of how long an opponent could live with him; how many of his blows they could absorb before they fell.

He could take a punch. He showed that in his seventh fight, against a Scot with a huge weight and height advantage over him, who dominated the first round by using his reach to jab away at Conlon's head, and on three occasions followed it up with short, rapid combinations which sent him back into the ropes, gloves up. By round two, Conlon had worked him out and stepped inside repeatedly, his huge body blows eventually sending the Scot to his knees. When he was up, Conlon knocked him out with a straight right over his sagging gloves.

Conlon had a name now. People came to see him fight. Men recognized him in the street. There was talk of him going to England or even America to try his luck in a bigger pool.

But in Dublin, money was a problem. He could not devote as much time as he needed to his training if he was laboring. His purses were not enough to keep his ma and himself going—not yet.

Xavier entered his life in the form of Jordan Devereaux.

Conlon left the gym after training one rainy Monday evening and there he was, leaning by the door, in a sharp black suit and hat, boots shining, smoking a cigarette with a certain style—the same style that meant he wore a mustache that twisted itself around at its points like the horns of a bull.

"Mr. Conlon. My name is Devereaux. Would you happen to know who Mr. Francis Xavier is?"

Conlon looked at him a few seconds before answering. Already, he knew that this was one of Xavier's men...and not a minor one. Somebody with some importance. He had a posh Dublin accent, the kind that barely sounded like a Dublin accent at all. Some British vowel sounds in there, words finished, t's left undropped.

"I would, yeah."

"Well, then. That makes things slightly less complex. Mr. Xavier would like the pleasure of your company, Mr. Conlon."

"Now?"

"Indeed."

"Why?"

Devereaux laughed at this, silently. "I would imagine he has a proposition for you, young man."

Conlon just stared at him, waiting for more. He had no intention of matching verbal wits with this man. He was all too aware that he would lose.

Devereaux seemed to wear a smirk as his default expression but, after ten or fifteen seconds of Conlon silently staring at him, it faltered.

"Well?" he stammered.

"Well what?"

"What shall I tell Mr. Xavier?"

"Tell him when I asked why I should come, you wouldn't answer."

Devereaux nodded seriously. "Mr. Conlon. The best way I can put it to you is to ask you this: would you like earn yourself considerable sums of money for very little work?"

"Of course, I would."

"Well. Come with me to meet Mr. Xavier. He will show you money, shelter, perhaps a roof over your head, a warm bath—everything you need. I would suggest that you pay minute attention from this point onwards, my boy."

"It can't be that simple. There'll be conditions."

"Aren't there always?"

————

CONLON HAD HEARD OF XAVIER. Everyone had. He was the most feared gangster in the city, and he was a local boy. From Stoneybatter, it was said. But that part was all a bit hazy. He had risen from the shadows to sudden prominence with a reputation forged over the course of a single day, a trail of corpses.

Conlon knew that he was infamous for the extraordinary violence of his gang. Men were nailed to walls for betrayals. Fingers were removed with shears. Eyes were burnt out with red-hot pokers. A runner named Shay who Conlon knew distantly had double-crossed Xavier, it was said. His body was found in a butcher's shop. His fingers had been minced, his feet, and genitals removed with a cleaver.

In a city where crime and gang warfare were common, Xavier had changed the landscape entirely, introducing a new level of brutality and terror. And it had worked. His rivals had been vanquished and now all he had to deal with were the young pups working on smalltime scores. Those he could control. Other than that, the city was his.

The Dublin Metropolitan Police dealt with petty

crime and were, supposedly, obsessed with the rebels, but they had no way into the gang scene in the city which was tight knit and based around families and areas. A stranger, any stranger, was instantly suspicious in this world. So they could not use agents. Xavier had made the penalty for disloyalty not just death but torture, agony, then death. And nobody wanted to cross him.

Conlon thought about all of this on the way to that first meeting. He knew he should feel afraid but he did not. He was curious to meet this man, to see what he was like, to hear exactly what he wanted. He was also smart enough to realize that if Xavier wanted him harmed then that is what would happen. This was something different, something interesting.

Xavier was in room above a pub in Christchurch. Before he could be introduced to him, Conlon had to meet his guard dog. This was a man named Finch. There was absolutely nothing about him that could inspire intimidation or fear. He was short and slight, balding, and weak-chinned. His face was a little bulbous above that chin, what hair he had was so wispy it looked like twists of browned straw and he wore a tight brown suit, had a matching hat upon the table beside him. When Conlon followed Devereux into the pub, he was sitting there surrounded by four younger men. One of them was up instantly, his hand inside his coat until he recognized Devereaux.

Finch was already watching Conlon. He had been since the instant he stepped inside. Finch stood up to continue his appraisal. Up close, Conlon could see he had dark brown eyes that seemed almost edged with gold; his most distinctive and memorable characteristic.

He stood directly in front of Conlon and stared into his face. "I've seen you fight," he said. His voice was a whisper, his accent Dublin but without any obvious marks of class or neighborhood.

Conlon said, "I hope you enjoyed it."

Finch made a noise of agreement in his throat.

"Frisk him," he said, and two of his men patted Conlon down while Finch stood back, observing impassively. After about ten silent, endless seconds of this, Xavier said, "Bring him up."

Six months later, Finch killed three men who attacked Xavier. He killed them with a knife and a witness claimed he had done it in under twenty seconds. A month after that, he beat Archie McDowall to death with his bare hands. Nine weeks after that, he killed Val "Shark" Waters in his own place. He did that with a hatchet. These were the stories about Finch. Conlon knew that at least half of them were true.

Finch was one of the first men Conlon had ever really feared.

————

AFTER HE HAD MET XAVIER, nothing much changed. Conlon knew he had just been judged. The man wanted to look into his eyes, to see what he was made of, like a bookie checking on a horse before he backs it. Xavier was calculating whether Conlon was a good bet. All Conlon had to do was keep winning and show his face at the odd event: drink in a few specific pubs, attend a certain party here, a gathering there. Then he would be paid for his trouble.

He agreed to all this. And he did it. It was easy. It was

fun, even. People knew who he was and wanted to chat to him about boxing. Some of the ol' lads at the parties really knew their stuff, breaking down his fights for him with deft understanding, shocking him into impressed silence. He could go into any one of a few different bars and be served with a free drink and some food. He had his photograph taken, for the first time, posing with his gloves and trunks on, staring determinedly at a spot just above the camera. When he saw the picture, he did not recognize himself, looking stiff, young, and handsome.

One was hung in McClean's, another in his gym, where the other lads made ceaseless jokes about it, ribbing him mercilessly. After a brief sulk, he, too, found this funny.

What was not funny was the cash that showed up in an envelope under the bar at McClean's each week. It wasn't much, but it was more than he had ever made in wages in his life before.

McClean's became vital. It was where he got paid but also where he checked in, where he was seen.

He met her in McClean's.

She looked unlike anybody he had ever seen outside of the picture shows. That first time they had met, introduced by McClean himself, he had been brought up short by her face.

She was working, busy, moving and stooping and fetching, talking over her shoulder in a country accent he would later discover was Cork city and McClean had said to her, "Orla. This is Tommy."

Conlon had caught sight of her as soon as he came in. Her hair was like gold, shiny and made straight somehow. She was tallish and, even from behind and from a distance, something about her was arresting—

something in her carriage and the way she swung her hips. He was by no means a ladies' man, then. He was a bit too quiet, a bit too reluctant to express himself in conversation. But as soon as he saw her face, he knew they would be together. He felt it go through him the way a solid punch will; traveling up his spine like a current.

Only this was just her face. She turned to greet him and, when their eyes met, he felt like a butterfly pinned beneath glass in a case, her face filling his view, the world shrinking away and leaving them alone there together. Her eyes were a startling cold blue, and she had cheekbones like knives, high and sharp and beautiful. She was almost frightening in her icy beauty until she grinned, and Conlon saw her teeth weren't perfect. Warmth crept into her expression and, like that: he was in love. Orla.

The funny thing was that he sensed, instinctively, that she had felt it, too. Something had passed between them, something wordless—a recognition, an acknowledgment. They both said hello, their eye contact lasting perhaps a beat longer than it should have. Then McClean was moving on, Conlon was following him, and Orla was resuming her labor.

———

HE DID NOT SEE her again for some months after that even though every single time he entered McClean's he obsessively looked for her—even though he thought about her face in his quiet, solitary moments, even though he went over in his head subtle ways to ask McClean about her, even though when he walked the streets, he searched every female face for hers. Despite all this, he did not see her. Worse; he thought about her in this way without ever acknowledging it to himself. It was as if he was in complete denial: That he had ever even seen her; that he had felt the way he had; that it was real; and finally, that he would never see her again.

He began to wonder if he had imagined it and imagined her. Such a creature could not have been working there, he mused; she had stood out, sparkling like a gemstone in a bedpan.

And just as he was beginning to think about her less, there she was.

Xavier had asked that he attend a party in the Gaiety. Some businessmen were there, supporting a pair of young actresses who had appeared in a play. Xavier turned some of the rooms off the lobby into a mini-casino, with cards and roulette, and stuffed the place with his more respectable friends. Conlon knew all of the faces well from Xavier's circuit. They nodded in rueful recognition.

He had not attended the performance, sloping in some time after it had ended and the crowds had cleared, and he did not see her enter, either. People recognized him and shook his hand and he was chatting to some well-wishers when she passed by in a devastating line of odor and magnetism. It was an older couple he stood with and, when his eye found the side of her face, he was instantly deaf to their voices.

He watched her move through the crowd. She had changed. She seemed altered—more sophisticated, more comfortable, more at home in this crowd than she had been, even in McClean's. More beautiful, if that was possible.

She was on an arm and he had to step sideways to see whose it was. Finch.

He felt a series of tremors in his face as he struggled to contain all of this, what it might mean. He wanted to leave, now, straightaway. He wanted to run out of this place.

She turned now and he saw her face fully. Damn, she was beautiful. It made his breath quicken. He felt almost sick at the sight of that face. Finch was speaking to her, his face a mask of dispassion. She nodded, then greeted somebody Conlon could not see with a smile. And then he saw it—brief but unmistakable, in the instant after saying hello to that unseen stranger—fear. She looked assured and relaxed but he was certain it was an act. Somewhere inside, she did not want to be here. She hated it, just as he did.

She looked over at him then, perhaps thirty feet away, a dozen heads separating them. Their eyes locked and she stared at him for a moment and he stared back and neither said a thing or made any expression. The band in the next room played "She Moved Through the Fair". A man stood before her and their eye contact was disrupted. Conlon, feeling shaken and sick in a way he had never before experienced, left.

Walking through the drizzle toward home and lying in his bed that night he could not think of a thing beyond those crystal blue eyes and the feeling that hung in their depths.

He would not see her again for months.

———————

FINCH CAME TO HIM, which was unusual. They had rarely spoken. He was waiting by the water closet when Conlon finished his training. His usual lapdogs were nowhere to be seen and he seemed diminished without them. Again, Conlon was surprised by how normal the man appeared. You would not notice him in a small crowd. He seemed as if he might work as a barman or a waiter, perhaps, nothing too physical, nothing too intellectually demanding. And yet he was so feared. Conlon studied him for signs of that fearsome cruelty, the mind capable of barbarism, the body which had broken so many people. All he saw was that mousey hair, which was beginning to recede, and the soft lack of character in the face. Nothing strange or memorable until he spoke and his voice was a silken whisper, intelligent, and seductive.

Every time they had spoken, Conlon had felt the same way: on his guard, aware that anything he said could be taken by this man and used as a weapon. This time was no different.

When he had seen Finch with Orla at that party, he had feared that she was with him, but a few overheard details since then had made it plain that she was one of Xavier's women now; he was known to have a few. She no longer worked in McClean's, and that meant that Xavier had put her up somewhere and was paying for her or that she had her own employment and he was merely an extra source of income for her. Conlon tried not to think about it, which meant of course that he could not stop thinking about it.

And she was the first thought in his head when he saw Finch: you have spoken to her, he thought, you know her, you have had her on your arm and spent time in her company.

"Tommy," Finch said. "We have a job for you." He saw the look in Conlon's face and he almost smiled. "Nothing like that. We need you to go get somebody and bring them back here."

"Who?"

"Her name is Orla."

———

THEY THOUGHT she had returned to Cork and Xavier had already sent somebody down to dig around and see if he could find her. Conlon's job was just to talk to her.

"She doesn't know you, Tommy," Finch had said, unnervingly reasonable as ever. "But she'll probably know who you are. She'll know you're not one of our boys. If you were, she probably wouldn't even talk to you. She's a headstrong girl."

He said this as if he were discussing an animal of some sort, its tempers and moods a matter of humor.

"But you; be nice to her. Talk her around. She's better off here. She'll see. Don't come on too strong. Let her think she's making her own decision."

Conlon had nodded and agreed and all the while his mind had raced. She had run away. Whatever he had thought of her and her situation, real life was complicated and she had run away from Xavier and Dublin and the life she had somehow gotten herself into. He was never going to say no to this job.

Finch gave him money and a telephone number to call if he needed more. The man they had sent was staying at the Imperial Hotel and he would arrange a room for Conlon, too, if needed.

————

HE TOOK a train the next morning. It was February and snow chased them along the railway line, buffering and shaking the carriages in raging flurries every twenty minutes or so. The passengers smoked and sank down into their coats. Women clutched shawls and blankets around themselves to keep warm.

Soon, the windows were cloudy with the fog of their breathing. Conlon used his elbow to paint a patch so that he could watch the land as they passed through it but, once they had cleared Dublin, the weather was so bad he could scarcely see a thing. Occasionally, a stretch of white would rise up from the gloom, broken only by the thin fingers of trees bending beneath the wind, tattered hedgerows crouching on pale hillsides, and the odd dark little house naked to the cold and the spite of the elements.

He thought of what he would say to Orla and how the conversation could possibly go. He watched the young couple who sat across from him. Their affection and closeness was obvious in the way their bodies turned toward one another, the way they laughed at quiet words he could not hear, the way they looked at one another with a shining joy in their eyes.

What could he say? How could he persuade her to return to Xavier when he did not want her to return to Xavier? He was not sure he could even speak to her; he was not sure his voice would not entirely desert him in her presence. He imagined conversations in his head but abandoned that when it occurred to him that he had no idea what she was like. How she spoke, what her personality was, how she saw the world—all of these things were utter mysteries to him.

He resolved to stop thinking about it. It would happen. He would react when it did.

———

HE HAD NEVER BEEN to Cork before. In the driving wind and snow, he could not get a fix on it now, either. A river, hills. It felt small to him and there were few people on the streets as he made his way to the hotel, head down against the hard sprays of ice that clawed at his eyes.

In the lobby, he was just about to enquire at the desk when an older man approached him. He had a strong, nasal Dublin accent and heavily oiled hair.

"I didn't think they'd send you, Mr. Conlon," he said, almost bowing as they shook hands. "I'm a big fan. Big fan. Seen your last three fights with me own eyes. Sure you move like the wind; they can't lay a hand on ye."

Conlon thanked him and they went to the bar to talk. The man, it emerged, was a cobbler named Bennett, but his business had folded two years before and, ever since, he had struggled for work and had started taking contracts as a sort of detective.

"What do you mean? You solve crimes, like the peelers?"

"No, no, no, no. The things normal people need doing, but can't do themselves, I can do."

"Like what?"

"It's dirty work, I won't lie to you Mr. Conlon."

"Give me an example."

"Like I find people. People who've run away or people who owe money or just people who disappear. That happens. Or, I spy on people. People don't trust each other in this world. So I watch them. Cheating wives, now, I've seen plenty of them. It's not easy to watch a man's face when you tell him that all the things he was worried about are true, I'm telling ye. And I dig up dirt on people. That's the easiest. Research."

"How's the money?"

"Depends on the client and the job. But I get by."

"This client?"

"Mr. Vincent Francis Xavier pays very well, yeah. But I'd do these jobs for free. For the contacts I'm making and the acquaintances I've met. They'll come in handy one day soon."

"Have you found her?"

"I know where she is, yes. I was instructed not to approach her but to let you do that. Has there been a change of plan?"

His speech became far more formal and labored once they discussed business. It made Conlon feel tired. "Not that I know of, no. Where is she?"

"She's in a town called Clonakilty. Staying in the hotel on Main Street there."

"Why? Has she got family there?"

"I don't think so. I'm assuming it's a sentimental thing for her or she might've picked it for remoteness. It is another train ride from here. Do you know this lassie, Mr. Conlon?"

"No. We've never spoken."

"She is a very good-looking girl."

Conlon nodded. "I need to get a room in that hotel."

"You already have one. Under your name and all."

"Good work."

He bowed his head.

"What does she do with her time? What's she doing there?"

"I watched her for a day. She wandered the streets, talked to strangers. The men of Clonakilty are taking turns to introduce themselves to her. She is very polite and very firm when she rebuffs them. She had cream tea in the café near the hotel but usually she eats lunch and dinner in the hotel. I paid a cleaner a shilling for that information. She reads, too, an awful lot by the looks of it. Newspapers and books."

"Is she all right?"

"She seems to be in good health."

Conlon laughed. "No, is she ok. Nothing unusual about her?"

"I don't know the lassie." He held his hands up, baffled by the question.

"And she doesn't seem to be meeting anyone?"

"She could be, all right. Perhaps they haven't shown up yet."

"But you don't think so."

"No, I don't. I think she's hiding out."

"All right. I suppose I'll go and see her tomorrow, then."

"What then?"

Conlon shrugged, genuinely perplexed. He had no idea what he would do or say.

"Your job is to bring her back, hah?"

"It is."

"Well. The trick with persuading anyone to do anything—in my experience, anyhow—is to let them think it was all their idea."

Conlon studied him. "That sounds good, yeah. But I have no idea how to do it."

Bennett chuckled. "I'm sure it'll come to ye."

———

HE TOOK the train to Clonakilty the next morning. It only had a couple of carriages, with only a couple of passengers each, and its progress was slow across the soggy green of the Cork countryside. The snow of the previous day had become a drizzle and, aside from a solitary farmer mending a fence, they passed nobody for almost the entirety of the journey, as if the country had emptied out. There was nobody at the small station, either.

After a short walk up the main street and across the square, which were relatively bustling, he checked in to the hotel. His room was small and laced with mahogany. The dark brown of the wood was oppressive and, after ten minutes in the room, he had to close his eyes rather than have it pressing down on him. He wondered if hers was the same.

He unpacked his few meager belongings into the mahogany dresser and wardrobe. Then he paced and lay on his bed and sat upon his mahogany chair and tried to force himself to go back out.

It was a pleasant town, small but agreeably busy. You could smell the sea on the breeze. Horses and carts sagged past, clattering as they went. The weather had improved and the world was visible without the use of a telescope, the gray skies emptied of their snow and rain for now. Every so often, he would rise and stand by the window, watching people go about their daily lives.

He knew he would have to do it, approach her, but, at the moment, it seemed absolutely beyond him.

It was hunger that finally drove him out; he had not eaten since he had some toast in Cork for breakfast and the pangs made him grit his teeth and leave his room. She was, of course, sitting in the hotel restaurant. He saw her before he had even entered. She would have stood out anywhere. Her beauty was startling, her hair so vividly golden and cheekbones so cruel and sharp, but she was wearing fashionable clothes, clothes that could only have come from Dublin or London. Compared to the ladies of East Cork, she looked like a visiting princess from some exotic tribe. She wore a long, periwinkle skirt and brown boots and a sort of tunic in a darker shade of brown. A small hat, in a bluish gray, hid some of her hair, which made what fell free below it only look brighter.

His entrance made her turn her head to look at him and, not knowing how else to approach it, he made straight for her. "Do you mind if we share a table, Miss?"

"Francis sent you."

Francis. For an instant, his brain groped for who she might be referring to before he realized she meant Xavier. Of course, she would use his first name.

"Is that a yes?" he asked.

She nodded, a sour expression crossing her features with a crease.

He sat across from her while she conspicuously studied the menu in her hand.

"So, how are you going to do this, then? Are you going to hit me over the head and throw me unconscious into a car? Or have you got a gun and you'll force me to get on a train back to Dublin with you?"

She said this all without raising her eyes to him, the level of contempt radiating from her staggering him. At the same time, he was disappointed. He had hoped she would remember him. Hoped that those two brief glimpses had not been entirely imagined by him and that she had felt the same way.

"I think you have the wrong idea, Miss."

She looked at him. "Do I, now?" Her Cork accent was strong, full of character and ferocity.

"I'm not muscle."

"You look like muscle. One of Finch's boys."

"I've spoken to Finch once in my life. I don't work for Xavier."

"Then why are you here?"

"I'm doing this job because it doesn't involve violence or anything illegal. I'm not a criminal or a killer. I'm just here to talk to you."

"To talk to me. To charm me. To persuade me."

He laughed. "I can see it'll be easy."

She said, "It's not funny. This is my life."

"I know. I'm sorry."

She studied him then. He looked back at her and he could feel his pulse in his throat and hear it in his ears. He thought she must be able to hear him panting so labored were his breaths.

"What do you do, then, Mr.—?"

"Conlon. Thomas Conlon."

"Mr. Conlon."

"I'm a fighter. A boxer."

"And Francis likes to wheel you out at his parties, doesn't he? Impress his pals. He always has to be into everything."

"What do you do for him, Miss?"

She gave a bitter laugh. "Oh Mr. Conlon. You disappoint me."

She stood without warning and left him sitting alone.

———

SHE KNOCKED on the door of his room that night. When he opened it, she said, "I'm tired of eating alone and of the men here thinking that is an invitation. Take me to dinner, Mr. Conlon. I'm sure Francis has given you some spending money."

They ate in the same hotel restaurant where they had earlier spoken. There were a dozen other diners and, as soon as they walked in, he could feel everybody monitoring them, people watching them out of the corners of their eyes, whispering comments. The menu was mainly fish. She ordered whiting, he turbot. They both had mashed potatoes and greens. She told him what wine to ask for.

He watched her whenever he could steal a glance. Her face was hard for him to look at it was so delicate and fine. He could see why Xavier was exercising so much caution in his efforts to get her back.

"Are you from around here?" he asked her once the waiter had retreated.

"Cork City. I had an auntie who lived here. Nice memories of coming here in summer."

"It's a bit different at this time of year, I imagine."

She smiled; the first time he had seen her do so. He felt his heart leap. "I also forgot quite how strong the smell of horse droppings can get on that main street.

Isn't it funny the things we leave out of our memories of people and places?"

"This is the first time I've ever been this far away from Dublin."

She laughed. "Really? Ah sure, why would you leave. You Dubs all think it's the center of the world."

"You came there, too."

"I did. Cork wasn't big enough for me, as a young girl. I wanted more glamour and more excitement."

"Did you get it?"

She met his eyes. "I wouldn't put it quite like that, no."

"He obviously wants you back an awful lot; to try to do it this way."

"Without force, you mean?"

He nodded.

"He likes owning things. People are just things to him. He owns me. He owns you, too. Some things you have to be gentle with. So he's being gentle with me. If I keep running, we'll see how long his gentleness lasts."

"How did you meet him?"

"I worked in one of his pubs. He saw me. I was impressed by all the money and all the power. People act differently around him, like he's a king—you must have seen it, too—and I was young and foolish and impressed. He made me feel special. He is very clever. He doesn't care about people but he knows how to manipulate them. Until you see what he is. I've seen what he is. I can't un-see it, I can't pretend. He can't manipulate me anymore, so here I am and here you are, Mr. Conlon."

"And what happens now, Miss?"

"Well that depends on you."

"No, it depends on you. I'll go back in a day or two, with or without you."

"Will you?"

"I will. You don't get it. I'm not going to hurt you. I'm not going to force you. I'm just here to talk. Then I leave."

She was quiet a moment. "It's interesting. Why you? He has some real talkers working for him. They could sell you Spanish Flu if they wanted."

"Devereaux."

"Yes, that horrible man. But he chooses you. I don't understand."

Conlon shrugged.

She said, "Because you're normal? Decent? Did he think I'd be stupid enough to think that reflected well on him?"

"I doubt anyone has ever thought of you as remotely stupid, Miss. And—are you saying I can't talk?"

"Oh, you're doing fine, Mr. Conlon. But you know what I mean."

"Maybe he thought we'd get along."

"Maybe he did."

The waiter had returned with the wine. Conlon sipped it and pretended to approve, trying to ignore her amused grin.

"So you're a boxer. You punch other men in the face for a living."

He laughed. "Only when I can. A lot of the time I can only punch them in the body or their arms."

"Do you like it?"

He had honestly never considered it in those terms before. "I'm good at it. I like some aspects of it."

"When you were a little boy, stealing coal or whatever it was you Jackeens were up to, what did you want to do?"

He shook his head. "I had nothing in mind. I wanted to keep me ma safe and fed."

"Your ma? Is she still alive?"

"She is."

"And is punching men in their arms keeping her safe and fed?"

"It's helping, yeah. What about you. Glamour and excitement? What were you hoping for?"

"I don't really know. It's harder for a woman than a man."

"Even one who looks like you?"

"How do I look, Mr. Conlon?"

"You're the most beautiful woman I've ever seen."

Her cheeks flushed and she gave him a new look, then glanced away. She said, "My family had nothing. I stayed in school as long as I could but, then, it was work as a maid or a waitress or maybe in a shop, if I was lucky, or find a rich husband. Or get one of those jobs and find a husband I could actually love, then struggle through life for nothing, like my parents did."

"You're not going to marry Xavier?"

She laughed that bark again. "No, no. He has a wife already, though nobody ever sees her."

"And if he didn't?"

"No. But what else can I do? And he knows—he knows, damn him—that I'm getting used to these clothes, and fine food, and parties. It'd be hard to go back to living with my mam's friend in Oldtown."

"Do you love him?"

"No. But he treats me well, he does. I just can't look at him sometimes."

"Why?"

"You know the things he's done. Everybody knows. He treats me well but he's a monster. I can't forget that. I can't and I shouldn't allow myself to forget that, should I? It wouldn't be right. My mam and dad...they reared me to do the right thing. I know people might say that even being with a married man is wrong, I know that, but that's a little thing. But this...this would be about who I am and what I believe in. I couldn't do it. I have to remember what he is or I'll lose some part of myself. And I've done enough of that."

Conlon nodded. He could not take his eyes off her. He had never wanted anybody the way he wanted her. He felt a wash of emotion in him while she was speaking, like her words and the way they made him feel had surged over something within him, and he was changed afterwards.

"That's why you ran away," he said, surprised to hear his voice sounding just as it always did.

She nodded. "It's so seductive, living that life. I can read all day. I've read more books in the last six months than in the rest of my life up to now. Go shopping, go to galleries, the theatre, eat in nice restaurants. I only see him once or twice a week. The rest of the time is my own. I had to get away. If only to think, if only to see things from a different perspective."

"A Clonakilty perspective?"

She laughed and so did he.

"I just ran. Cork." She said that last word with a shrug, her accent never more pronounced.

"Are your parents still alive?"

"No. My father died when I was nine. My mam died last year. I have aunties and uncles and too many cousins to count, though, so I always have a bed in Cork City."

"It's not really a city, is it..."

"Here we go. Snobby, sniffy Dubs, always up your-selves. It's the true capital."

They laughed again.

"Where are you from, then, Dub?"

"Stoneybatter."

"Ah, so should I start on the Northside, then? That usually gets a Dub going."

They were laughing again when their food arrived, presented with a hushed solemnity by their waiter, and then they were silent for a few moments. He dared not look at her now but he was intensely aware of the musical clink of her knife and fork against her plate and the whisper of her glass on the tablecloth.

She was the one to break the silence. "So, you know who he is. You know the things he has been responsible for. And here you are anyway. You seem like a good person. So why? How do you justify it to yourself? What do you tell yourself?"

"I don't think about it. I show up at the odd party and smile and shake hands. This is the most I've ever had to do with him and this won't happen again."

"So why say yes to this? Were you that desperate to see Cork?"

"Honestly...I thought it'd be helping you."

She laughed with delight. "You thought you'd come and save me?"

"No. It's like you said: he's being gentle. I'm the gentle. I thought if I could talk you around, then you wouldn't have to experience what happens when gentle doesn't work."

She was looking at him with sad eyes that were impossibly blue.

"That's not a threat, you know? He won't give up. You belong to him. Either you keep running, so far that he can't find you, or, eventually, you'll be back there, one way or another."

"I know. I know that. Thank you, Thomas."

He nodded. Thomas. "So what are you going to do?"

"I don't know."

They were silent again, eating.

"What are you going to do?"

"I'll give it another day, then I'll head back to civilization."

She laughed. "I've never heard Stoneybatter called that before."

———

THAT NIGHT, he could not sleep. Her face appeared before him each time he closed his eyes and he went over and over the things she had said, hints at her past. He had never met anybody remotely like her. He was planning things to say to her, ways to make sure that he saw her tomorrow, how to make her laugh again. He was in love.

———

SHE APPROACHED HIM AT BREAKFAST. "Morning, Thomas. Would you like to be my chaperone on a trip to the beach today? It's a fine day for it."

He looked outside through the window as a way to stall her. The winter sun had that fake smile look to it, overcompensating for the chill wind streaming down Main Street with an unusually strident light.

"Where is this beach?"

"Not far. We can walk there."

"All right, yes."

"I'll meet you in the lobby at eleven."

She had arranged a picnic basket from somewhere and he carried it as they strolled along the road toward the coast. The sun was bright but the wind off the sea was forceful and had teeth whenever they were not sheltered by hedgerow. Both wore heavy coats; she had donned a scarf and a heavier hat than the one she had sported the day before. She wore gloves but he had forgotten his and had to change hands every five minutes or so as the cold eroded his grip.

They were talking as they walked. Not the serious personal conversation of dinner but the easy chat of people who were comfortable together. He realized he had rarely felt quite so happy. Talking as they walked made the time disappear. He looked around as they crested a hill and saw that the sea was on both sides of them.

She said, "It's a headland. Inchydoney. At high tide, the very tip gets cut off and becomes an island."

There were a few ugly squat houses, crouching and hidden behind the beginnings of dunes and gray stone walls. The inlets on either side of them were a rich dark blue and he could smell the sea now, strong and living. It reminded him, oddly, of Dublin.

Dunes rolled up and down, long grass stubbling them in patches, and they forged through.

On the beach, Orla took off her shoes, encouraging him to do the same. He looked around. They were alone. The sea stretched out to the horizon, the coast-line's green pulling away on either side. His life had never felt as remote to him. He pulled off his shoes and socks and rolled up his trouser legs slightly. She let out a giggle to see this. Harsh and cool, the sand felt pleasant beneath his toes. She was running toward the water, her shoes forgotten beside the picnic basket. He followed her.

———

LATER, they carried the basket back up over the dunes and laid out the blanket in a deep hollow. They were in the sun but out of the sea breeze. They ate ham sandwiches and apples and a little sponge cake. She had a bottle of stout and glasses, too, and, when they were finished, he lay back and enjoyed the feeling of the sun warming him. She sat up and fixed him with a look.

"I've enjoyed myself today, Thomas."

He squinted at her, the sun in his eyes. Her hat shaded her face but her hair was shining the way water will shine under sunrise, a shimmering, magical effect.

"So have I," he said, feeling the stupid inadequacy of his words and his own cowardice. "Thank you for inviting me, Miss."

"Thomas. Call me Orla."

"Orla. Thank you."

"Do you have to go back tomorrow?"

"I think I do. There's a difference between trying to persuade you and being on holiday."

She laughed. "Yes. Today felt like a holiday."

"Have you ever been on holiday?"

"With Francis. We went to Salthill. Never before that."

"We'd go to the beach for a day when I was a boy. Loughshinny was my favorite, but it took so long to get there, we'd leave at dawn. Usually Clontarf."

"Northsiders never want to leave the Northside, hah?"

"Sure, why would we?"

She laughed again. She had laughed many times today and each time it had given him goosebumps. He never wanted to stop making her laugh.

They were silent for a moment and he could feel her eyes on him. He liked that, too. He said, "You know I don't want to go back. If every day could be just like today, that would be just fine. That would be lovely."

He didn't look at her.

"It would be," she said. "It would be lovely."

———

THEY HAD dinner again that night, and though they talked and laughed and stayed there until the waiting staff could no longer hide their impatience, there was a strain between them now. A new tension. He could feel it even if he was unable to articulate what it was or why it had slipped between them.

He escorted her to the door of her room. There she turned to say goodnight and leaned in to kiss him on the cheek. He could smell her, the rose sweetness of her perfume, the warmth of her hair. Her lower back was soft beneath his fingers.

In the morning, she was waiting for him in the lobby. Packed. Ready to leave.

"What are you doing?"

"I'm coming with you. You win. You've persuaded me."

And, in that moment, his first impulse was to shake his head and tell her no, Xavier did not deserve her and she herself deserved so much better, and he would rather see her free and happy...but he was selfish. He only thought that it meant he would get to spend more time with her. And there was the prospect of seeing her in Dublin, even if only fleetingly.

All he said was: "Are you sure?"

"I'm sure."

———

THERE WAS A SHYNESS, then, between them. It lasted through a rushed breakfast and all the way on the train from Clonakilty to Cork. They chatted a little waiting on the platform at Cork Station. She recalled a few incidents from her youth but, even then, he felt she was almost performing for him. The balance kept tilting one way or the other and it felt as if neither of them really knew how to keep it stable.

When the Dublin train pulled in, they realized it was composed of small cabins with four seats facing each other. They sat on either side and shared the cabin with an old lady until Charleville. When she got off, the silence that her presence had ensured remained.

At Thurles, a young couple looked to enter the cabin and he found himself silently willing them not to, to stay out, find another cabin. He wanted these last minutes with her, alone, even if they sat in silence. They chose another cabin and he and Orla shared a glance. Relief, he thought.

A few moments later, he mustered up his courage and asked her, "Will I see you again? In Dublin?"

"Would you like to?"

She was looking at him with those blue eyes, eyes that were so deep and pitiless.

"Yes. Yes. I can't imagine not seeing you again."

She made a face as if she were about to cry then covered her mouth to hide it.

"What?" he said. "Are you all right?"

"Oh, Thomas Conlon, you are a fool."

"What? Why?"

"Did you think I didn't remember you? When you walked into the hotel restaurant? I remember you. I remember when we met in McClean's. I remember the way you looked at me and the way it made me feel just to see your face."

"I... I thought—"

"Because I wanted you to think that. What if somehow Francis knew about that and sent you to use it somehow. I had to be sure."

"I'm sorry."

"Why are you sorry? You weren't to know. I'm a good liar. But it was hard. I remember seeing you at that party, in the theatre. Stupid party. I felt so ashamed, so ashamed, that you knew what I was now, what I'd done."

"You didn't need to feel ashamed. I was happy just to see you."

"Oh Thomas, stop, stop saying things like that."

"No. No, I won't. I said yes to this job because it was you. It meant I could talk to you and maybe I'd never get that chance again, so I had to say yes. And I'm so glad I did."

She laughed and then she did cry. He stood and moved over to sit beside her and put one arm around her shoulders and took her hand in the other. She leant her head into his shoulder and wept and then they were silent for a few minutes, both thinking, calculating what this all meant, what might come next.

Her voice was small when next she spoke, fragile and unsure. "So. You understand why I've come back. Not for him or because I'm afraid. I could run. But then I wouldn't see you again, ever again. And I can't imagine that, Thomas. So I've come back for you. Even if I only see you once in a month, at least I'll see you and be near to where you are. I'll read about your fights in the papers and hear people say your name. I'll be where you're from. And that will be enough for me."

"Orla," he said. And kissed her.

5

McPHAIL AND HIS PALS STOPPED OFF AT A NEWSAGENTS on Fleet Street. Conlon tagged faithfully along on the other side of the road. What his plan of action was he had not yet quite decided. It depended on where they went and what they did.

McPhail was definitively the leader of the group, striding at the front down the streets, bestowing remarks out of the corner of his mouth, nodding, and cocking his head in response to the comments of the others.

There was a part of Conlon that just wanted to take the direct approach. There was always that part, urging him to abandon subtlety and charge at any obstacle head-on and trust in the power of brute force. But he had learned not to heed it except when he could reason that it was the most effective option. And right now, he knew that he needed more information. He wasn't sure what McPhail's part in all this was or what use he could be. So he needed to wait, and watch, and poke around.

And if an opportunity presented itself, at some point, be ready to step in.

They crossed College Green then headed up Grafton Street, turning off to eat oysters in the Dive. Conlon went into Davy Byrnes, ordered a pint, and nursed it near the window, where he could watch them laughing, heads back, McPhail's lips always, always moving, the others nodding along in perpetual agreement. How much he had missed Dublin pubs when he was in France and now, already, he was taking them for granted, barely noticing the people in here, the snatches of conversation which fell his way, the rich scent of oats and wine.

They went next door into the Duke and Conlon had finished his drink and eaten a corned beef sandwich by the time they emerged to a sky beginning to darken. They crossed Grafton Street and headed southwest, up Camden Street, before eventually disappearing into a house not far from the canal in Portobello.

He followed them all the way. The Duke was interesting—it had long been a meeting place for Republicans, and he wondered if this had been their reason for visiting. Gun-running, BOD had said. He remembered conversations with Podge about gun-running from years before. Podge had had friends in the Brotherhood then. He had been the most political of them, the only one who would spend time pontificating about a free Ireland, who hated Brits, who prayed for the cause. Conlon had a sick feeling in his stomach as all these thoughts began to coalesce into something in his head.

A link or the vague beginnings of one.

He could not stand outside the house and keep watch so he did laps around the block. An hour or so had passed when one of McPhail's friends left. Conlon saw the chance he'd been waiting for and followed him.

He was a young man but built like a farmer—wide at the shoulders and chest—and he carried himself heavily, without guile, long strides giving him a slight dip in his walk. He walked back through town and across the Liffey. The atmosphere had changed with the fall of night. It always did in Dublin, which was a nocturnal city if ever there was one. Conlon loved it after dark. For all the threat and the violence, it was his.

They saw none of that tonight. It felt like a nice stroll across the city on a clear, temperate evening. The pools of gaslight on corners had always excited him as had the squares of light in windows and the brightness of the shops—it made the city feel grander somehow, a shining palace with secrets and hidden beauty around every corner. But shadows, too. That was the Dublin he knew—a city of shadows and whispered conversations in alleyways and hushed gardens. Plots in the darkness, forbidden love, the hunter, and the hunted.

The young man kept a steady pace, eventually coming to a house on Bolton Street. As he climbed the steps to the front door, Conlon made his decision and his move. He was on him at the door as he struggled with his keys.

"How's it goin'?" he said.

The man jumped and his eyes went wide. "Who the fuck are you?"

"I just want a little chat."

The man had kept at the door and, now, it swung heavily open, away from them.

Grasping his arm near the softness of the elbow, Conlon asked him, "Is there anyone else inside the house?" He gave the arm a hard squeeze and the man shook his head sharply.

"Let's go in, then." He gestured into the hall and the man warily half-stumbled inside. Conlon closed the door behind them and for a second, in the darkness, they regarded one another.

"What do you want?" the man asked him.

"Just to ask you a few questions. Get a lamp going, will you."

"You don't have a gun..." the man said, incredulously.

His face changed like a little boy's; a sullen anger suddenly seizing it. He reared himself up, like a bull, and took a few steps across the hall toward Conlon. Conlon realized that the man had only co-operated because he had assumed that Conlon was armed. Now that he saw that he was not, he was determined to take control of the situation. He was about a foot taller than Conlon and probably two stone heavier. Conlon watched him come, adjusted his feet in an instant then hit him once, a straight right to the nose. The man went over backwards, crying out, and then lay curled up cradling his face on the floor, moaning in pain.

Conlon left him there for a moment, lit a lamp in the front room, fetched a towel from the kitchen, wet it in the sink then carried it to him. "Here. Your nose is broken; there'll be a lot of bleeding for a while. This'll help."

The man groped for the towel. Conlon helped him sit then pulled him up and steered him into the front room, where he melted into an armchair.

Dabbing at his face with the towel, he squinted at Conlon. "Who are you? What did I do to you?"

"You started that; you were charging at me. I just defended myself. But if you want to try again, this time I'll break your jaw. I said I just wanted to talk, didn't I?"

Instead of replying, the man let out a strangulated whimper. Conlon watched him in silence, allowing him to collect himself.

Finally, the man looked at him again. "What do you want to talk about?"

"McPhail."

"I've only been working for him for a few months. I don't really know anything."

"Some friends of mine have gone missing. I have a feeling he's involved. Does that sound like the kind of thing he's involved with?"

The big man shrugged. "Yeah? I dunno. He's got his fingers in a lotta pies. Gamblin', money-lending, protection...he does anything for a profit."

"Have you seen him kill anybody?"

The man looked at him almost pleadingly.

"I'm not Dublin Metropolitan, man. I'm not going to have you arrested."

"I know he's been involved in things like that. I haven't been around it yet. He carries a gun at his ankle and a knife on his belt and I've seen him cut a man up fucking bad, like he was a rabbit, just slashin' his chest to bits...but I haven't seen him kill anyone. That man survived."

"He runs guns for the rebels."

"Yeah, but he keeps that really quiet. Even he knows not to fuck with them."

"Is that why you were in the Duke earlier?"

The man nodded, his eyes wide.

"Give me a name. Who does he deal with on the rebels' side? Who's his contact?"

"Somebody he calls the Long Man."

"Cormac Long?"

"That's it, yeah. I've never met him."

Conlon nodded. He knew Long. That was good.

"That house in Portobello—he lives there?"

"Yeah. He's got another place out in Monkstown but he spends most of his nights there all right." He shook his head. "He's gonna kill me when he finds out I talked to you."

Conlon shrugged. "Don't tell him. That would be in both of our interests, wouldn't it? If I was you, I'd give McPhail a miss for a while. I've a feeling his life is about to get a lot more complicated. You got anywhere to go he won't know about?"

"Yeah, home."

"Where's that?"

"Mayo."

"Go. Leave in the morning. Don't come back for a while. You don't seem like you're able for this kind of thing."

The man nodded and hung his head. This was plainly not how he had expected this evening to play out. The towel Conlon had given him was saturated with blood and from his nostrils to his lips stretched a red stain that looked like an odd, crazed moustache.

"One more thing," Conlon said.

"Aye."

"You ever heard the names Sean Murray or Podge O'Riordan?"

"I hear a lot of names, Mister."

"I know. They're not familiar?"

"Maybe? But I can't say for sure, I'm sorry."

Something had been thrumming in his head for a few moments and he realized just then what it was; "What's his address—in Monkstown?"

"Tivoli Terrace. I don't know the number. Second house from the corner."

"Tivoli Terrace."

"That's it."

"Right. You ok? You need a doctor for that nose?"

"No, no, it hurts like fuck but I'll be all right."

"Right. I'm going. Remember, get out of here for a while."

———

FEARFULLY, George answered the door to him this time. "Tommy! Jesus, she wasn't lying!"

They shook hands and pulled off a sort of half embrace, arms on one another's shoulders, then withdrew at the same time. Conlon felt genuinely moved to see his old friend. And life with Theresa was evidently good for George, who looked as if he had not aged a minute in the years since they had last seen one another.

"Come in, come in!"

"I can't George, it's late and I've already bothered that wife of yours enough today."

"Ah don't be stupid, Tommy, come in for God's sake."

"I promised me ma I wouldn't be too late back."

He wanted to go in; he wanted to see her again and, for that very reason, he was determined not to.

George threw up his hands at that. "How is your ma?"

"She's very well, thanks for asking. How is yours? I was hoping I'd see her this morning."

"She's grand, she was upset not to see you, too. She always had a soft spot for you, Tommy, you know that."

"Well tell her I was asking for her, George, would you?"

"I will of course. And the same to yours, Tommy."

Conlon nodded. They looked at one another and he picked up the wariness in George's eyes, this time, feeling an edge of irritation that he had initially missed it.

"You know why I'm here, George?"

"I was hoping you were here to see me?"

"I am. And we'll go for a pint soon, I swear."

George nodded, head down. He seemed unable to meet Conlon's eyes now.

"Where are they, George?"

"I don't know, Tommy, I swear to God. I don't know."

"What do you know?"

George shrugged. "They wanted to invest some of the money. Sean—Sean knew somebody who would give it to the rebels somehow. I'm not sure, I swear to God."

"Who did he know?"

"I don't know. Once I heard what they were doing I kept out of it. I was just married; she'd kill me, wouldn't she. They were all right with that; they didn't slag me off about it or anything. I think they were buying guns."

"Why do you think that?"

"I'm not sure, like, but just some of the things they said. Things I picked up, Tommy, you know. There was definitely a delivery coming in. I had the feeling they were paying for it. It was a lot of money, wasn't it?"

"It was. Where's your share?"

"Most of it's gone. The rest is for a rainy day."

They looked at one another in silence and Conlon accepted it there and then; his friends were dead. He would never see them again. He reached out and put his hand on George's shoulder, letting him know that it was all right, that he was not to blame.

George hung his head and peered at him from underneath his brow. "I wasn't sure you'd ever come back."

Conlon held his hands out, palms upwards. "Neither was I, but I did. Here I am."

"What are you going to do? For money?"

"I still have some left. I'll find work, I'm sure. First, I'm going to find out what's happened to the boys."

George nodded.

"Is there anything else—any detail—you can tell me? Anything at all could help. It doesn't matter how minor it seems."

George shook his head faintly, eyes distant then focused and said: "They used to talk about a house in the East Wall."

"The East Wall. Sure?"

"Yeah. They had to go there a few times. Always went a bit funny when they talked about it in front of me."

"All right, thanks. I'll let you know what I find."

"Yeah, do, please." He looked lost for a moment. "It was hard, Tommy, without you. I knew something was wrong but what could I do? What could I do?"

"You couldn't do anything. I probably couldn't've either. It's all right, George. It's life. Bad things happen and, sometimes, you just have to watch."

George nodded glumly. Conlon offered his hand and they shook warmly.

"I'll see you soon," Conlon said.

"You will." George said, sadness a shade in his voice. "You will."

———

HE WENT HOME AFTER THAT. His ma had made a coddle for him and, as it always had, it transported him straight back to his childhood even before he had tasted it—the first tentacles of its smell as he opened the front door and moved up the hall into the warmth of the living room. It sat still cooking in the pot over the lowest of flames. He killed the flame and ladled some onto a plate. He had dreamt of this in France, this feeling: the smell rising up to his nose in steamy ribbons then, the actuality of the peppery flavor. There was brown bread, too, and he mopped up plenty of the broth with it then sat alone in the kitchen, the women sleeping upstairs, mulling things over.

For all his feelings about what had happened, he wasn't sure how that affected what he would have to do. He would still have to find proof that Podge and Sean were dead. But he knew that they were. He had known since the first day back. He had felt it in his gut; a turning, tightening feeling of unease. And while he felt complicit somehow—as if his being here would have had any influence on the outcome—he was not sure what his next step would be.

But he had a vague feeling that it would involve him having to hurt some people. And deep down, a part of him was excited at that prospect. Whoever had done this had killed his friends. He didn't have many friends and he would make them pay for it.

———

CORMAC LONG WAS a hard man to find. That hadn't always been the way. Only a handful of years before, he could always be found in one pub or other, falling off a stool, raging about politics.

But now, he had risen sharply in the Brotherhood or the IRA or whatever Rebel faction he was in these days and his name would be known at Dublin Castle, placing him on watch lists at the very least. More likely, Castle spies watched his every breath, had his friends under surveillance, and basically haunted his every moment. So he lived partly in the shadows, always on the move, people guarding him and watching his back.

Conlon understood all of this the first time he asked for Long in one of the old pubs he had frequented. People denied all knowledge of him or his whereabouts. By the time he got to Shalvey's, Conlon was getting grumpy. The barman said he didn't know him—which Conlon knew was a lie—and he felt something alter in the room's chemistry. There was a shift as if the air in the room had changed. People were watching him now and other people were watching the people watching him and everybody knew something was about to happen.

It was a small pub. One room, basically, and he turned to look at the two men who had stood.

"I don't want any trouble, lads."

"Why would ye be asking for Cormac, then, eh?"

They took a step toward him. One had a hand in his

pocket. Conlon was calculating whether that would be a blade or brass knuckles or a blackjack.

"I know him."

"We don't know you. How would he?"

"He had a life before he joined the cause."

One of them had a thick Northern accent, the other was a Dub. Like most of the members of what had been called the Volunteers and now seemed to be the IRA, Conlon knew, his accent suggested that he hadn't come from the slums but was a bit more well-off, probably educated by the Christian Brothers, perhaps even University. Conlon felt that bitter thought rise up in him and washed it away. Focus.

Conlon focused on him. "My name is Tommy Conlon. I knew him."

The Dub looked at the barman. "That name mean anthin' to ye?"

The barman nodded. "Aye, he was a boxer."

"That you?" the Northern Irishman asked.

"Yeah."

"British Army, I heard," the barman said.

Conlon looked at him as if to say help me out here. The barman shrugged.

"I don't want to fight you," Conlon said.

"Sure, what would a British soldier want with Cormac? You've been asking in pubs all day, we're told."

"I'm not a soldier anymore."

One of them was edging sideways.

"Did you get promoted?"

Conlon was running out of patience. He dropped the conciliatory tone and let hardness come into his face. "Stop moving sideways. You think if you flank me, you can both come at me at once." He nodded at the

Dub. "But you'll still be closer. I'll break your nose first. Then you—" he looked at the Northern Irishman "—Your head goes into the bar."

The two men laughed but there was doubt and nervousness in the laughter.

Conlon said to the room: "Did anyone here ever see me fight?"

An old man sat near the door said, "I did, a few times."

"Was I good?"

"You were, son." He spoke to the other two. "Fastest I've ever seen. Punch on him like a bleedin' hammer."

Conlon said, "Don't be stupid here. I'm not a fucking spy. I'm an Irishman and, yeah I was in the Army, but I never fought Irishmen. I'm looking for Cormac. I just need to talk to him. If you want to fight me, then the only way you win is if one of you has a gun."

"You're so sure?"

"I am. It's the only thing I'm good at. So let's sit down like men and talk. I don't want to fight."

The men looked at each other. The Dub nodded. They started to walk backward and gestured toward the table they had just left. Conlon moved in the same direction, all three of them watching one another, eyes flicking from face to face.

Conlon said, "I'm going to need to have my back against the wall here, boys. You understand. This being your turf, these being your friends."

The Dub nodded again and indicated the chair against the wall. Conlon edged sideways toward it. He let them sit first then he lowered himself into the chair.

There was still silence in the barroom and they sat

for a moment before the Dub said, "Will you have a pint?"

"I will, yeah, thanks."

"A pint for the boxer, Bren," he called over his shoulder. At that, people turned away and began to talk again.

"I'm kind of jumpy, now," the Dub said to nobody in particular. "Thought there was gonna be a fight there. Me blood's up."

Conlon nodded. "Feel like you need to do something now, don't you?"

"I do. Like run up and down the stairs or beat the shite out of some fucker or ride me mot. Do you feel the same?"

"Yeah. Have to learn to control that, use it. Makes you skittish otherwise. Then you'll be knackered later."

The Dub nodded. There was silence between them for a minute. The barman brought Conlon's drink. He took a long, slow mouthful.

"So, what do you want with Cormac?" the Northern Irishman said.

"He's a busy man nowadays. Maybe we can help instead," said the Dub.

"I believe he's doing business with a man who might have something to do with a few of my friends disappearing."

"Why don't you just ask this man about your friends, then?"

"He's not the kind of man who would be happy about a chat like that."

"You don't seem to be the kind of man who would be worried about what anybody else thinks."

"When I say 'chat', I mean the kind of chat one of us doesn't walk away from."

The two men laughed and, after a second, Conlon joined them.

"This man..." the Northern Irishman said, "What's his name?"

"McPhail."

They exchanged a look.

"You know him," Conlon said.

"Never met him. He's around though."

"I'm not sure what that means. If he's the man I'm after, am I going to have trouble with you boys?"

The Dub looked glum. "You might all right. You probably do need to talk to Cormac."

They all drank.

The Dub said, "You think he was involved in your friends disappearing, you said."

"Yeah."

"You think he killed them."

"I think they're dead. I think he was involved."

"Who were they?"

"Nobody. They had some money, which I think he wanted. Does that sound like the man you know?"

"It sounds like what I've heard of him, aye," The Northern Irishman said. "He likes blood, I've heard. Got a bad temper. Not a pleasant combination unless you're a fighting dog."

The Dub said, "I'll have a word." He went to the bar and came back with a piece of paper with a phone number scribbled on it. "Call this number later on. Ask for Gene. We'll give you a time and a place. Or, if Cormac doesn't want to, we won't. Either way, you'll have an answer."

"If I don't get a time and a place, how's that an answer?"

"Well if that's what happens, you need to understand that McPhail is useful to us."

"And if I need to deal with him?"

"Then you can consider yourself a traitor to the new Irish Republic."

"There is no new Irish Republic," Conlon said, standing.

"There will be, pal. Wait and see."

6

THE DUB HAD BEEN RIGHT; CONLON LEFT THE PUB WITH his blood raging within him, the need for action and exertion burning in his chest. He stood in the sunlight in the street outside, feeling like he did not belong around these people. Like he should be in a cage.

Control it. Remember the Major's words. Breathe. Breathe. Focus. Use it. He could not just wait to make a phone call. He needed to do something. He needed to be moving. He needed to be involved, and trying, and to keep his mind active. The part of him telling him to go back into the bar now and tear them apart—he had to ignore that. Use that anger. Direct it. Focus.

Taking the notebook he had lifted from Sean's place out of his pocket, he looked at the four addresses. The Monkstown one had to be McPhail's other house. He would hold back on that. The others were Crumlin, the East Wall, and Glasnevin.

A tram was passing at that moment, the 19, and, without really thinking, he trotted along and swung himself on at the back. The pole he grabbed was warm and greasy from other hands. The tram was busy, a saloon filled with people, heads and hats bobbing and swaying as the vehicle moved them through the streets. He was feeling better already. He paid the conductor and watched the city, Phibsboro—which he knew well —reel by, and then they were on the edge of Glasnevin.

Houses had been built here since he had last visited as a boy, coming to the Botanic Gardens with his ma. Then it had lain on the edge of the little village, only the huge cemetery and the countryside beyond. He remembered the greenhouses had seemed immense to him; the musty smell of them was like the jungle was in the air itself. And Glasnevin had been quaint to his inner-city eyes; big houses and cottages, trees on wide roads, the sky blue above. Now, lines of tall new redbricks stretched off the main road. New trees had been planted. It was disorienting; how much his city was changing, growing. But it was exciting, too.

He jumped off the tram in the center of the village and had to ask a man in a bowler hat for directions. It was one of the new houses, down a street that had not even existed a few years ago. He walked past once. The curtains were drawn. Some of the other houses were not yet occupied and, about a hundred meters away, more still were being built, a din of banging and activity carrying on the light breeze down the street to him. He turned around. Focus.

He walked up and knocked on the door, still unsure of what he would say, how he would proceed. A man answered the door, wearing only a shirt and trousers, his bare feet making him appear instantly vulnerable. Conlon recognized him and, for an instant, he groped for the identity of this man. He was middle-aged, balding, his dark hair greased flat to his head, and he had what looked like a large purple stain across his chin and mouth—a birth mark. As soon as he saw Conlon, the man was backpedaling, alarmed, calling out. Another man appeared in the hall behind him, his voice loud, and they grappled there for a moment. He was wearing a suit, his hat in one hand.

Conlon was trying to understand what was happening. He took a tentative step forward, his foot in the doorway. Both men were moving back into shadows of the house. Conlon saw the one who had answered the door pointing at him, his face a desperate, contorted mess. Both of the men were shouting at one another. And he remembered.

Donegal. This was one of the men who had found them. This was the one who had pulled the trigger. And the man's response made perfect sense. He was afraid Conlon had come for him, for revenge. And, suddenly, he forgot why he had come, what he was doing there. He forgot Podge and Sean and McPhail and the money and the guns and all he wanted was to be standing over that man—the Birthmark—with blood on his fists.

Conlon moved forward into the house and the man turn and ran. He saw the sudden flash of light as the back door burst open and the figure moving barefoot across the yard. The other one was between them, in the gloom of the backroom, and as Conlon entered, about to explode into a sprint of his own, he saw that the man was pointing a pistol at him.

Conlon stopped.

"What the fuck? Who the hell are you?" the man asked.

"This has got nothing to do with you. This is personal. Me and him."

"Sit down a minute. Let him go." The man's nerves were jangled. His speech was rapid. He stammered, the gun shaking in his hand.

"Mister, I don't know you. Don't do this. I need to get—"

"I don't fucking care what you need. He's one of our boys, no way I'm goin't' let you beat the fuck out of him. Sit down!"

One of our boys? "You work for Xavier?"

"Sit down!" He shouted it.

Conlon said, "That's not going to happen. My name's Tommy Conlon. You might have heard of me. If you think you can shoot me before I can cover two steps across this room to make you eat that fucking gun, then let's see how that goes." He moved straight across the room toward the man, light on his feet, ducking as he went.

In the end, the man tried to pistol-whip him. It was hard, pulling the trigger that first time, Conlon knew. He came up from his dodge under the swing and, for a second, he was distracted by movement on the stairs near the door to the kitchen. That gave the man time enough to clip him with a clumsy punch.

Conlon was on him though, and one punch threw him back into the fireplace, blood flicking in a neat fan shape across the mirror over the block range. Conlon went for the gun hand then, smashing the wrist into the mantelpiece. The gun clattered onto the floor and then another man was on him from behind; the movement he had glimpsed on the stairs—an arm around his neck, a hand at his elbow. Conlon went with it for an instant to give himself space and then he speared a kick into the gunman's groin. His scream was like a guffaw and he doubled up as Conlon butted backwards, his head connecting with the nose of the one behind. Conlon wrenched himself loose and turned in the same movement. This one was younger, Conlon's age perhaps. He raised his fists and Conlon recognized some training in the stance and in the way his feet moved. But he had no time for this so Conlon shook his head and moved straight at him, throwing a rapid, brutally destructive three punch combination that left the man on the ground, blood and teeth slipping between his lips.

Conlon bent, picked up the gun, and followed Birthmark through the kitchen and into the yard. There were three walls and Conlon pulled himself up to look around. Identical yards stretched left and right, a series of red brick walls jutting up one after another like dominos, the backs of houses impassive in front of him. Birthmark could have gone anywhere, in any direction, could be out on the street and running, or crouched down only feet away, hiding. Already, there was no sign of him. Conlon lowered himself down slowly, hearing his own breathing thick through his nostrils. He forced himself to slow down. Relax. Focus. Another time, he thought. He's in Dublin, working for Xavier; it's not that big a city. It's just a matter of time.

Funny to feel so terrible about missing out on something you didn't even know you wanted ten minutes before.

He went back inside. The gunman was getting to his feet; the other one was still down, moaning almost imperceptibly. Conlon sat in the armchair by the door and looked at the older man who was still protectively shielding his groin. The man looked back at Conlon, his eyes drawn to the gun in his hand, the one he had already forgotten he was holding.

"Howya," Conlon said. He leaned forward and put the gun in his waistband at the small of his back. Sitting there, watching this man look at him with fear in his eyes, feeling the cold hard shape of the pistol press against his kidney, he felt sadness swoop in low over him—that this was his life. Memories of bright moments with Orla blossomed in his head for an instant. That was what Birthmark had taken from him. But there was a point to all this, he remembered. It meant something.

"So this is a safehouse, is it?" he asked the man who was now sitting against the wall by the fireplace.

"Yeah, yeah."

"Somewhere Xavier's soldiers come when they've nowhere else."

The man nodded. The other one was starting to sit now, dragging himself tortuously into a semi-upright position, a crimson delta across his face and chest.

"See, I'm not here for you. I wasn't even here for him." He nodded out at the backyard. "I just want to know if this place is ever used for anything else."

"No. Men sleep here. That's it."

"That's it?"

"That's all I know. It's a new house. But as long as it's been ours, that's what it's used for."

"All right. You've been very helpful. I assume our friend who runs for his life at the sight of an unarmed man has spent more time here than either of you?"

The men nodded.

"What's his name?"

"Rossa."

"Rossa. Thank you."

He stood up, again conscious of the gun against his back.

The one with the napkin of blood dribbled at him, "Xavier is gonna kill you for this. You don't know who you're dealing with."

Conlon said, "Ah, but I do. And he's tried to kill me already. Maybe, if I'm lucky, he'll send one of you next time, eh?" He laughed and stepped into the hall, then turned back and looked at the man again. "Tell Finch Tommy Conlon says hello. Tell him exactly what I said. See you around, lads."

––––––––

HE HAD to walk back into the city. Blood felt as if it was surging around his head in thick lines. He could hear his own pulse, like a wave rising and falling in him every few minutes. Energy was still coursing through him, and he recognized these symptoms—times in France when attacks had been postponed, when there had been shelling but his unit had been absolutely unscathed. Then, he felt something like this: like his body had responded to the stress and then the nature of the situation had altered, only he had not altered, not one little bit. It meant that he had to pretend that everything was fine while his body was prepared to run mile after mile, fight man after man after man, and he just had to smile through it and pretend it wasn't so.

This was worse, somehow. He wasn't at the front, surrounded by hundreds of men who understood. No, he was in the city, passing plumbers and postmen and cooks—none of whom had a clue—walking with his head down, feeling increasingly desperate.

If Birthmark had wandered into the street in front of him now, Conlon had no doubt that he would be unable to restrain himself and he would kill the man. For a moment, he lost himself in a twilight of memory and daydream: his fists swinging, ribbons of blood in the air, the soft sound pulverized flesh made beneath his knuckles.

The Major had been an educated man and fond of sharing his erudition. Conlon recalled a conversation when the man had identified his fury and explained how he could use it. He talked about bear cults and warriors in Germany and Scandinavia who fought the Romans with Bear hoods on their heads. He talked about the Viking berserkers who would become so frenzied and maddened during battle that they were virtually invulnerable and would kill dozens of enemy soldiers, only to find themselves weakened and placid afterwards. As a proud son of Ulster, he talked about Cuchulain and Ríastrad, when his eye would pop out of his head and even his hair became a spiked weapon and opponents fell in swathes. But through all of this, he stressed control and discipline and channeling these feelings. How Conlon was a weapon and, if pointed in the right direction, a brilliantly effective one.

He never spoke about how Conlon was to deal with these feelings when they came upon him back home, in the street, on a sunny afternoon. He never mentioned this was even a possibility. The Major was not the type to give much thought to the civilian world. He believed he was born for war and he took little else so seriously. Although Conlon had loved the man, and appreciated his guidance and protection, he had been relieved to escape him and his smothering world. Only now did he realize that a part of him missed it. He missed the attention and the assumption that he was special, missed the way other soldiers looked at him, the aura being one of the Major's boys bestowed.

Conlon looked up. He was near the Quays now, he had walked all the way in a sort of trance, wrestling with himself. He did not know what he could do, what he needed. He felt lost.

———

SHE ANSWERED the door and he saw surprise give way to something else within an instant, before she had even spoken.

"Tommy, are you all right?"

"Theresa, I'm sorry, I'm sorry—is George in?"

"He's on tonight. You don't look well. Come in, come in."

"No, no, it's—"

"Come in and no more arguing."

She ushered him inside and into an armchair and, within a few minutes, he had a cup of tea in his hand. She sat across from him, quietly waiting for him to tell her what was wrong. She had only lit one lamp and the fire was low. Trying to save money, he knew, and he felt guilty for coming here. But then, seeing her face had made him feel better. Hearing her voice, being in this room with her; he felt calmer already. How could he explain that?

"I'm sorry," he said. "I didn't mean to put you in this position."

"What position? What happened? George won't tell me what you're up to, so I know it must be bad."

"I shouldn't have come, I'm sorry. I didn't know where to go."

"Stop apologizing. Why did you need to go anywhere? What happened?"

"I had a run-in with a lad I haven't seen in a while. It brought back bad memories."

"Always mysterious, Tommy."

"There's things I can't tell you, I'm sorry."

"I think there's things you need to tell somebody, Tommy. Who do you have to talk to?"

He shrugged. His friends were gone except for George. And their lives were so different; it was as if there was a wall between them now. And her. Her between them, not that George knew that. The boys from the unit. Dalton. Mossy. But they had never talked that way. Wilkins, Robson, Charles, Bright—they were all dead, too. So many of his friends were dead.

"Nobody," he said.

He did not look at her face then. He did not want her to pity him; he did not want to know that she felt this way about him.

"Well then, I 'spose that means you have to talk to me, doesn't it?"

He was silent. He would not be telling her about Orla, or the War, or the feeling of blood-lust that had overwhelmed him. But he could tell her about what he was doing. She was intelligent. She could perhaps see something he had missed.

"Did you ever meet Podge? Or Sean?" he asked her.

"No, but George mentioned them enough when we were first courting. Not for a while though."

"Podge is my best friend. I've known him since I can remember. We grew up together so, when I got back, he was the first person I went to see. But he was gone. He has a shop and I went there but he was gone, and the man working there now says he bought it off Podge. Then later, some lads are waiting to welcome me back to town and the only way they could have known that I'm even here is if he's told them."

"What does all that mean? They wanted to what? Batter you?"

"Yeah. But the point is, he told them I was here. He knows them, he has something to do with them."

"Who are they?"

"A gang. Criminals. Don't worry, George has never had anything to do with them."

"But you have?"

"Sort of. Boxing isn't the cleanest sport, Theresa."

"And why would they want to hurt you? What did you do?"

"I offended their boss."

"How? You called him a mean name? Jesus Mary and Joseph, you have lived an interesting life, Tommy."

"No. A woman...came between us."

"Ah." There was a light in her eyes at that.

"Anyway. So somehow, they're connected to Podge and wherever he's gone. So I go see Sean, only he's gone, too. And I ask around and there's a man been asking around about them. A gambler, but he's connected to the Brotherhood or the IRA, too. And I reckon somehow, they've gotten themselves involved with this man and this gang and they've ended up dead because of it."

"How would they have gotten involved? How does that happen?"

"Podge was a believer. Always political. I think they were buying guns."

"How could they do that?" Then her face changed. "The money."

"George told you about the money."

"Of course, he did. Would they have?"

"Maybe, I don't know. I don't know enough to do anything about any of it. It's all gaps and guessing and I fucking hate it—I beg your pardon."

She laughed. "This gambler—can you ask him? What's he like?"

"A bad man. When the time comes that I have to talk to him, that will probably be the last conversation one of us ever has. No, I need to figure it out myself."

She was silent then, alternately looking at him and off into the middle distance. Then she said, "You don't know that any of this has anything to do with your gang. Podge might have gone missing and they took the shop because it was free and easy to take it."

"I just visited a house that's belongs to that gang. I got the address out of a notebook in Sean's coat. There's a connection."

"Have you talked to anyone else that knows them? Other friends or family or something? Podge had a girl-friend, didn't he?"

"He did." This had never occurred to him.

"Did you speak to her?"

"I don't really know her."

"You don't really know what she might tell you, either."

"You're right. Thanks, that's a good idea."

She was looking at him coldly, frankly. "When you're finished."

"Yeah."

"What do you do then? What's the plan? If this gambler has...whatever he has done. What do you do with the information?"

He looked at her. Her eyes were shockingly green. He didn't want to stop looking at them.

"What do you think I should do?"

"Bring it to the law. Let the courts deal with them."

He rubbed his eyes. "That's...I've been obeying for too long. Doing what I'm told, bowing and scraping, running away, being a good little Irish boy. The world wants us to obey, poor people."

"Ah, none of your Socialist shite, Tommy—"

"No, no, no. I'm not political. I couldn't give a fuck, Theresa, they're all just men in suits to me. You hear so much shite in the trenches; socialism, communism, anarchists, libertarians—I couldn't be arsed with any of it. I just want to try to live my life. But one thing that I heard over and over that did make sense to me is that the world wants poor people—and that's most people, in this country, definitely, in this fucking city, you know it is, but it's the same in England, in France, too, probably in Germany and America, I don't know—the world wants us to bow our heads and do what we're told. Be happy with what we can get. Obey. Join up for King and Country. Get a job, pay taxes, send your chislers to school so they can learn the same shite you learned and learn to obey, too..."

She nodded solemnly. "I understand."

"Be happy you can get a few lumps of coal so you don't starve, you know? Be happy you could pick blackberries and make jam. Well, I'm sick of it. Other people in this country feel the same. Fighting the Brits—

fighting the Empire—that's the same thing. That's standing up and saying I won't do what I'm told anymore. And I can do that. I went off and I got better at the only thing I was any good at anyway. And it means I don't have to obey, sometimes. I can stand up and say fuck you. Pardon my language. But I can. And when I find out who killed my friends—and I know they're dead, I just know it—then I'm going to fucking kill them. Not let any judge or court decide anything. Sorry." He laughed weakly.

She was almost panting, her eyes shining and wet. "Tommy," she said.

"I'm sorry," he said. "You bring something out in me. I don't usually talk that much."

"Be careful. It's dangerous here now. If your friends disappeared and basically no-one noticed, what does that tell you? Anarchy indeed."

"I will be."

He drank his tea. She sat back and did the same. There was a faint sense of embarrassment between them at how intense the feeling had been a moment before.

She said, "You need a job, Tommy Conlon. You've too much free time. That head of yours is just buzzin' with all that thinking you're doing."

He laughed loud at this. No woman had ever made him laugh before, not like this. "You're probably right," he said.

"You'll find I'm always right."

"Nobody's always right."

"Wait and see."

"I will."

"Good."

They both looked away from one another then. Eye contact between them would have to be rationed, he realized. And knew, at the same instant, that he should be away from here, from her.

"I should be going," he said. "Thank you, for listening. I appreciate it."

"Anytime, really. You've no idea how exciting your life is to me."

"Is it?"

"It is."

They went to the door and he thanked her again—for the tea, for the advice. When he was outside, in the darkness of the landing, he turned back to her. She was silhouetted in the crack of the door, a pale light from within behind her, and he could not make out her features.

He said, "It's funny, Theresa. You say my life is exciting to you. But the most exciting part of my day has been seeing you. Bye."

He turned away quickly.

"Goodbye, Tommy," she called after him.

———

IT WAS dark now and he was crossing the street when he heard a voice call his name. He recognized the voice but, at that moment, could not place it. He turned around and searched the dark doorway shapes, looking under the unkempt trees. A figure leaned against railings across the road, a few doors from George's house. It was sloppy of him not to have noticed that. He was distracted, lost in his head, in the conversation with Theresa, in his feelings. That could not happen again.

He took a step toward the man against the railings, peering at the figure in the gloom. This man had chosen the spot furthest away from the lamps, a spot mostly darkened by the canopy shadows. It was a spot most conducive to violence, to illegality, he thought. Conlon was instantly ready, his blood starting to roar again. He suddenly connected the body language—the tight shoulders, the tilt of the head—with the voice he had heard a second before.

The man spoke again and confirmed it. "Hello, Tommy."

"Hello, Finch."

Conlon approached slowly. "You on your own?" he asked.

"I am. You expected a crowd?"

Conlon shrugged. "Might have seemed safer to you."

"We tried a crowd with you already. Didn't go that well."

Conlon stepped onto the path and stopped. There were perhaps ten feet between them. Finch had not changed. He had his hands in the pockets of his long coat, his hat perched near the back of his head, his eyes as flat and empty as a basilisk. A horse and cart clattered down the street behind Conlon, the driver chatting through a cigarette to a boy sat behind him. He and Finch kept their eyes on one another until it was gone.

"That a gun in that hand?" Conlon nodded at the right pocket of his coat, bulging slightly.

Finch laughed. "I almost forgot the way you are. You never miss a trick unless there's a woman in the picture." There was the slightest incline of his head toward George's door at that.

"I haven't forgotten you."

Finch nodded. "So, what are you doing, Tommy? Beating the shite out of those boys we sent to see you; that was almost understandable. That made us laugh, to be honest with you. But today, you bust up one of our safe houses? What the fuck are you doing, son?"

"I didn't know it was a safe house."

Finch guffawed without any humor. "So, what? That was a coincidence?"

"It was, yeah. I was there for another reason." Tommy could feel the gun, still in his belt.

"What reason was that?"

"A couple of my friends are missing. I'm trying to find them. I found the address in one of their things."

"Who are these friends? Maybe I can help."

"I doubt it. Did you think I wanted a war, Finch?"

"That had occurred to us, yeah. You might think you have reason."

"If I wanted a war, you'd already be dead. Xavier, too."

Finch said nothing for a moment, just looked at him. Tommy looked back.

"So if it was a coincidence," Finch eventually said, "Why'd you cause so much trouble?"

"The one with the birthmark—I remembered the face and it brought something out in me."

Dawning awareness on Finch's face. He had not known. Conlon could see him struggle for something to say. He had never seen Finch unsure before and it gave him immense satisfaction.

Conlon said, "Tell him: if I see him again, I'll kill him."

"I have no doubt you will. Hopefully, you won't see him again."

They were silent, watching one another. Finch began speaking and, as he did so, he took his hands from his pockets to help him gesture. Empty. The gun remained in his coat. He was signaling parlay.

"I wondered why you hadn't come for us, you know? You come back and you've obviously done some...difficult things over there. You've learned how to fight in different ways, but then you come back and it's like you don't care anymore. So then I thought maybe war had made you renounce violence. But that would be confused by your two scraps with our boys when you seem like you actually enjoy it. You hurt people in ways that are vindictive, I'd say. I know you're good enough that you don't need to so that tells me that there is a part of you that loves the violence, eh, a part of you that loves the power, maybe. And most people, I'm sure, would say that you must be aching to hurt us, too. So what is it, Tommy? What exactly is stopping you?"

"There are people here I care about. A war would hurt them. That doesn't mean I'll hesitate if you get in my way. Any of you."

"As long as you're not interfering with business, then we have no interest in you."

"He said that?"

"He did say that. Nobody should be getting in your way. If they do, then you're probably interfering with business. And that would be bad for everybody."

"Is he afraid of me, Finch?"

"He's not afraid of anything."

"Everybody's afraid of something."

"Oh yeah? What are you afraid of, Tommy?"

"It's already happened—you saw to that. How about you?"

"Maybe I'll tell you when I figure it out."

"You should. I could help. I know a lot about fear now."

"You offering to do me a favor, Tommy?"

"You offered me one. I'm just being polite."

Finch nodded, a tight grin splitting the bottom half of his face. It didn't look quite like a regular, ordinary grin. It looked like he had learned the expression and jerked it into place whenever he felt it might be appropriate.

"I have a question for you, while I have you here. It used to bug me when I was over there, thinking about things—which I tried not to do too much, you understand."

"Go on."

"When did you realize I wasn't dead? And why not send someone to finish the job?"

"That would be two questions."

"So it would but they're tightly linked, aren't they?"

"You were seen. You signed up in Cork, right?"

Conlon nodded.

"Somebody recognized you. It got back to us."

"And you let the one with the birthmark live? After fucking that up?"

Finch shrugged. "There were three of them, you'll remember. An example was made of one."

"That sort of thing is out of character for you, isn't it?"

Finch shrugged and looked thoughtful, putting on the act of remembering for Conlon. "By the time we knew you were alive, you were in basic training somewhere in England. Too much manpower, too much money, too much bleeding effort to get to you. And he admired that you'd survived. We knew you'd be hard to kill, even with Orla there distracting you. So we sent three of our best. You battered one of them, crippled another, and survived a bullet to the chest from the last. How many times did they shoot you? They said five or six. We never knew. Fair play to you. You're a fucking tough fucker. So he said to leave you alone. Don't get this wrong, I wanted to hunt you down and kill you. Didn't want you coming back some day and biting us on the arse. But he's the boss and he said to leave you alone. I knew you'd be back some day. Just like I know that even though we're having this chat, someday I'll have to tell somebody to kill you. And then somebody will come and tell me that you're dead. These are the realities of this life, Tommy. But for the moment, the boss says to keep an eye on you but leave you alone. So that is what I am doing."

"This isn't leaving me alone, Finch."

"This is letting you know the rules, bud. Not fair if you don't know and then you break one."

"You can do me a favor."

"Can I?"

"Yeah. Do you know a gambler called McPhail?"

"I know him. Friend of yours, is he?"

"We've met. Could you let him know that I'm back in town? He was looking for me, a few months ago..."

Finch laughed at that. "Ah, that kind of friend, yeah. A word of advice, Tommy, on Mr. McPhail. He's sneaky. He carries a set of brass knuckles in his pocket and a knife in his boot and he's not shy about using either of them."

"I'll remember that. Can you let him know?"

"I'll make sure he hears, yeah."

"Thanks, Finch. Have you anything else to say to me or are you still just admiring my handsome face?"

"Hopefully I won't be seeing it again for a long time."

Conlon smiled. "Now, you don't really mean that."

Finch stood, "I'll see you around, Tommy."

"Bye, Finch."

They walked in opposite directions.

7

MᴄPʜᴀɪʟ ᴡᴏᴋᴇ ɪɴ ᴛʜᴇ ᴀғᴛᴇʀɴᴏᴏɴ. Aʟɪᴄᴇ ᴡᴀѕ ѕɴᴏʀɪɴɢ beside him and the room was muggy with the smell of their sex and the sunlight held back by her thick drapes. He scratched his belly, enjoying the coarse sound of his fingernails on flesh. Something about the light and the noise of the Monto beyond the window and Dublin beyond that told him that it was late. He elbowed Alice sharply in the side. Her snore ended suddenly and she gave a little hiccup of surprise, then silence. He elbowed her again.

"Get up and get me a cup of tea."

"Wha?"

She was always confused when she woke, like a child, baffled by the world beyond her eyelids. When they had met, he found that endearing. Now it only irritated him.

"Get out of bed and get me a cup of tea," he said again, deliberately.

She groaned something and slid sideways off the bed. She stood there naked for a moment, casting about for her robe. He admired her lithe, slender form, her small breasts, and hard belly. He didn't care for too much flesh on a woman. He liked them small and tight. He liked to feel how weak and fragile they were beneath him.

The robe was balled up under his leg and, when she tried to pull it free, he slapped her hand away. "Why the fuck do you need to get dressed? Go in the nip."

She began to roll her eyes but remembered herself, faked a smile for him, and opened the door. She was back a few minutes later with tea on a saucer for him. He lit a cigarette as she began to dress silently.

They didn't speak as he drank and smoked and thought over the night before and the evening to come. The tea was perfect; sweet and milky the way he liked it. She knew him as well she ought to. She had been his since he had taken a liking to her one night in an alley off Mecklenburgh Street two years before. He had needed to go see her Madam but he had enough of a reputation in Dublin by that point that she let the girl go for a small sum. He rented her this flat on the edge of Talbot Street and gave her the equivalent of a wage. She had a place to live and money to feed and clothe herself. She could do as she wanted most of the time. All he asked was that she was here waiting for him every night, should he care to spend the night.

After asking around, he had discovered that she was still on the street some evenings and that her Madam sent a few of her old regulars her way but it wasn't all that often. He supposed she was saving her pennies, maybe planning to go back to Limerick or wherever she was from. He appreciated that and appreciated that she wasn't fucking British soldiers or sailors and sleeping in a crowded, disease-ridden kip like most of the other few hundred girls on these streets. She was his. She washed, ate well, and kept herself well-dressed and clean. He liked walking in to see her waiting, all pretty and nice. He liked ripping her clothes off and holding her down and making her scream.

They spoke rarely, before or after. He came here to get away, to turn off his mind, to sleep and fuck and eat. He had no interest in telling her about his world. He spent one or two nights a week. He had three other girls in other parts of the city but Alice was his favorite. Tonight, he would probably either spend at his house in Monkstown or at Blathnaid's, a few minutes away. He hadn't seen her in a fortnight or so.

He told Alice to fetch him a bowl of hot water to wash himself in. She nodded, scurrying out of the room again. On her return, he set the deep bowl of swishing water before the mirror and he washed his face and his hair and under his arms and his hands. He held his hand out and she placed a towel in his palm. He kept a full wardrobe of clothes here and, after lighting another smoke, he went through it and selected the right suit, a dark brown tweed, then a yellow shirt and a burgundy tie.

Clicking his fingers in the direction of his shoes, he sat down on the bed once more. She brought them to him, and he pulled her to him and kissed her hard, forcing a finger inside her as he did so. He stopped abruptly, and she fell back away from him. His laces were tied in a few seconds then he was standing, retrieving his hat, and on his way out the door.

She lived on the top floor and the neighbors used the staircase as a playground or city street and so it was full of children and women gossiping and laughing as he moved down the steps. They fell silent at his approach and watched him pass. Some of them were prostitutes, he surmised, something about the tired and empty look in their eyes. Most of the population of the Mondo were working girls, "poor unfortunates", living either in the stuffed and fetid kips or in the classier, more expensive brothels that served the city's wealthy men. These few must have been lucky enough to find benefactors willing to pay for them to live somewhere a bit nicer but not so nice that it would cost real money. Like him.

The babies—"Monto babies"—were a probable reason.

He had considered a more thorough study before because any situation where men paid for secret vice instantly suggested blackmail to him. But he had too much going on, at the moment, and he let the idea percolate deep down in his mind. He had many such notions down there. Each of them would one day float upwards, arriving fully formed for him to execute. Last year, he had been struck with the idea to kidnap the child of a wealthy gentleman. To hold him for ransom. He chose a victim, very carefully, and began reconnaissance. But during that reconnaissance, it had come to his attention that a few young men with no real experience, knowledge or protection were intent on buying into an arms shipment, and so he had postponed the kidnapping. Now, it was next on his list.

The day had that still, dead heat odd for this time of year with wind rushing off the Liffey, only the burn of the sun from above. He squinted into it then adjusted his hat the better to shade his face as he walked. He crossed the river and headed for Ringsend. He liked to mentally check his books as he walked. The numbers and the certainty of different streams of money, of income, had a calming effect on him. He had so many concerns, so many things moving in his interest that all he had to do with many of them was stay as he was and the cash would come his way. He found this immensely satisfying.

He went over them systematically. At the end, he estimated that he was involved in twenty-seven distinct forms of enterprise from racketeering to gun-running to pimping girls to handling stolen goods to blackmail to good old-fashioned robbery and murder. And yet gambling was still probably his chief form of income.

In Ringsend, he made his way to the upstairs room of a pub where he had a regular game with a bunch of dockers and a revolving cast of Sandymount Brits. The room was transformed into a bordello once a week with girls imported in from the Monto, a roulette wheel, and whisky running freely. A great deal of money changed hands here and McPhail was cute enough to ensure he always left with more than his share.

Today, a Brit who he assumed worked in the Castle was at the table with a large mess of coins in front of him. McPhail had played him before and lost, something that was rare enough to be notable. This Brit was tall and thin and utterly expressionless. He played poker as if he were hollow on the inside—no emotion, no tells, barely a pulse. He would join in their ribbing and chat on occasion, his accent clipped and cut like crystal.

McPhail sat down at the table and several of them acknowledged his arrival with nods. The Brit met his eyes for an instant and held the look and McPhail knew this was his acknowledgment. He suddenly realized that he wanted to kill this man; he wanted him bleeding at his feet to see if an expression cracked that pale, plain face of his. He watched the man gamble for a few slow minutes all the while allowing this fantasy to spread between his ears until he was certain it would happen. Then he signaled the dealer and joined the game.

———

THE ENGLISHMAN TOOK HIS MONEY, again. But McPhail felt strangely magnanimous about this; he felt that the man should have his little victory, should enjoy it even, if the ghoulish fucker ever enjoyed anything. For soon, he would be dead.

The Englishman left the game. He would return later; McPhail knew his habits well enough to know this much.

He stayed on and won most of his money back from the others. He did it almost mechanically with little pleasure or joy. This was a job and one he enjoyed a lot less than he enjoyed leaning on somebody to pay a debt or even shanking somebody who had betrayed him. Those activities still gave him a surge of adrenaline and risk. Gambling was almost easy, everyday, casual.

Fletcher was at his shoulder suddenly. He had a way of doing that—of ghosting around the world silently, materializing inside rooms, leaving them without seeming to open doors or windows. He was under five feet tall, slight, and startlingly red-headed. From a distance, he looked like a child. And then you saw him up close and he had the angry, pinched, stubbled little face of a middle-aged man who believes he never gets his due. He had his cap in his hands in this company but still he stood out in an embarrassing way.

McPhail turned his head to regard him in a way he hoped communicated how little this man meant to him. "What?" is all he said.

"Thought you'd want to know."

"Know what?"

"Remember last year you had me looking for those lads—with the money."

"Of course."

"The one who was off in the army, the boxer, Conlon. He's back in town, I hear."

"Do you, now?"

"Yeah, I heard it off one of Xavier's boys."

"Well, that is interesting, for sure."

Fletcher stayed, watching him wordlessly.

McPhail narrowed his eyes and spoke without regarding him, "Get out of here. You look like a fucking knacker."

Fletcher melted away as was his way.

Conlon. He remembered the name, certainly. When he had gone after that money, Conlon was the one they had worried about. He had a reputation, and Xavier's favor, it was said. But he had lost that somehow and gone off to fight for the King. The others had been easy enough to deal with but most of the money had eluded him.

Conlon being back raised the prospect of him getting his hands on it again with the idea that perhaps Conlon had been the one with all of that money and that McPhail could salvage something. As for Conlon's reputation, no reputation could stop a bullet.

He felt excited at the prospect of all of this. And hungry. He went off to eat.

———

HE WATCHED the Englishman for the rest of the evening, dipping in and out of games, nursing a few drinks slowly. He marveled at the manner of the man. He had spent hours in this place, an establishment dedicated to illicit pleasure, and yet he showed no signs of any pleasure whatsoever. His face remained a mask with no trace of emotion crossing it over the time McPhail observed him. In that time, the Englishman won, and won, and won. He was one of the best gamblers McPhail had ever seen. But, finally, he began to look tired and McPhail gathered himself. He was ready when the man left and followed him out at a distance and an interval.

It was late now, near midnight. A wind shook off the bay into the streets, juddering the streetlamps, rattling trees. The Englishman lit a cigarette in a doorway and began to walk, holding his hat onto his head, smoke pluming from his collar.

McPhail followed the trail it painted in the dark air and strolled after him. They passed two people and a single automobile in this time. The city was sleeping.

He allowed his quarry to walk for five minutes or so then increased his pace just past Bolands Mills. He waited until they passed an alley then he rushed the man from behind, slamming into him, driving him into the shadows, a bull rushing a gate. The man was light; his limbs were surprisingly loose. He made no attempt to defend himself and the only sound he uttered then was a startled little "oh."

McPhail grasped one of his wrists in the darkness and moved closer. His knife was already in his hand and he was a surgeon with it. A series of rapid stabs and cuts and the man's stifled scream was dead in his throat, blood bubbling from his belly and chest, his eyes losing their light. McPhail stood away to avoid the blood which burst in a gout from the hole in his throat. He cleaned his blade on the man's trouser leg.

Then, when the Englishman was dead, he took the money from his pockets, pocketed his knife, and calmly, as if he had just pissed in the alley, he walked away.

———

CONLON RANG the number from O'Neill's. He had not spoken into a machine like this for some time. In Turkey, he thought. The odd delay between replies, the echo, the sense of time and space bent by technology, all of it came back to him as he asked the operator for the number.

A woman answered with a husky voice and a strong Dublin accent. Conlon asked for Gene. There was a pause. He could hear sounds in the background and he strained to identify them. Then a man's voice came over the line.

"You were meant to ring yesterday."

"I was busy."

Silence.

"Sorry?" he said.

"He'll meet you. There's a game at Dalymount at 2:00 p.m. Be by the gates before kick-off. Don't be late, now."

And they hung up.

Conlon laughed at the entire exchange then consulted his watch. He had time.

———

HE CAUGHT a Donnybrook tram and jumped off near the canal. He remembered the way from here. Podge had called in to see her once, years ago, with Conlon tagging along. It was one of only two occasions when he had met her and he remembered her shyness as she stood inside the back door of a big house in her uniform, Podge's laughter, and the way she had wrapped scones in wax paper for them to eat on the way back into town. Podge had seemed so in love with her although he would never have said it in so many words.

The house was on a smart residential street of similarly smart houses; a gleaming automobile stood in the road a few doors down and sweating gardeners worked in two of the gardens he passed.

It was warm and he had removed his jacket and rolled up his shirtsleeves. As he struggled to recall exactly which house he was looking for, he had a moment of sudden and utter dislocation. Had he ever adjusted to being back here, to the cavalcade of memories, the swirl of emotions so many shop fronts and pubs and street corners evoked in him? Dublin, he had dreamed of it in Turkey and France, he had yearned to be here with her. And now on coming back, he had thrown himself headlong into this search for his friends and never really considered why or had any doubt that it was the right thing. But everywhere he went his past was waiting for him and, at times, it was hard to bear; the way it assaulted him, booby-trapping a simple walk across a neighborhood with memories of her, or another life, of hopes and dreams that had been crushed.

He finally identified the house after walking up and down the street three times. It had a sprawling chestnut tree in the garden that threw shade onto the path—he remembered that vaguely.

He rang the bell. She opened the door and plainly did not recognize him.

"Mairead," he said.

She looked instantly suspicious, her hand going to the door again as if to close it on him.

"You don't remember me, I'm a friend of Podge's. We met a few times. Tommy."

She was squinting at him. "Tommy. You went off to the War, did you?"

He nodded, smiling, making his face as safe as he could make it. "That'd be me, yeah. You gave me a scone once, in that kitchen."

"I remember that, yes, sir."

"Can I come in? I'd like to talk to you."

"Let's go in the garden, so," she said. "Walk around, sir, I'll bring you out some tea. Or—it's hot, would you like a lemonade?"

"That sounds lovely."

"There's a bench. Go and wait. I won't be long."

"Can you do something for me, Miss?"

Her face was open in anticipation.

"Don't be calling me sir. Sure, I'm the same as you."

She smiled warmly and turned away.

He followed the path through the shade around the house, taking in the flowerbeds, already violent with color, the odd ornaments scattered through the vegetation, a glimpse of a pond, sparkling through the fence. The bench was set in a wooden arch with a view of the house with small stone tables by its corners. He sat carefully, watching her approach bearing a tray a moment later. Mairead placed the tray on one stone, poured two glasses of lemonade, handed him one, and then sat.

"The Lord and Lady won't mind?" he asked.

She gave a snort of half contempt. "Lord bless us and save us, they aren't here. Away in London this last week."

"You've the house to yourself?"

"Chance would be a fine thing. Gardener is in most days. There's a cleaner and a butler on part-time. The only time it's quiet is at night."

She sat and took a long swallow of her lemonade. He picked up his and did the same, surprised at how sweet it was.

She was looking at him when he finished. "So, what can I do for you, Tommy? I'd be right to assume that scone wasn't that good that you came back just on the hope of getting another one for yourself?"

"I'm looking for Podge. I thought you could help me."

"What do you mean you're looking for him?"

"He's disappeared."

Her face was a network of round shapes, eyes, mouth, nostrils. She looked stunned.

"You didn't know?" he said. "When did you last see him?"

She shook her head. "Months ago, sure I can't remember the date."

He wasn't sure how to ask her the next questions that occurred to him, not wanting to embarrass her or make this conversation any more awkward than it already was.

"What happened?" he blurted.

"He changed. He changed so much, so quickly."

"Podge?" he had to ask, out of surprise.

"Oh aye, Podge. First, he stopped coming around. I barely saw him, like. He said he was busy with the shop but...I just knew there was something else. I thought he just didn't fancy me anymore. I thought he might've found somebody else, somebody prettier."

She looked at him. "This isn't easy."

"I know, I'm sorry. You don't have to say anymore. I just want to know where he is."

"So this could be important, couldn't it?"

"Yeah, it could be, yeah."

She shrugged. "When he was with me though, I knew he still felt the same. I don't think you could fake those feelings. He'd always been such an ol' dote. Well, maybe you could fake that, could you? But you'd need a heart blacker than night. And Podge wasn't like that, was he?"

"No. No, he wasn't."

"But then that started to change, too. He was colder; he was cruel sometimes. He was always angry about politics. He was almost like a different person." She stopped and drank some lemonade. He watched her throat move as she gulped it down. "And then he said that it was over, he didn't want to see me anymore. Just like that, sudden as a sun shower. One night, when we met at Cleary's, he told me. He told me there, just after saying hello. And he couldn't wait to get away then; he was climbing out of his skin to be away."

"And you haven't seen him since?"

"No, no I haven't. Is he all right?"

"To tell you the truth Mairead, I don't know. I doubt it. From what I'm finding out, I doubt it."

They were silent for a moment. He drank and looked at her again. "Do you think that change in him you mentioned...do you think it might have been because he was afraid?"

She looked at him with those big eyes filled with confusion and hurt and Conlon felt terrible for her. She said, "I wish I could be more helpful, so I do, but I don't know. We didn't talk about it or anything but I just noticed it one day, so I did. He was different." She shrugged, her face hopeless. "He was just different."

He let her recover herself in silence then before he spoke again, trying to make his tone gentler, easier. "Did he ever mention anyone? From work, or friends, or anything?"

"No. That was part of it. He used to talk to me about people and things and then he stopped. And I was thinking to meself that I ain't imagining this. I should have known then."

Conlon thought. Podge had never been "cold" in all of the years of their friendship, never withdrawn emotionally. That was not him. He had seen him afraid. He had seen him mourning, had seen him angry. But had never seen him cold. Something felt wrong about this but he could not say what.

Mairead was watching him and he became aware that his face had reflected his confusion.

"He used to talk about you all the time. The things you'd do together when you were chisellers. This fight you were in. Some ol' wan who used to chase youse down the stairs."

Conlon gave a soft little laugh, more of appreciation at her effort than at the words. "Thank you for saying that."

"It's true! He was awful fond of you."

"You, too, when I saw him last."

She nodded and looked away, her face controlled now. "Ah sure. It's life. There's no escaping a bit of pain, is there?"

"No. Not that I've seen, no."

They were silent and, after a moment, he found it was pleasant to sit there in silence with her and sip his lemonade.

"Are you courting at the moment?" he eventually asked her.

"Are you asking?" she said with a leer.

He laughed. "Not wanting to offend you, miss, but no. I'm just nosy."

"Well then sir, yes I am. A nice young man who works at Hoyte and Son has been taking me out."

"Dublin lad?"

"Oh no. Son of Galway."

"You'd be as well-off avoiding Dublin men from now on, I reckon."

"Oh, I know that. Can't trust a one of you."

———

Conlon was approaching Phibsboro when he noticed the crowd beginning to form in little dark knots on the paths, all men, all headed in the same direction. He felt a familiar throb of anticipation, one he hadn't felt in years. When he saw the back of the stand over the houses and heard the first wash of actual crowd noise—

a babble of voices moving on the wind as one—he felt excited. He hadn't really considered it before but now that he was here, he felt a sudden need to watch the game. It was literally years since he last came and stood, buffeted and squashed, high up in the stand, men all around jostling and cursing, smoking and shouting. He had seen Bohemians play here countless times but also watched a team of Englishmen destroy Ireland 6-1 a few years before. Those Englishmen had seemed like giants, springing onto the pitch like stags, all energy and superiority.

He knew a half dozen young men who had played for the club, too. It had been in the background of the last few years in Dublin before everything and the War. And now here he was again; this time it felt so different. He was edgy, worried, his head a buzzing clatter of ideas and doubts. But beneath that edginess, the sight of the ground had given him a little surge of optimism and excitement.

Life was strange.

Cormac was waiting all right, standing, smoking furiously near the gates. He broke into that shy smile when he saw Conlon.

"Tommy fucking Conlon, I never thought I'd ever set eyes on you again."

Conlon laughed. "I'm not sure how to be taking that, Cormac."

"Ah, it's a compliment. Too good for this kip, you are. Should be off fighting in America."

"I think me fighting days are over."

"Who are you tryin' to kid, hah?"

Men were still streaming past them and into the ground.

"Will we go in?" Conlon asked.

"Might as well. Watch an English game," he said this with a hint of mischief. Conlon was reminded of his habit of dropping in such references to annoy or test people.

"Stop being a bollix, Cormac. I've played football with you. You were shite."

Cormac chuckled. "I'm not the best athlete, that's true."

They wound their way up the short terrace. Most of the crowd was drawn to the pitch near the front but Conlon and Cormac lingered near the back where the crowd was much thinner, mainly made up of older men smoking and chatting quietly.

"You're a Bohs fan, aren't ye?" Cormac asked.

"I am. Grew up just up the road, sure I did. I'd've thought you were Rovers."

"You'd have thought right. But Dalymount is better for this."

Cormac lit another cigarette and offered Conlon one. "Ah, I forget about your lungs. How are you, anyway? How was fighting for the King?"

"Like fighting for Ireland, probably, only I got better pay."

They both laughed. "Yeah, Ireland doesn't pay much at the moment, you're right. Is it as bad as they say over there?"

Conlon shrugged, his head down. They were quiet for a while watching the players emerge onto the pitch.

"I haven't been here in years," Cormac said quietly, almost to himself. They waited until the match had kicked off, the noise from the crowd reaching a decided pitch, and then Cormac looked at him and said, "So what can I do for you, Tommy?"

"McPhail," Conlon said.

Cormac's eyes did a strange little dance: he narrowed them at the mention of the name, then they flicked downward and left, then he rolled them, making some sort of tutting sound as he did so. "What about him?"

"Is he protected?"

"It's not quite that simple, now. He does business with us, let's leave it at that. What concern is he of yours?"

"Some of my friends have gone missing. I think he might know something about it."

Cormac frowned.

The crowd exploded. There had been a chance at the far goal, a Bohemians player had skipped into the area and clipped the crossbar with an instinctive shot. They both joined in the applause.

"McPhail. He's an...entrepreneur, so he is. He doesn't work for us; he deals with loads of people. I've heard stories I don't like about the man, I can't lie to you. But this is a war we're fighting, Tommy. And we can't afford to be squeamish about our friends, especially ones who can supply guns at the prices he can."

Conlon nodded. "I understand all of that, Cormac. I just need to know: if I have to do what I might have to do...am I gonna be dealing with you and the boys as well?"

"Jaysis, Tommy, I don't know. If you bollix up one of our operations somehow then yeah! Of course you will, for fucks sake. These things have consequences. People die. But maybe not. It depends. It always depends."

They watched in silence for a few minutes, then Cormac said, "Don't you have fucking Xavier on you anyway?"

"That seems to have sorted itself out."

"You must be joking!"

"I'm not. I've been back a few days and here I am."

Cormac smirked at him. "Is it true?"

"What?"

"Why he tried to kill you? Why you left?"

"Probably, yeah."

"Jaysis, Tommy. Fair play, you always had fucking balls. The fair-haired one, yeah? She was a right beauty, her."

Conlon felt acutely uncomfortable. He had not spoken to another human being about her like this, ever. It had been a secret then it had ended so violently and then he had been in the army. He felt the emotion of it in his throat all of a sudden as if acknowledging it would make it more real and some defense against the pain would be washed away.

Cormac said, "First time I heard you were back was word that you'd smashed a few of Finch's boys up. That true?"

"It is. I think they were just reconnaissance."

Cormac shook his head in admiration. "You been carrying a shooter?"

"No."

"Tommy Conlon doesn't need one, wha?"

Conlon laughed at that. "I've got one. Just doesn't feel right walking down Sackville Street with it in me belt."

"That's because you weren't here during the fighting. Nothing about that felt right. But, then it felt so right, too. First time it really felt real. Like we could actually do it, y'know what I mean?"

"Yeah, I know. Violence has a way of..."

"Making it feel real. Yeah. Jaysus. Wish you'd been with us, Tommy."

"I'm not sure I would've been any use at all to you."

"Ah come off that."

The crowd noise soared again and they both watched. The Bohs winger was on the ball and had taken it around two players with a surge in acceleration that looked somehow superhuman, even from up here. He shaped to pass it inside, then swerved again into the penalty box. The crowd roar was visceral, the movement of air violent and almost perceptible. The winger—skinny, snake-hipped, and balding—suddenly slowed, making to shoot, and a defender clattered both him and ball right off the pitch. Tommy was watching but he was far away and she was in his head, again. Men all around them were howling in outrage.

Cormac chuckled. "That was my kind of tackle."

"I think I remember a few of those off you."

"Fuck off, ye bowsie. You used to kick the ankles off people."

Conlon laughed. He had forgotten how much Cormac made him laugh.

Cormac said, "Remember what Grattan used to say, when he was going on beforehand? Loved the sound of his own voice, Grattan. You have to fight to earn the right to play."

"He got that in the Army," Conlon said. "Officers are always talking like that."

"I'm sure they are. How'd you stand it?"

Conlon thought for a moment. "I was angry. I

wanted to hurt people. They put me in the best place to do that."

Cormac looked at him silently for a moment. "I could still use a man like you, Tommy. There's an actual war coming."

Conlon looked at him. "I'm done with war, Cormac."

"This one doesn't work that way. You'll have to pick a side."

"I know. Let me know when it's about to happen. We'll see."

Cormac nodded.

Conlon said, "McPhail."

"I'll try to protect you when it comes to it but really, it'd be out of my hands. Is it going to come to it?"

"I've a feeling it will, yeah."

"Poor fucker," Cormac said.

Cormac lit another cigarette. "Right. I've things to do. You staying?"

"I think I will. See if there's a goal. For old time's sake."

"Fair enough. I'll see you around, Tommy."

"Cormac."

And he stood there until the referee blew the whistle for half time, watching the game, and seeing only her.

8

After they had parted at the station, he did not see Orla for over five days.

On that train, he had kissed her, and she had returned the kiss instantly and, all in all, it had given him a feeling unlike anything he had ever experienced before. He had kissed girls in the past, and sometimes it had been exciting, and sometimes it had felt good, and sometimes he had wanted to do it again, but this was like opening a door he had not known existed to a joyous oblivion he had never glimpsed or considered might be real. As soon as that kiss had ended, he wanted to kiss her again. The need to put his mouth upon hers blotted all else out as they sat together in that cabin, her body fragile in his arms, her hand light upon the back of his neck.

It was only when the flickering light changed—the gray and brown and red blur of the city outside the window—that they came apart and looked at one another, laughing nervously.

She was a realist about it: "It'll be awful hard to see

each other. You won't see me for days."

"As long as I do see you."

"You will. I promise you will." And they kissed again. "It'll be easier, later, when we have a routine or a system." She seemed so sure, but the prospect of losing this the same instant he had found it was horrifying to him.

"How will I contact you? When will I see you?"

She shook her head. "No, don't do anything. Do normal things, be yourself. I'll find a way to get to you."

"I can't do that. I—this—I..."

"I know. I know, Thomas." She put her hand to his face and he felt that sensation move straight up his back like a feather, soft and silken.

"You don't know him like I do," she said. "Xavier trusts nobody, nobody at all. Me coming back like this, with you—he'll be watching you for a while, I'm sure. We have to let that pass, hard as it'll be—for me, too, for me, too."

He nodded. His stomach was a rolling ocean of euphoria and terror, and he really had no idea what he was feeling from instant to instant.

"I'm sorry," she said. "I'm so sorry it has to be like this." She looked as if she would cry and he held her tight to him and kissed her again.

"It's not your fault, is it? As long as I get to see you again. As long as I know that'll happen and that you want it, too, I can take it."

"Can you? I'm not sure I can, so," she said with a despairing croaked laugh.

They kissed again, a desperate kiss now, as if that, too, was about to be taken from them forever.

"I'll find a way to see you. In a few days, or a week or

two. Don't forget me now."

"I've never stopped thinking about you since the first time I saw your face in McClean's. Don't you worry about that."

The railway lines were fanning out like tail feathers, the stationary carriages plentiful, lonely, and still on rusting tracks. They were nearing the station.

She held his hand tight. "How did this happen?" she whispered. "I never thought I could feel like this, I felt so foolish about it. I don't want to say goodbye now."

"Neither do I. But we have to."

"I know. I know."

He kissed her again and when they came apart, the train was coming to a halt. They looked at one another and stood, her hand still in his.

He pulled her bag down and helped her from the train, and they walked up the platform together, and through the smoky, crowded station. Although they were not touching now, it felt to him as if they were moving along in a bubble. Everything and everybody else was outside it and only they were within, close together, connected, breathing the same rarified air.

He looked at her and she looked at him and then they were outside. A short line of Hansom cabs greeted them. Eagerly, one of the drivers was already approaching.

"Can I take that for ye, sir?" he asked and Conlon nodded and handed him the bag.

He moved with her toward the cab and helped her up, desperately wanting to kiss her again. As she sat, she gave his hand one last squeeze and a sort of sad smile, her eyes wide and wet. He felt that in his throat, too, a hard knot of emotion.

The driver said, "Will ye be comin' yourself, sir?"

"Just the lady. She knows the address."

He looked at her again as the driver climbed up. They didn't say anything, just stared. The drivers whip cracked, the horse jerked away, and she was gone.

———

WHEN HE AWOKE the next morning, it all seemed as if it had to have been a dream. Those feelings and events could not possibly have been real, she could not have felt like that, said those things, kissed him that way. But he knew it had been real and as he reflected on that, he allowed the euphoria of it to carry him through much of that first day apart.

But by that night, his feelings were different. He missed her. They had had so little time together and he was hungry for more. He was having difficulty holding her face in his mind. It haunted him all day long but, whenever he turned his full attention to it, it would flit away like a butterfly, frustratingly just out of sight.

He kept on thinking of things he wanted to say to her, things she didn't know about him, things he didn't know about her. It got so much that he had to bite down on the urge to scream her name into the sky that first night as he walked back from training. And then, he started to think about what she was doing, who she was with, the reality of it. Once he let these thoughts in, there was no fighting them and he wondered how he had ever spent any time not obsessing over it. She was with Xavier. If not now, then an hour ago, or in an hour. She was his. His property, virtually. His toy.

It was jealousy, yes, certainly. But much worse than

that. He was terrified for her, for what it must be like to be in that situation. He was jealous of the man she was with. He spent hours wondering what exactly she was seeing and feeling. Was she in bed with him? Was he showing her off? Was she alone, thinking of him? Had she thought of him at all? It was maddening; a torment the likes of which he had never experienced before.

He endured it each day they were apart until their next meeting—an hour or two a day of angst and agony regarding where she was and what she was doing and who she was with and was she thinking of him. And then he would think himself into accepting it and would get beyond it, be stronger than it. And then, the next day he would have to go through the whole thing all over again.

He trained like a madman. He ran, he punched a heavy bag, he sparred with such ferocity that nobody at the gym dared get in the ring with him, anything to quiet the voices in his head that was whispering about her.

————

ON THE SIXTH DAY, when he was beginning to believe that she had been lying, that he would never see her again, a young boy came into the gym looking for him.

He was a typical Dublin urchin—tattered shorts, a white shirt gone yellow, dark jacket, cap and scraped shoes—and he was smiling cheekily as he handed Conlon a folded piece of paper. The note told him to follow the boy and do what he said.

He read it and looked around, suddenly certain that he was being observed. But the gym was as it always was, an oblivious clatter of raised voices and the slap of fist on leather, on flesh, on canvas, feet tapping and thrumming on floor, the splash of water, all comforting sounds for him now.

The boy was regarding him without curiosity. Conlon raised his chin at him, wordless enquiring.

"She told me to wait," the boy said.

"All right. Wait then."

Conlon trotted off, washed quickly, and changed his clothes, then was back with the boy who led him out and into the streets.

It was a long walk, right across town and the Liffey. He let the boy stay ten or twenty feet ahead, watching him bobbing and feinting through the heavy crowds, his head always moving, watching people, scanning for opportunity. He was light on his feet, ceaselessly active and busy. Conlon recognized all of this because it had been him and his friends only a few years before. Life in Dublin was hard and it demanded that children were alert and hungry for any chance to take anything that might be available to them or lucky enough to survive without being alert or hungry. He had always been alert; that had never left him and he had taken chances when they came. Luck was a different matter.

The boy led him across College Green and around Trinity then far on, through Merrion Square, before finally stopping in front of a house on Mount Street. These were more well-to-do areas of the city, where the ladies wore expensive dresses, many of the gentlemen in shining shoes and fine hats, and people from Conlon's part of town stood out. His suit was his best and he looked otherwise unremarkable—he didn't look like a laborer or docker. He was still young and fresh and physically vital enough that the poverty he had grown up in didn't quite cling to him, like an odor, as it did to so many. He had escaped at just the right time before he could be claimed by it. He could pass here without drawing much attention. Just about.

The boy pointed at the door. "In there."

"You already been paid?"

"Don't you worry about that," he said with a little grin and then he was off, running down the street past Conlon.

Conlon climbed the steps and went inside. The house was silent; the kind of silence that was almost oppressive. He had the fleeting impulse to run away. But she was here. She must be here.

Quickly, he searched the downstairs rooms. There was no furniture and no carpets. There were varnished floorboards in some rooms and gleaming tile in the kitchen but one room where carpet had obviously been torn up, dust motes clouded in the sunlight from his passage.

Then her voice came from above, calling his name.

"Orla," he said and ran. He climbed the stairs and she was in his arms before he could turn onto the landing, her lips on his, their bodies pressed together. They didn't speak for a moment or two, kissing, again and again, his hands in her hair, hers on his shoulders and back.

"Oh, I've missed you," she whispered. She was crying, he saw. He felt unaccountably close to tears himself, a rawness in his throat he had trouble identifying until he realized it was emotion. He felt utterly happy to see her, moved beyond his ability to articulate.

"I've missed you, too."

She broke away and took his hand and led him into a bedroom, empty of all furniture save for a four-poster bed, its dark red curtains shut on all but one side. She took off his jacket, then began to unbutton his shirt. She had a fierce little look of concentration on her face and he watched her for a moment. He realized there and then that he was in love with her, that this was love, and that it was the most amazing thing that had happened to him.

He stopped her, taking her hand as she worked at the second button. He had no idea what to say. He cocked his head and struggled for words.

She smiled. "Don't worry. It'll be fine. I want this more than anything."

He nodded. She kissed him again then stepped back and began to undress, her eyes never leaving his. He stood stock still, just watching for a minute or so, and then he finished his own disrobing. She took his hand again and they walked side by side to the bed. She climbed in first and he followed her, unable to take his eyes away from her pale beauty, not quite believing this was happening.

"Pull that cord." She pointed. He stretched out and took it and when he tugged, the curtains dropped shut with a heavy slap. Soft light fell from above, and she moved against him again, seeking the cocoon inside his arms, her face a few inches from his own.

"Hello," she said, softly.

"Hello," he echoed.

She kissed him again. This. This was love. This.

THEY NEVER REALLY HAD ANY proper routine. They would meet once a week, sometimes twice in a week, sometimes in public—a park, the National museum, church, even—or sometimes in a flat or house she had arranged. She seemed to have a steady line of venues for them. Some had a bed, some did not. But as much as he enjoyed it, indeed, and thought about it obsessively when they were apart, the sex was not the part of being with her that he enjoyed the most. No, that was the moments before and after, when they lay together and just talked or held one another, her head on his collarbone, his finger tracing circles on the skin at the small of her back. This was the way they gotten to know one another, lying in the gloom together, entwined and spent. They talked of their childhoods, their dreams, politics, food. Anything. Just to be there, so close to her, being allowed into her world. They talked of how they met, how it had felt, errors and misunderstandings. They went on about their few days in Cork, how beautiful it was, how she had felt when he walked in, how he had felt on his way to see her. And finally, when they could no longer ignore it, they talked of what was next.

She loved to idly fantasize about the things they would do together, the places they would visit. He was more realistic but he found it impossible to resist the fantasies she spun and the warmth they spread in him. So, he did not force her to confront reality. Neither wanted to break their delicate spell. Neither wanted to acknowledge the truth of the situation. When they were together, their love was all, though neither spoke of it. He had not told her that he loved her and she had not told him. But they both knew.

A room in Clontarf, one wet afternoon

They were both tired, and after they had climbed into bed together, they simply lay there, enjoying the way their warm bodies felt up against one another; the everyday thrill of it. She felt so small in his arms with her fingers knit tightly between his. He could smell her hair, too—rose petals and the light, clean scent of her skin. It was, perhaps, his favorite smell in the world.

The constant thrumming of rain on the skylight and hiss of carriage wheels in the road outside were the only sounds as he squirmed down beside her and put his forehead against hers, their eyes locked tight.

"I've never been this happy," she said softly.

He felt tears in his eyes. "Me either. Never."

He kissed her so that he would not cry.

It troubled both that they could not really be together in the world. Snatched moments in a park or a gallery felt momentous due to the threat of discovery. Because they had to restrain themselves, they could not touch or even really relate to one another in the way that both had come to see as normal. This meant that memories of their time together in Cork began to shine in recollection—the ease of it, the way they had existed in banal surroundings, moving around and interacting with other people without fear or anxiety. He loved every moment he spent with her but it was always rarefied by their separation from the world beyond the walls of whatever room became their universe. He wanted to test them against life, against people, against Dublin.

And then, almost six months after that first kiss on the train, they found themselves at the same event, in the same room, and something changed.

It was a Francis Xavier evening in the Metropole Hotel on Sackville Street. Conlon, who had been told been told only an hour beforehand that his attendance was expected, rushed home, dressed in his smart, evening suit, then made his way to the hotel, where he was simply expected to be seen, to chat to anyone who might want to chat to him, to look happy to be there. Usually, this meant awkward conversations with Dublin Castle gentlemen and businessmen with pompously affected country accents and the seriously neglected wives of such. This night was shaping up to be more of the same until he saw her entering the room on Finch's arm.

He felt the blood drain from his face in a rush, felt a sudden inability to control his expression, felt a sudden nausea rise in his chest. He watched her as he pretended to listen to a story being told by the fat businessman he was standing with.

The party was in the big ballroom and there must have been over two hundred people there, so he could watch from across the space. Finch was leading her around knots of people and she was saying hellos and nodding and smiling. But, all the while, her eyes moved quickly over the room, and he understood that she was searching for him. After a minute or so, she found him and there was a moment when their eyes locked and she gave the very faintest of grins—just a slight tug at one end of her mouth—that made his heart surge. Then she was turned away and chatting to someone else and he was left with a kind of panic.

Part of him wanted to stay here, just to see her and glory in the beauty that was his, his girl, and feel the pleasure of her glowing across the room like a star, let her warm his skin. But he knew that the risk of pain was too great. He had felt the tip of that dagger pressing lightly against his flesh at the sight of Finch's hand on her arm. Her smiling for men who leered at her in that manner that brought out the violence he contained in his heart every day. Already, he was imagining his fists smashing faces.

He had to get out.

The fat businessman was still talking: something about a recent trip he had taken to France. French food. His terrible French. He had fastened on Conlon once he realized that they were both from the North Inner City. "Northsiders have to stick together," he had said.

Conlon had nodded as he searching for any trace of the Northside in the man's accent, which sounded thoroughly polished, the better to do business with the English and Anglo-Irish.

He was still thinking of what to say to excuse himself when there they were, Orla and Finch, obviously intent on joining their conversation.

Finch said, "Mr. Cassidy. This is Orla. I think you and Mr. Conlon have already met, dear."

Orla nodded and said something Conlon could not make out over the thunder of blood in his ears. She looked fine except for the panicked light in her eye and the suggestion of terror he could clearly make out there.

Conlon could not understand why Finch would bring her over this way, at this party. And then he saw the way Finch had steered her toward the businessman who was already leering at her and had one hand at her lower back. He was trying to make her laugh, his head bent forward, seeking out her eye.

To Conlon, she looked sick, her smile forced. Of course. Of course. They had never spoken of it. She was Xavier's but, of course, he would or could use her as he pleased, as a favor for a business partner, as a makeweight in a deal. She was essentially a piece of cattle for these men.

He had to get out of here but he could not leave her. He could not let this happen, whatever her arrangement with Xavier and Finch was.

He managed to stammer, "Excuse me," and made for the lavatory.

Inside the water closet, he stood and held his face in his hands for a moment, thinking desperately. Then he went back out and ordered a double whiskey at the bar. He carried that to the cloakroom. There were no staff in attendance, though they had been here this evening, he was sure. On the way, he had picked up an oil lamp from one of the halls beyond the lobby. He poured the whiskey over a line of heavy coats, then flung the oil lamp at the wall above them. The flames were instant and stronger than he had imagined they would be. The surface of the wall belched and cracked and the flames raced down toward the coats, following the strands of oil. The whiskey went up in a blue cloud and he was already turning and moving away. He went into the lobby and asked the porter: "Is that smoke? I can smell smoke."

It took about half a minute for the man to find the blaze and, by that time, the cloakroom was a box of raging flame. There were staff racing around, ringing bells and shouting within seconds, and people were soon pouring out of the ballroom through the lobby and also through the exits onto the street. Conlon went out with the crowd and watched from afar as Cassidy cursed and tried to get back into the building, having utterly forgotten about Orla, who stood shivering beside Finch, peering around, trying to locate him, he knew.

The Fire Brigade arrived soon after but the crowd had already begun to disperse, people giving up on their coats as soon as they were told that the fire had begun in the cloak room. Conlon watched as Finch led Orla away, her head still craning around to see if she could spot him lingering in the shadows.

It took the Fire Brigade perhaps ten minutes to bring the blaze under control. It had been largely confined to the cloak room, which was now a charcoal cube, the reek of it thick even out in the street, near the doors to the hotel.

Conlon approached Cassidy, who smoked a cigarette while casting continual forlorn glances toward the hotel entrance, still guarded by firemen, others nearby gathering up hose.

"Still here?"

The businessman looked at him and Conlon could see him struggle to recognize the young man who stood before him. Awareness came with a jerk and he said, "Ah, yes, yes. My wallet is in my coat."

"It was in the cloak room?"

"It was."

"Ah."

"Yes. It's—Yes."

"You didn't have a lot of money in it, did you?"

At that, the man just looked at him and Conlon retreated, nodding, palms up in apology.

———

SHE WAS APOLOGIZING as soon as he walked in, the next time they were together, all breathless and more emotional than he was used to, and he could see that the four-day wait to see him had been even harder on her than usual.

He took her and held her to him and said it was all right as she shook her head. She apologized and he shushed her. After they had made love, with her lying in his arms, she returned to the subject.

"Did you start the fire?"

He laughed. "I did. I didn't expect it to be so ferocious. But it did the job."

"I didn't know what to say. I didn't know you'd be there and then, as soon as we got there, I knew, of course, you had to be."

"Is that something that happens a lot?"

"What?"

He knew she knew what. "You having to be with other men."

"Do you really want to talk about this?"

"Probably not." So that's a yes.

"It happens, sometimes."

Silence between them. Distance in their bed for perhaps the first time ever.

"Don't let it be like this," she said. "You know I'd be with you if I could be."

"Would you?"

"You're being cruel. I get enough of that with him."

"Now who's being cruel?"

"I'm sorry. Thomas..."

"Sorry, it's me. Sorry."

"I know it must be hard, knowing what I'm doing or who I'm with…"

"I don't think about it. I can't think about it. I saw you there and then I had to think about it and my instinct was to…to just destroy something."

"Which is what you did."

"Yeah, sort of. But…"

"I was so relieved."

"We need to get away."

"What do you mean?"

"We need to run away. Just me and you. Fuck this place. Just us."

"How could we. Where would we go?"

"I don't know. America."

"Ah stop joking. You needn't be thinking that this is funny."

"I'm dead serious."

"How? How could we…"

"I've money. We just—I have money, now. Enough."

"What about your ma?"

"She'd be fine. I'd take care of her."

She was silent.

"I love you." He had never said that before. He could feel her heart beating against him suddenly.

"I love you," she said.

"Then come with me. All I need is you. You make me happy. I'm miserable without you. Come with me. I want to marry you and I want your face to be the last thing I see before I die. Please, Orla."

"Yes. Yes. Yes."

9

HE HAD TEA WITH HIS MA, JUST THE TWO OF THEM IN THE dining room. She loved cooking for him, and he liked the happiness it gave her. So they ate her champ, one of his favorites from childhood, and lemon plaice, together with fresh soda bread, washed down with tea. They talked about a stream of inconsequential things and then she asked him a few questions about the war. She did it in a quiet, offhand way as if what she was asking was nothing of import. And she listened to his answers, which he was sure to keep short and factual, striving to avoid anything too emotive.

Finally, he asked her: "Were you worried about me?"

"Of course I was, I'm your mother. But it was good that I didn't know where you were for sure. I could pretend you weren't really there."

He nodded. That made sense to him. "I used to pretend I wasn't really there, too," he said.

"And now, here you are, thanks be to God, and I'm still worrying about you," she said slowly with a cold and emotionless tone. He recognized the significance of this; this was her making a point.

"What are you worried about?"

"Whatever you're up to now, I know it can't be good. Sure you haven't got a job. You're not courting. But you're out all day, doing God knows what."

"Ma…it's not what you think. I'm not doing anything…"

He shook his head.

"I don't know if you think I'm some poor unfortunate ol' one, here with me rosary and me tea, but I'm not stupid," she said.

"I know that!"

"I heard things when you disappeared. I'd walk into the grocers and all the talk would stop. Nobody could look me in the eye. People said you were dead. I know you were hanging around with a bad lot but you've always been a responsible boy—"

"Ma. It's nothing like that. I'm looking for my friends. I can take care of myself now, God knows."

"Is it dangerous, is it?"

"Probably, a bit, it might be. But—it's not France. Most of the time, I'm walking around town, talking to people. The biggest danger is sore feet."

They were quiet, finishing the last scraps on their plates, the scrape of fork on delph.

He said, "I won't let anything like that happen again. I'm sorry. I was young, I didn't really know what I was doing. It's different now."

She looked at him in silence for a moment, then nodded, stood, and lifted his empty plate across the table. "Do you want sweet?"

"What is it?"

"Apple tart. With cream."

"You know I'd never say no to that."

There was a knock on the door. The look they exchanged told him that she was far from fully reassured by the conversation they had just had.

"I'll get it," he said. As he stood, he fleetingly wondered if he should fetch his gun from upstairs, but he went to the door unarmed, confident in his own quick thinking and reactions, ready for anything. A doleful, little middle-aged man stood there, long drooping bags under his dark eyes, scraggly dark hair peeking out from under his hat, an expression on his face like he had just lost his wallet and missed the last train, and now it was raining.

"Thomas Conlon, is it?"

Something in the way he said it told Conlon what he was. Some sort of sense of assurance.

Conlon said, "It is—is it Inspector? Constable? It's hard to tell when you're not wearing the funny little hats."

A flicker of amusement, perhaps, showed in the man's eyes at that. "Barry'd be my name and don't you concern yourself with rank. Would you mind if we had a little chat?"

"Just a little one?"

"It won't take too long, I swear to God."

"Well, my ma has just made us some apple tart. Would you like some?"

"That sounds lovely, if she won't mind."

"She'll be delighted, I'm sure. Come in, Mr. Barry."

He led the policeman into the back room and introduced him to his mother, who welcomed him as if he was an old acquaintance. If anything, he was given an even bigger slice of tart than Conlon, with more cream, and he entertained her with a few tales of the larger-than-life characters who were regulars around Capel Street station.

When she was busy washing dishes in the kitchen, Conlon asked, "Is that where you're based, Capel Street?"

"No, I was but I'm over in Exchange Court now."

"G-Man, what?"

Barry nodded.

"So. What do you want to talk to me about, then?"

"Well. One of my jobs is to keep an eye on your old friend Mister Francis Xavier and his somewhat nefarious activities. I've been doing that for a couple of years now. But I missed you, the first time. There is a file on you but we thought you were dead."

"Sorry to inconvenience you."

"Ah tis no inconvenience. I had to dictate a report. One of the girls in the pool had to type it up but that's the only excuse I have for talking to a pretty girl these days."

"You had to write a report to the effect that I wasn't dead?"

"I did. You are a known associate of Mr. Xavier and Mr. Finch, too. One of the lads had this mad theory that you had done a runner with Xavier's girl, because she disappeared, too, but most of us just thought you were dead in a ditch somewhere."

"Are you asking me a question?"

"No, no, not officially. I'm just curious."

"I was in the army. The War."

"I thought so, from looking at you. Anyway, imagine our surprise when we hear from a few people that you're back in town and causing some problems for Mr. Xavier. Boxed the heads off a few lads now, haven't you?"

"They started it."

Barry laughed. "I'm sure."

"You're the strangest peeler I've ever met. Are you ever going to ask me a question?"

"I like a chat. I'm a sociable chap. How do you think I get on with some of the gobshites at the Castle?"

"The pay packet can't hurt."

"It's probably a lot smaller than you think."

"You're a Dub."

"I am. Just up the road in Cabra. I heard of you back when you were fighting. Northside is always proud of a son doing well. And now, what are you doing, Mr. Conlon? I hear these things about you and then one of my friends at the Castle informs me you've been seen with some notable Rebel figures. Nobody ever had you down as the type."

"Maybe the War politicized me."

Barry laughed at that and his laugh was infectious, so Conlon joined him.

"We're all politicized now, aren't we, so?" Barry said. "But no—I don't see it in you. What are you doing? And will I have to write any reports about it?"

Conlon liked this man. His decency seemed plain and he liked the way he spoke, always aware of his own ridiculousness, self-mocking but serious when he needed to be. Conlon liked few enough people that he respected this response.

"I came back and some of my friends have gone."

"Gone? To war?"

"No. Disappeared. No explanation, no trace, nobody knows where. So, I've been looking for them."

"Which has meant that you've become friendly with some interesting people..."

Conlon shrugged. "Some of them I knew before. Some of them knew things I needed to know."

"And what have you found out? If it'll keep you out of trouble, there's a chance that I can help you, you know."

"You know a gambler called McPhail?"

"I do, unfortunately."

"He's involved, somehow."

Barry made a face and Conlon instantly read it.

"You think they're dead."

Barry said, "I have no idea what any of the circumstances are so I can't say either way. Do you think they're dead?"

"Probably."

"So what is this about, then?"

"I have to make sure."

"And if you make sure?"

Conlon shrugged again but it was a different shrug and it made Barry frown.

"It's one thing for me to be writing about rumors of you cracking heads in some street fight, but I can't be cleaning up bodies. This country has seen enough blood lately."

"We both know there's a lot more to come."

"So is that it? You've come back, the War has scrambled your nerves the way it will, and you need the blood to make yourself feel better? Is that it, Mr. Conlon? Like one of the many drunks we pull out of the Monto every night, back from the War, and they can't stop the shaking in their hands or the tic in their face until they're battering some whore. Some of the lads from the

Rising are worse. You can tell that it isn't over just because there are so many of them who are in love with the violence now and the blood they get to spill. Is that you, too?"

"My nerves are fine. I don't need violence; it's just a tool. I'd prefer to talk to McPhail. But I've a bad feeling he won't feel that way."

Barry slumped back in his chair, resigned. "You need to be careful. He's in business with some bad people."

"I will be."

"You can't have been over there. Did you get invalided out? Or did you desert? If I send a letter to them over here, would you be picked up the next day, I wonder?"

Conlon laughed dryly. "I didn't sign up under my real name. They don't even know who I am. And no, I didn't desert. I'd done my time."

Barry's eyes were narrow, calculating. "You should think about working with us. The Metropolitan needs good men."

"Who said I'm a good man?"

"I've been doing this long enough to tell."

"Well. I've taken enough orders for this life, thanks very much."

"Mmm. That never gets any better, it's true. Was poxy during the fighting, told to sit on our hands. And now the city is full of guns and black with secrets and we're supposed to uphold law and order? Jaysis."

Conlon laughed and, after a beat, Barry laughed with him.

Eventually, he stood. Conlon stood with him. Barry called in thanks to his Ma who was still in the kitchen.

They made their way out into the hall.

"Well. I've a feeling I'll be seeing you again, Mr. Conlon."

"You can call me Tommy."

"All right. Just call me Barry. All me friends do."

They shook hands, there, in the hall, at the end of their first conversation.

"Try not to do anything too interesting, if you can."

Conlon laughed. "I can't be promising anything."

Barry rolled his eyes and opened the front door. "Nice apple tart, that was. Tell your ma. See you around, Tommy."

"Barry."

———

CONLON WAS awoken by rain upon his window the next morning. It was a hard Dublin rain, falling with vengeful force onto the city out of a sky of low, dark gray.

There was a telegram for him. It came while he ate his breakfast. A sodden boy handed it over and Conlon absently gave him a few coins while he read it. The boy splashed off across the street and Conlon stepped back into the hall, away from the rain, and scrutinized the sky, considering. BOD wanted to see him. He had forgotten BOD's love of telegrams, but it had been his first thought upon hearing the news of the General Post Office during the rising: what will BOD do without telegrams?

There had been talk among the Irishmen in France that the Rebels had specifically targeted the GPO because it was a hub of telegram communications to

London. But then there had been a lot of talk among the men. Mossy and Dalton had both professed disdain, he remembered. Neither of them cared what happened to a load of Dubs, they said. They had laughed about it.

But he had been thinking about BOD, and now BOD wanted to see him. BOD who was somehow involved with McPhail. That was something Conlon needed to pry into in more detail, anyway. What could be gotten out of BOD, how could he be useful? He was sure he could be. But he was less sure that BOD could be trusted.

The last time they had spoken, at the hotel, he had almost forgotten about BOD in the rush to follow McPhail. But the whole exchange had felt off. BOD had known that his friends were missing. BOD knew McPhail. BOD knew everyone and everything that was going on in Dublin. He must have known that the two things were linked. Which meant that he had hidden something from Conlon.

That was possibly what he wanted to see him about now. Or, just as possibly, Conlon could be walking into a trap. Perhaps McPhail had gotten wind of his return and wanted to tie up loose ends. Either way, Conlon knew he had to go. He was growing impatient with the slow progress he has been making and he wanted this all to be over.

But thinking about all this, he was aware that he was precisely where he had hoped he would never be again: living in this paranoid Dublin of grudges and guns, unsure of what people knew and what people wanted, nervous of taking a wrong step in case the floor fell away beneath him. He much preferred knowing what he was fighting. Then he could dictate the terms of engagement and prepare himself. This way meant he had to be constantly alert and always ready. He found it exhausting.

His first thought on awakening—before he had even registered the rain or that it had woken him—was of Orla. That was the way on most mornings. And now, he thought of her again. She had hated the way involvement with Xavier had made Conlon so suspicious and careful. She had said she wanted to be away so she could see him living a carefree life; she wanted to see what that would be like.

And here he was, right back in it. And she was gone. Which meant that all he had to worry about this time was his own neck. And that was easy.

————

IT HAD STOPPED RAINING by the time he reached the hotel. He shook himself off in the lobby and took the stairs. BOD answered the door, all smiles and happiness to see him.

"I'm just on my way out, Thomas. Would you come and walk with me?"

"Of course, BOD."

They made for a tram, BOD prattling on for a minute or so about some acquaintance he presumed Conlon knew. Conlon had no idea whom he was talking about.

"Where are you going, BOD?" he finally interrupted.

"Rathmines."

"What's in Rathmines?"

"You'll see."

So they took the tram together and, eventually, BOD

settled down to reminiscing about some of Conlon's old fights, the details of which he seemed able to recall intimately—punch by punch, round by round. It began to disturb Conlon when he realized how encyclopedic BOD's memory of his short career was, how he remembered the fights as though he himself had fought them.

It rained once more as they crossed over the canal and BOD seemed annoyed. "Ah for God's sake, I was hoping we were done with the bloody rain for the day."

Conlon said, "When I was in Turkey, some of the Irish lads used to talk about missing the rain. It was so hot there, and dry. You could never get enough water down you. So they'd go on about wanting it to rain and missing slow days in Kerry or whatever bogtrotter part of the country they came from." He looked at BOD, who nodded, smiling at the insult. "But I never missed the rain. Or I thought I didn't, anyway, until I got home and was caught out in it again. And I realized I missed the way the street smells just when the rain is starting. You know that smell?"

"I'm not sure."

"Sort of a dusty smell, almost. And that wasn't me missing the rain, that was just me missing Dublin. Anyway."

BOD caught Conlon's sudden embarrassment and tried to help him skirt it. "Ah sure didn't dirty old Dublin miss you, too? I never miss Limerick. Dublin is my town; Dublin is where I became who I am."

"Who were you before, then?"

BOD laughed. "Somebody very different, Thomas."

The rain stopped before they disembarked, which visibly cheered BOD. At Rathmines, he led them through a series of residential streets and squares until they arrived at a park. They went in and made for the far end.

As they approached, Conlon saw a large area fenced off and people moving inside it, surrounded by trees and bushes and the odd garden shed. He realized what it was; "You have an allotment?"

"Of course, I do, Thomas. I'm sure your dear old mammy does, too."

Conlon shrugged. It was the kind of thing she would enjoy but she had never mentioned one.

"The food shortage has been worse lately so a lot of people grow their own food. We're Irish, working the land is in our blood, isn't it?"

"I've never worked the land in me life."

"You're a Dub. It's different."

They were inside now, and BOD nodded and waved greetings to the half dozen people bent and kneeling in various plots. They were all different ages: men and women, one lady working with three children. Each of them was armed with a trowel, and there was a pair of old women filling a basket with what looked like celery. One man sat in a chair in the doorway of his shed, reading a newspaper and smoking.

BOD's plot was in the far corner. He had a small shed, which he unlocked, and then presented Conlon with a deck chair. He donned a pair of heavy, muddy leather boots and thick gloves before dragging out a clanking bag filled with tools.

Conlon sat and watched him clipping and digging for a few minutes before asking, "So. You telegrammed me, BOD."

"I did. I feel a bit guilty, Thomas. I wasn't entirely honest with you the other day."

"I had a feeling that you weren't."

"I wasn't expecting to see you so I hadn't really thought through what I said. But having had time to consider it, I feel I owe you some honesty."

"I appreciate that. I was going to come see you again."

"With your fists primed, eh? Well, much as I appreciate your pugilistic skills, Thomas, I am relieved to be spared a first-person demonstration of your continued ability."

"So...?"

"Yes, sorry." BOD stopped what he was doing and looked at Conlon. "Your friends, Thomas. They're dead, I'm afraid."

Conlon nodded. BOD watched him closely for a reaction.

"You're not surprised?" BOD said.

"No. I've been asking around, BOD. I thought they probably were. What I need are a few more details."

"Ah, yes. What do you know?"

Conlon shook his head. "That's not how this is going to work, BOD. I'm not in the mood. Tell me what you know, then we can compare notes." He was staring levelly at the older man who looked a little shaken now. "How did they die?"

"I'm not sure. Their bodies were dumped out at sea. I know that."

"Was McPhail involved?"

"He introduced them to the gun runners. He was a broker for the deal. But the deal went wrong. I don't know if he was directly involved in their deaths."

"Who are these gun runners?"

"I don't know. Guns come from all over. Most of the

Volunteers guns were taken by the British after the Rising and they're desperate to re-arm themselves. If you know where to go, there are people from all over Europe willing to sell rebels guns, Italians, Serbs, Germans, Belgians, even the Brits. Most of their guns come from Brits over here who need the money, imagine that, ha?"

"I can imagine that, yeah. Who does McPhail usually deal with?"

"Anyone he can. Plenty of Yanks willing to give us guns, too. They love to help out the motherland."

"But this must have been a specific group?"

"I have a feeling it didn't even get that far, Thomas."

"They were betrayed before that."

"That's how I see it, yes."

"Killed as soon as the money had changed hands. That makes sense. But they must have met somebody beyond McPhail. Who would he introduce them to...?"

BOD shook his head, indicating his ignorance.

"How do you know all this, BOD?"

"I listen. I keep my eyes open. Sometimes, people tell me things that they shouldn't. Nobody's said anything direct, but I know what all this means."

"So why did this happen? Why the lads?"

"They were stupid, Thomas. Trying to just get into a world where they didn't belong, really."

"That can't be it. Half the rebels in the country are just farmers. They don't belong either."

"But they're just asking to be used like weapons, aren't they? Give me a gun and tell me who to shoot. Your pals wanted to be involved in a different way. There was money in it, too. People in this town will do anything for money."

Conlon nodded. That money had been trouble from the moment they had come into it.

BOD, as if reading his mind, asked, "Where did youse get all that money? Your friend, Podge...he owned a shop, didn't he? But you grew up with him. So how'd he afford it?"

"It's a long story. We got lucky. Or maybe it was unlucky, based on everything that's happened since."

"Was it dirty money?"

"Yeah, probably. But we came into it fairly. Does it matter, BOD?"

"No, I'm just a curious old boy, that's all. Do you still have any?"

"No. That's what McPhail was looking for when he was asking around about me, isn't it? So he knew about the money. But we didn't tell anyone."

"One of you must've told somebody."

"No. We talked about it. You're right; people here will do anything for money. Especially a lot of money. So we were careful. Which means he found out by asking them, maybe..."

"You don't know this, Thomas."

"No, but it fits with everything I've heard about the man. Would he be above torture if he thought he could make a fair few bob?"

BOD didn't answer and looked away. The sun had come out, and Conlon had to squint to make BOD out, crouched amidst his runner beans.

Finally, after the silence had stretched out, BOD said, "You don't even know for sure how involved McPhail was. You don't want to be going off and doing anything stupid because you're assuming it was him."

"You're right. Before I do anything stupid, I'll be sure."

He stood. BOD looked at him, shading his eyes from the sun with a gloved hand.

"What are you going to do, Thomas?"

"Same as I have been doing—ask a few questions."

BOD nodded with a relieved, "All right, so."

"What they need to worry about is what happens when I run out of questions, BOD. I'll see you around."

———

CONLON GOT off the tram in town; he ate a sandwich, drank a half a Guinness, and read a newspaper alone in Bowes before heading home. The sun was filling the streets with a warm yellow light and there was a pleasing haze over the Liffey. His conversation with BOD and the resolution he had made gave him a feeling of lightness, so he walked home. His mother was waiting for him at the door.

"There was a lassie here for you, a Mrs. Byrne. George's wife. I hadn't met her before. Very upset, she was."

"Why? Did she say why?"

"I sat her down and gave her a cup of tea but her hands were shaking, the poor thing, and she could barely sit still."

"Why, Ma? What did she say?"

"She said she had to talk to you."

"That's it? You didn't get any details out of her?"

"I think George hasn't come home but she didn't exactly say that."

"Why wasn't Molly here? Between the two of you, you could get anything out of anyone."

"She's at her Aunt Rosaline's."

"I should go and make sure she's all right."

"You should, you should. She was awful upset. A very pretty girl, isn't she?"

He was already out the door when she said this and he ran most of the way, growing increasingly worried as he did so. Theresa seemed so sensible and unflappable. If she was upset enough to show up at his door looking for help, then things had to be bad. Something had happened and she was scared. With these thoughts came an unmistakable feeling of guilt as if he had gotten her into this. Which was not true. George had, by marrying her. Or nobody had and this was life. Bad things came out of the darkness, terrifyingly, at random, and caused pain.

But still, Conlon felt guilty. And worried. He did not want anything to happen to her, did not want her to feel any of that pain.

He was unsure if the sudden sweat on his brow came from his jog through the sunny afternoon or his sudden realization of how much she meant to him, and he disliked the ambiguity.

He saw her at her window as he approached the house. She was in the doorway when he got there and she came sobbing into his arms like a child as soon as they were close enough to touch. He held her, feeling her shudder as she coughed out great racking heaves of grief into his chest. George's mother appeared in the hall behind her. He had known her for years. They had always got on well but she was keen on propriety; he knew she would not like this. He saw her expression harden but he gave her the kind of stare few people ever got to see from him and she nodded, flustered, and retreated.

He guided Theresa up the stairs, and helped her into a seat, gave her his handkerchief and knelt beside her, holding her hand, one arm still around her shoulders.

When he felt she was ready, he said, "Tell me. What's happened?"

She could not speak for a moment. She put her head back, her eyes closed, trying to control her breathing. He squeezed her hand.

"It's fine. Take your time."

She looked at him. "H-he was due back yesterday. Yesterday morning. He's never even been late before! Always on time. But nothing. Nothing, Thomas, and I couldn't help of thinking of your story about your other friends. I haven't been able to get it out of my mind. I didn't sleep last night. I know that something's happened to him, I just know it, I know it."

"Is the boat in? Did you try the boat company?"

"Yes, I talked to Brian Sharp. He's his best pal on the boats...he said it docked on time. George was on it. He left at the usual time. He was coming home, he said. It was just another day. But where is he? Where could he be?"

She started to cry again. And, as he had known with the others, Conlon felt it in his gut: George was dead. He held her and let her cry.

She said in a rush into his shoulder, "Those people you talked about, they're the types that'd just kill him, aren't they? Aren't they? It wouldn't mean much to them either way. But he's my husband and he's young and so gentle. Oh Tommy, please tell me they haven't killed him. The world can't be that cruel. He doesn't deserve it —not George, not George..."

He felt an extraordinary tenderness toward her then. She was so small and vulnerable and afraid. He rubbed her back and held her until she had stopped shaking and it felt as if she had almost fallen asleep.

Then he said, "I'll go and see what I can find out. He might have fallen ill, Theresa. There are a few explanations. Try not to worry."

Those words felt less than pointless and inadequate in the face of this reality. But she nodded.

He helped her up and led her back downstairs to George's mothers' door. The old woman answered and Conlon took Theresa past her and directed her into an armchair near the fireplace.

At the door, he turned to George's mother and said, "I'm sorry, Mrs. Byrne. Has this ever happened before? Anything like this?"

"No, you know George, Tommy; he was born two weeks early for God's sake. He's never late, he plans everything."

She put her hand to her eyes.

"I'm sorry, I know this must be hard for you, too. But she needs you now. You can help each other."

"Are you going to find him?"

"I'll try. I'll be as quick as I can."

"Lord have Mercy on you. I'll say a prayer."

He nodded with no idea how to respond to that. Then he was gone.

———

THERE WAS a DMP man at the Gate of Exchange Court and a handful of soldiers inside the gates, in the courtyard. This DMP man was a big man, late-middle aged, and he looked as if he would win a fight with a rhinoceros.

He looked at Conlon with a kindly, vaguely patronizing air. "Can I help you, lad?"

"I need to see Inspector Barry. Detective Barry. I'm not sure of his rank. I know he works here."

"What'd it concern?"

"It's important."

The DMP man looked at him for another five seconds or so then nodded and returned to the guard box by the gate. He picked up a telephone, had a short exchange, then looked at Conlon. "What's your name?"

"Thomas Conlon."

The conversation resumed. Conlon eyed the soldiers through the gate.

The DMP man returned to his side. "He'll be right down, he said."

"Thank you."

He followed Conlon's gaze to the soldiers. After a moment, he said, "Imagine, right? You grow up in Grimsby or Stoke or Rotherham. Fuck all education. Not much chance of a decent job. So you join the army for some adventure, want to see the world. And they send you to this shithole full of diseased peasants, whores and drunken fucking priests, where most people hate your guts. Not only that but the weather is shit and there's as much chance of being shot or blown up as there is in India or China or wherever. Joke's on them, isn't it?"

Conlon made a noise. Then thought. Then said, "Or

maybe they're just really fucking happy that they didn't end up at the Somme."

"Fair fucking point, Thomas Conlon."

Barry was as good as his word and was at the gate quickly. "Tommy. I didn't think I'd be seeing you again so soon. I take it that there isn't a happy reason for your visit."

"I've a friend gone missing."

"Another one? You think something's happened to him? Was he involved in—"

"Not at all but they won't know that. He's a married man. He was due home yesterday morning. He wouldn't do that. Something's wrong."

Barry nodded. "Let me make some calls. Don, let him in the gate, would ye? He's with me."

The DMP man gave a little nod and a grin and waved Conlon through.

Barry said, "What's his name?"

"George Byrne."

"Description?"

"Five feet six, dark hair, clean shaven."

"That doesn't help much."

"He's the type that doesn't really stand out, George."

"All right. I won't be long. Don't punch anyone."

The soldiers watched him. Could they tell that he had been one of them, just weeks before? Did he still bear that mark, give off the scent? He felt so different already.

George. George was dead. He knew it and he knew it was connected; everything was connected. He had to calm down. Think. He leaned against a wall, closed his eyes, and willed his mind still, the way he had done so many times in France, when he could feel fear and anger gnawing at his nerves.

Time telescoped. He was not asleep but all thought had ceased. He had no idea how much later Barry interrupted by coming back to tell him what he had discovered, "The Mater. We'll drive, come on."

He led Conlon through a courtyard and out of the complex via a smaller gate to a garage in a yard manned by DMP men. Shining black automobiles stood in a line. Barry signed a ledger at a desk and then they were climbing into a car. Lurching out onto the road, the growl of the car's engine filled Conlon's hearing so that he could not make out the words Barry was shouting at him. The policeman made a face that passed from annoyed to amused in seconds and they drove the rest of the way without any attempts at communication.

Conlon had never ridden in a motorcar through Dublin before. People actually looked to see who could be in the vehicle, which was an occurrence he disliked, though Barry seemed not to notice. At the Mater, Barry parked it with a jerk. They both heard the rheumatic sputter of the exhaust before it was still and silent. Conlon's ears rang.

"I should have chosen another one. That one's a loud fucker," said Barry as they walked away.

"So what are we here to see?" Conlon asked him.

"Let me ask you, what do you think has happened to your friend, this George?"

"I think he's dead."

"Why do you think that?"

"Because I'm a pessimist. What are we here to see?"

"A body. A young man, found in the early hours of

the morning. They're not sure about cause of death yet, but it looks like he had his brains beaten in."

"Ah fuck..."

"It might not be him. You said he was married?"

"Yeah."

"Children?"

"No."

Confronted with the reality of it and what they were about to do, Conlon suddenly felt nauseated. He had seen so much death, so much gore and blood, images still occasionally opened up in his mind of horrors he would have once struggled to even imagine. But he had known George since he had been a boy. He remembered hours and days in his company, playing, laughing, talking. He did not want to see his ruined corpse. He did not want to tell Theresa that her quiet, respectable, lovely young husband had been beaten to death. He did not want to see that register in her eyes. He hoped his Ma's prayer would work.

———

THEY WERE LED to a room in the basement. On the walk down there had been no talking. Instead, Conlon had listened to the scuff and squeak of their shoes on the floor and the jingle of keys in the orderly's pocket with each step. There were endless doors on either side. That smell made him think of a tent in France, blood on his trouser legs, a nurse with kind eyes and a Scottish accent. Barry glanced at him once, checking he was ok, and maintained his deadpan face.

This room was brightly lit. Nevertheless, it carried an odd charge, something you could sense even before the door was opened. Conlon realized why as soon as they were inside: bodies lay on trollies in two rows, each covered by a sheet.

The one nearest the door was George. The brow on the right side of his face and around his eye had been damaged. It looked crushed, like wood that has been hammered, the skin swollen and yet crumpled inwards. Around his mouth was also burnished and misshapen. Conlon stopped staring and looked at Barry.

"It's him."

"Right so."

The sheet was gently replaced and they retreated from the room in silence. The three walked back the way they had come, then went into another room, an office this time, in which sat a middle-aged man with a luxurious head of silver hair above a body that seemed square in his dark suit. He instantly reminded Conlon of the busts he had seen of composers—Chopin and Mozart and Beethoven—all arrogance and grumpiness.

Barry said, "Doc. What can ye tell me?"

The Doctor looked at Conlon and said, "Who is this?"

"He's assisting our inquiries in this case. An expert witness, you might call him."

"I might. And what exactly is your expertise?" He swiveled his gaze toward Conlon who recognized the feeling of scrutiny. Officers had once looked at him this way, their assumed superiority as plain in their faces as the color of their eyes.

Conlon shrugged. "That dead man in there was my friend. Is that expertise enough for you?"

Barry drawled, "You should've just answered when I asked..."

The doctor visibly struggled with his feelings for a moment and then he began speaking as if the conversation had not even taken place.

"He was severely beaten. Perhaps as many as a dozen blows to the face and head."

"With fists?"

"No, a weapon. But I suspect something small."

"Blackjack?"

"Maybe."

"Truncheon?"

"Too large."

"Brass knuckles," Conlon said.

"Yes, that would be my guess."

Conlon and Barry looked at one another. They thanked the doctor and returned to the corridor. On their way back toward the car, Barry said, "So we both know that McPhail likes his brass knuckles."

Conlon said nothing. They were at the main door.

He looked at Barry. "Thanks for your help. I really appreciate it."

"What're you doin' now?"

"Telling his wife that she's a widow."

"Right. Do you want me to come?"

"No. No, I should do it. But thanks."

"No bother."

Conlon turned to go and Barry said, "You know that wasn't enough evidence, don't you? He's not the only thug in the city carries brass knuckles."

Conlon looked at him and nodded. "I know."

"So don't be doing anything too mad, now."

"I'll try not to."

"Right. See you."

"See you."

And Conlon was off, thinking of how he was going to break this to Theresa.

———

HE HAD one last card to play. Sean's notebook had contained five addresses. The one in Glasnevin had led him to Birthmark; Rossa, the safe house that he assumed must have been used for meetings or trades at some point in time. The one in Monkstown was probably McPhail's house, but he would have to confirm that personally. The ones in Crumlin and the North Wall had potential. So that was where he headed, straight from George's house to Crumlin.

There he had left Theresa, whose tears had stopped only a few minutes after he had told her and George's mother that George was dead. In truth, they told him, they had known as soon as they saw his face. He had approached the house struggling with himself—what words to use, how to dress it up, how direct and honest to be—and that had shown on his face. They had seen it and known it for what it was.

And yet, out of some nameless desire for something —emotion or empathy or import or finality—they had allowed him to tortuously tell them, hating his own fumbling inarticulacy, hating the pain he was causing them, all the while still trying to deal with the sight of George's corpse, lodged as it was in his brain. Finally, through tears that streamed down the sides of her nose, Theresa had stood and walked to him and he put his arms around her small shoulders and held her as she cried into him.

All the while, as he thought about how fragile she

was, how hot she felt beneath his fingers, how she smelled, even in this state, of cinnamon and rose and soap, another part of him was funneling down, preparing.

They had murdered George. George had been utterly, perfectly innocent. George knew more or less nothing. George was not a threat to them; he could not implicate or harm or identify them. His death was of no benefit to anybody. They had killed him because he was associated with Podge, and Sean...and with him.

He allowed the fury that came with these thoughts to cool, allowed it to settle into intent. He was going to hurt somebody.

This was the first definitive piece of evidence he had encountered, and it allowed him the luxury of revenge. He stayed with Theresa and George's mother until he felt she no longer needed his immediate presence. And then he left.

He was walking across the city and it wasn't a short walk. He knew himself well enough to know that he would start to lose faith in his own course along the way. He would become reasonable. His rage would burn itself out. So he refused to allow that to happen. Instead, he thought about George: George as a boy, when they had met; George breaking his arm climbing trees in the Phoenix Park; the first time George had ever eaten chocolate, the joy of it dissolving something in his round little face.

George. They had killed George.

10

HARRY WAS BORED. THIS WAS A FUCKING BORING JOB AS Dermot had said not ten minutes earlier. Nothing had happened, nor was it likely to and, if by some act of divine intervention, something did happen then there were five of them here most of the time and that was at least three men too many. They could handle anything that Dublin could throw at them. So they all sat around, trying not to get on each other's nerves.

The rest of them were still playing poker, but Harry had gotten pissed off with that after an hour or so, and he didn't have any money to bet anyway, having wasted most of it on floozies in the Monto two days earlier, when it was his turn for a day out. He needed to be doing things, that was the problem. He had too much energy to be sitting and waiting. This guard duty was not right for him at all and he would try to get that across to McPhail the next time the boss man was here. He shoulda been out and about, on the move. It was almost physically painful being in one place for so long, even with the conversation and the other lads to distract him—not that they did for long. They had been talking solidly for three days by then, waiting for these Wexford Fenians or wherever they were from, and he had heard all their best jokes and knew their personalities a bit too well. Tensions were starting to nip around their ankles over meals.

So now, he was wandering the house, trying to find anything to keep his mind occupied. It wasn't as if it was a big house with loads of wandering available to him. No, it was a typical terrace: kitchen and two rooms downstairs, three bedrooms upstairs, one of them the size of a wardrobe, and a toilet out in the backyard. But Harry was a tenement boy and, to him, that seemed an almost obscene amount of space if you were going to live in it. But not enough space, crucially, to keep Harry from getting bored, not enough to explore, not enough to do, not enough doors to open. The lads were around the living room, at the back, with their cards on a table that was a bit too low for the game so every time he passed through that room—which was a lot, because that room was at the foot of the stairs, so every single fucking time he wanted to go upstairs, he had to walk right through the game, which pissed everyone off. Then he had to do the same on the way back.

Right now, he was upstairs, smoking by the window in the front room, eying the street as if it held wonders, when really all he could see was a bunch of tenement kids from a few streets away playing barefoot with what looked like a tin can. It wasn't a warm day. Winter was just around the corner and it was testing the air in the city with its sharp little teeth, preparing to take a proper mouthful. But the kids ran around the street on their little feet as if the cold was nothing. He was one of those kids once, he thought. He remembered the ache of cold in his feet, the hunger, the fleas, and playing in the streets with friends. Even then, he had been constantly restless, unable to sit down for long. It had made school torture for him, despite his ma and da's persistence and strictness, and he could just about read and do simple sums when he left. He had always played sports as a channel for all his energy. He played football; he hurled and he boxed, a bit.

There were no steady jobs, obviously, for somebody like him. He took what he could, on the docks, on the canals, in a warehouse or two, working as a navvy all over the city. He always did physical work; whatever kind of work it was, it was always backbreaking and poorly paid. His workmates had been men like him. Some had been doing it for decades. They were old men with bent spines and aching muscles, faces coppered by working outside in all weather, hacking coughs each morning and rueful jokes all day. Many of them were Fenians. Some thought that an Irish Free State would be a socialist paradise where poor people like them would have greater rights and where life wouldn't be quite as grim and difficult as it was for them now. Others knew their history and hated the English, wanted them off the Island at any cost. Others still enjoyed belonging to a movement, to an organization. They liked being told what to do and where to go; they enjoyed the security of it.

Harry had been bored and the Volunteers gave him something to do. He didn't really believe in any of the shite he heard friends and workmates spouting. He doubted posh Irish people being in charge would make life for poor people any better than having posh English people in charge had done. Socialism was just a word to him, as was Fenian. He'd barely ever met any English people. It all seemed remote from his life: from waking up at half six in a freezing tenement room he shared with seven other people; from inhaling tar smoke that gulped from barrels while he labored with a shovel nearby; from never sitting on the couch in the French's room because it was jumping with fleas; from making a loaf of bread last a week between five people. But the Volunteers gave him something to do at night—training, maneuvers, meetings. So he went to a meeting and zoned out when their talking dragged on too long (which it always did). But he made some decent friends and he had a bit of fun so he went again. And again.

He tired of watching the children play. He sat down on the bed, stood up again and wandered over to the door. He crossed the landing and opened the door to the box room. The crates were still there, of course, the word HAMBURG painted on them. He wanted to open one but he knew McPhail would kill him if he did. Probably literally. He closed the door and went into the other bedroom. It smelled in here; a warm funk of sweat, socks, feet, and ass. He wrinkled his nose and walked over to open the window. He stuck his head out. A woman was pegging out washing in the yard a few houses down. She caught his eye and smiled. He smiled back.

He sat down on this bed. He felt like he had to get out of this house. He knew that he couldn't and that just made his need to get out even more pronounced.

He had a flash memory of Jacobs. The endless waiting there, waiting for the British to come, itching to fire his rifle, at least once. But that chance had never come. Instead, he had spent the week of the Rising keeping watch in a small room, eating biscuits, listening to abuse from the people in the nearby tenements. And then, afterwards, the British had arrested him anyway and sent him to Wales with everybody else.

In Frongoch, he had kept busy. He boxed more—he won a few fights, even—he ran, he played cards. But underneath all that, he had been bored on a level he had never experienced before. And now here he was, bored again.

He had followed some of his mates from Frongoch into this, working for McPhail. They basically provided security for gun-runners; they guarded guns and money, which was piss-boring, it turned out because nothing ever happened. The British never showed up, nobody ever tried to double-cross them; nobody tried to steal their loads.

He heard a knock on the door downstairs but stayed where he was. It wasn't worth going down and past all those fuckers at the table just to see one gobshite at the door. He heard the heavy rumble of one of them in the hall. The door opened and there was a murmur of conversation and then it went quiet. The door closed gently.

Nothing for a few seconds, and then, mayhem.

He heard what sounded like three of them start talking—shouting—at the same time. There was a crash which could only have been the table flipping, knocks and clatters, people crying out, and wet sounds. Then another cry. There was violent, sudden scraping along the floorboards and glass shattering. Dermot shouted, "Get a hold—"

Then there was more clattering.

Harry was standing now, on the landing, his pistol in his hand. He was terrified. He had no idea what was happening downstairs. He crept down the stairs pointing his gun at the gap, the space of the living room he could see. Each step brought more into view and forced him to turn his arm, keeping the room as a target.

Rory was unconscious on his back. He lay in the doorway. His head was in the kitchen and his body was in the living room. That was the first thing of any use he made out as he descended. Another step showed him that the table had been flipped and was upside down and covering Rory from the chest down.

There were more noises from the room: the hard slap of flesh on flesh, grunting, scuffing of feet on floor. One of them was hanging out the window, its glass gone, as if he was stretching to pick up something from the yard outside. He thought it was Breslin. Dermot was on his face on the floor beside the table.

And then he saw who was responsible. A man was standing, his back to Harry, between the stairs and the fireplace. Facing him was Gareth, that flick knife he carried in the air between them, waving slowly. He was so focused on the blade and the man that Gareth didn't see him on the stairs. Suddenly, Gareth made his move, flicking the blade at the man, who moved just like an animal, Harry thought, to let the knife slide through the air beside him and hammer a blow almost casually to throw Gareth backwards into the fireplace. Gareth was not getting up. His eyes were closed and he was unconscious.

It was a beautiful punch, Harry realized.

The man stood, five other men down on the floor around him, the room a mess.

"Don't move," Harry said.

The man was half-turned by now and he looked at Harry but kept his hands down.

"Hands up," Harry said.

"Which one?"

This stumped Harry, for he had not expected a response. "Both of them."

"No—don't move or hands up? You're confusing me."

Harry knew him from somewhere, he was sure. He had seen him before.

"Hands up," he said.

The man nodded and raised his hands. He had cold blue eyes, broad shoulders, and thick brown hair. Where did he know this man from?

Carefully, Harry took the last steps down into the living room. He had to skirt the overturned table. Playing cards were scattered like leaves in October. "Did you kill them?" he asked, indicating the men littering the floor around the room.

"No. I could have." The man's tone was reasonable and relaxed. He was not remotely afraid despite the fact that he was facing a loaded gun and a man with every reason to shoot him. He even said, "Don't make me kill you." Like he was doing Harry a favor!

Harry tried to laugh, to show how unafraid he was, to show he was in control here. "You're the one with a gun on you."

The man nodded. "What is that...a Bulldog? That'd do it, all right. But unless you shoot me in the head, it won't put me down. And once I close the distance between us, that's it. What'll you do then? I don't want to hurt you."

"I know you," Harry said.

The man cocked his head. "You're a Dub—where are you from?"

"Church Street."

The man laughed warmly. "Stoneybatter."

And that unlocked something in Harry. He made a connection and suddenly he recognized this man; he knew exactly where and when he had seen him.

"You're fucking Tommy Conlon! Aren't you? Tommy Conlon, what happened to you?"

Conlon laughed aloud at that, at the incongruity or the brass of the question, Harry didn't know. But he felt happy to have made this man laugh. "The Great War," Conlon said.

"Why are you—what are you doing here? You working for the Brits?"

"No. It's a long story."

"I used to train in your gym. I watched you sparring load'sa times. You were like a prince in that gym, just better than the rest of us. My mates and me just wanted to be like you, the way you destroyed people in the ring. I shoulda known from the way you punched him." He gestured at Gareth but he couldn't stop this sudden flow of words. "Once we went up to Wicklow with a load of ol' lads to get turf, you were there."

"With Roderick? I remember that. You were the skinny lad?"

"Yeah, yeah, that was me, yeah, you remember?"

"I do. Harry, is it?"

"Harry, yeah, Harry Shiels." Harry felt a burst of pride and gratitude to be remembered.

Conlon nodded, calm, as though they were in a pub. "You gonna put that gun down, Harry?"

Harry did it. Conlon put out his hand and Harry daintily placed the gun in it. It seemed ridiculous to keep hold of it, to keep pointing it at this man who had been like a God to him.

Conlon pocketed it and looked at him. "What the fuck is a good tenement boy like you doing working for McPhail, Harry? You do work for him, right?"

"Yeah. It's a job. I—I was in the Rising, I went to Frongoch, I came back...I just went along with me mates."

"What do you do?"

"We just protect the loads."

"What loads?"

"The guns."

"Guns that are brought in?"

"Yeah, yeah. From Germany and Belgium and America, even. We meet them at harbors and we bring them back to Dublin. Then McPhail moves them on. I'm still helping the cause. But I'm getting paid, too.'"

"There are guns here? Now?"

Harry nodded.

"Show me."

So he brought Conlon upstairs. Like he was showing him proudly around, Harry swung the box room door open and pointed at the crates. Conlon went straight inside and cracked one open. He pulled through the straw and came out with a small sack. He ripped a hole in it and Harry saw sand stream to the floor. Conlon rummaged once more.

"All sacks. Sand."

He moved on to another crate and did the same thing with an identical result.

"You boys are guarding sacks of sand, Harry. Did you see these come off a boat?"

"Not these ones, no. Sometimes we just pick them up in Ireland—they've already arrived. We got these ones out of a barn out near Lusk. What does this mean?"

"Are any of your friends likely to know any more about all this than you?"

"No, no. We came on together."

Conlon closed his eyes.

"Do you ever do any other kind of work for him?"

"No, he has other lads for that. They're with us sometimes. Gangsters, they are. They tell stories..."

"What kind of stories?"

"Well, they heard some of the lads talking about the Rising, right? And the lads who were there like to talk about it. It's something to be proud of."

"Of course, it is."

"And these lads hear us and they have to—sort of—compete with us because they weren't there, they weren't part of it. Their stories are all about killing people, only they sound like executions, not battles or anything."

"What kind of people?"

"They don't say names, really. Just sort of vague: where it happened and what they did."

"Like what?"

"Why do you want to know this? What are you doing, anyway?"

"Listen," he said. "McPhail is using his reputation as a gunrunner to make some money for nothing. Some friends of mine went missing when I was away. As far as I can tell, they tried to buy some guns to help the Fenians. I think McPhail didn't have any guns. He just pretended that he did and then killed them and took their money."

"How many of them?"

"Two."

"They talked about some lad who they shot out in Howth and dumped out at sea, weighed down with rocks, but not two lads."

"Did it sound like he was there for guns?"

"Yeah, it did; the way they told it, it sounded just like the way their guns come in. Only there were no guns."

"No. There were no guns."

They were silent then. Harry could see Conlon's eyes moving as he wrestled with something.

"Do you know who these are meant for?"

"Somebody from Wexford or Waterford, I think. Next week."

"What happens to the money?"

"His lads take it. McPhail's. They must keep it somewhere. It's not going in any bank, that's for bleedin' sure."

"Right. I think I know where."

Conlon looked at Harry. His stare was intimidating; Harry wanted to look away instantly.

"He'll kill you," Conlon said. "If he figures out you've told me anything, he'll kill you."

"I know."

"So what I'm gonna do is I'm gonna punch you in the face. Maybe give you a black eye. You can say I clocked you on the stairs. Then it'll look like I found the guns on me own. All right with you?"

"Yeah, yeah."

"All right. I'll count to three."

Harry braced himself. He closed his eyes and put out his chin slightly as if expecting a kiss.

"One—"

Conlon hit him. Harry bent over, holding his eye, the pain sudden and intense.

"You all right?"

"Yeah, yeah. Jaysis, remind me never to get into a proper scrap with you."

"Right. I'm going. Hopefully, if we meet again, Harry, it'll be in better circumstances."

"Yeah. See ye, Tommy."

"See ya."

And Harry sat there, happier than he had been for a long time as the skin around his eye began to swell and burn.

———

CONLON FELT NOW as if he had momentum, as though he was finally getting somewhere. Like he was close to ending this, whichever way that went. And though it was getting dark and late, and though he felt as if he should go back and check on Theresa, and though he was feeling tired as the controlled rage that pushed him through fights like that one ebbed away, he knew he had to use this momentum to see what he could accomplish with the rest of this day. He felt as if he was doing something good. It was a feeling he had never had in the War and one he had not even known he missed. But now it gave him a sort of ballast—he was on the right side here, and there was a strength that came with that. A strength he had never before known. So he headed for the North Wall.

Part of him was hoping that it would be like that house—filled with useless foot soldiers who didn't see him coming and couldn't fight worth a damn. Beating up those men had left him with a good feeling, one he had almost forgotten—the ease of it, doing something he did with such efficiency and poise.

He needed something now—proof? Leverage? A way to get at McPhail, at least. Much as part of him wanted to, he could not just walk up to the man in the street and kill him. He needed reasons. There needed to be a trail of breadcrumbs, something people could point to as explanation of his actions if he was not around to explain himself.

It took him a while to find the house. It was further north than he had expected. It was the last house in a line of terraces, all of which looked like tenements. The house was the exception to that, he thought, studying it from across the street for a while. There were lights on downstairs that were muted by the heavy curtains he could make out through the big windows in the front room. But unlike in the tenements, the other floors were dark. The door was painted and shining in the last of the light of dusk.

Children played on the front steps of the other houses; voices called down stairs and food smells billowed from windows open just a crack. This house was silent and hunkered down, trying not to be noticed. But the people inside, the people trying so hard not to attract attention, they weren't from around here. If they had been, they might have understood this place and known how to fit in to some degree.

Conlon watched for a full ten minutes, debating with himself. The rush that had gotten him through in the last house was totally spent, gone, and he felt exhausted. He didn't know how many men were in the house, or how many guns they had. He didn't know why they were in the house, even. It probably made sense to assume that if McPhail had five men guarding imaginary guns, he would have more men here guarding what Conlon assumed was money. But then, the men guarding the imaginary guns had partly been there to make the lie of the guns more convincing. So would McPhail have fewer men here, in the hope that anyone interested in his money would assume that he would never have so small a group guarding his cash? Was it possible, even, that the money was unguarded? Conlon had no idea. For all he knew, the money wasn't here. For all he knew, there was no money.

The Major would have ripped his bollocks off for even considering fighting an engagement on a field he did not know. It was, ordinarily, a recipe for disaster, for death or a beating. But he knew he could handle a few of them at once, and he knew they would be utterly unprepared for somebody like him coming at them as quickly and as powerfully as he could. He had been trained to put men down before they were even aware they were in a fight, and he had always done it very well.

Also, he knew houses like this one. He had grown up in a house just like it. Furniture could be moved—even used—during a fight. The layout of the rooms would be no surprise.

He considered for a moment and then he approached the children playing nearby. They wore rags, more or less. It was a chilly evening but most of them were barefoot. Some wore jumpers with holes in the arms and collars, others in ratty jackets too big for them. Their hair looked shiny with dirt. He had been one of them, fifteen years before—him, George, and Podge.

The children ignored him, riveted by an intense conversation between two of them, their heads down.

Conlon said, "Any of yis want to make yourselves a shilling?"

Their heads snapped round as one.

"I want yis to do a knick-knack for me. Do yis still call them knick-knacks?"

A small boy with a round face and a wicked grin was the one who spoke for them: "Why do you want us to do a knick-knack? Can you not do it yourself?"

"I'm playing a joke on a pal. I want to see his face the second or third time yis do it."

The boy considered, eying him.

"A shilling each," the boy said, his tone commendably even.

Conlon laughed. "I can't afford that. Two shillings between the lot of ye."

The boy maintained eye contact but Conlon felt the ripple pass through the rest of them. He could guess at how much the boy wanted to look at his friends. Two shillings was a massive amount for something so small.

"What house?" the boy asked as if he wasn't bothered.

"Last one," Conlon said. "Down there."

Now, the boy looked at his friends. "All right, yeah. Money first?"

Conlon nodded, dug in his pocket. He flicked the first coin at a girl standing near him, probably the oldest of them. It flashed in the light as it spun in the air. She caught it like a cat swiping at a bird, examined it and, beaming, nodded to the rest.

"You knock three times," Conlon said. "When they come out, the rest of you need to be invisible. Two minutes after the first knock, do it again, then five minutes after the second. Has one of yis got a watch?"

The girl said, "I'll count it."

Conlon looked at her, then nodded. He flicked the second coin at the boy. The boy was determinedly relaxed. He let the coin fall into his palm, without apparent effort.

"Give me a few minutes to get a good vantage point then start. Ok?"

The boy nodded. There was a giggly hysteria about the group now.

Conlon went to turn away and a voice said, "Mister."

He looked at the speaker, a tiny boy who was sitting by the railings. "What?" he said.

"You're weird, you are."

Conlon laughed. Then he nodded and moved off.

He walked around the corner and into the lane that ran behind the run of houses. It was dark here; night had come with a smothering suddenness and the lamps didn't reach this laneway, so he had to take it slowly and feel with his hands. He climbed over the back fence to the house in one easy motion and dropped down into the garden, hoping that the darkness hid no rocks or thorny bushes. He landed in thick, long grass. Of course, they didn't pay any attention to the garden. Why would they?

He crouched and moved toward the house, the posture as he moved reminding him of training, of missions in France with silence, patience, and death.

Something moved rapidly in the grass to his right. It had to be a rat, a bird, or a cat. He had no way of knowing which.

There was a light on in one of the back rooms and its glow gave some shape to the area immediately closest to the house. It was ghostly—dark shapes against pale air. He skirted around a couple, then paused just on the edge of the area which was most brightly illuminated. He crossed it in two steps and slid down to hunker right beside the back door and beneath what should be the kitchen window.

He thought about his breathing then controlled it and he listened. The sharp rap on the door seemed thunderous in the silence. He heard voices inside the house—a bass-like rumble. Men. Impossible to say how many voices here were—it could be two; it could be six.

He could not hear the door opening or any of the ensuing conversation but he heard it slam shut again a moment later. He could imagine them inside, grumbling about the kids and debating whether or not to sit down, knowing the kids would do it again. Conlon waited. His eyes had become accustomed to the darkness now. Stretching one arm up along the wall, he tested the back door. It was locked but it felt light, almost flimsy. He raised his head to check out the window. It was a clasp and it was locked.

He ducked down again. The second knock was just as loud and a little more prolonged. The children were enjoying themselves. This time, the sounds of movement in the house were different, the clump of feet in the hall firmer. The man shouted into the night sky: "Fuck off you little bollix!"

He heard a second man laugh.

He waited, counting. The girl had done her job well. When the knock came, Conlon tensed. He listened for the ripple of footfall in the house. Then he stood, turned, and kicked in the back door. He had the pistol he had taken from Harry in his hand. He was quickly through the kitchen and, in the hall, a man was emerging from the drawing room, confusion on his face. He had probably heard the back door go but had been confused because he had been listening for noise from the front where his friend had gone to deal with the kids. He went for a gun and Conlon savagely brought the pistol down on the man's nose. It exploded instantly, blood spurting out sideways. The man uttered a strangulated cry and pressed both hands to his face. Conlon followed with two rapid, powerful body blows and the man went down in the doorway.

Conlon stepped over him and had a quick look around the drawing room. Nobody else was inside. Outside, the other man was on the porch yelling down the street at the fleeing children. Conlon walked toward him and took him in a brutal chokehold, one arm tight under his chin, his other elbow pressed against the base of the skull. At the same time, Conlon pulled him backward into the house. When the man was unconscious, Conlon allowed him to slip to the floor. He closed the front door and dragged the man by his feet into the kitchen. The other one was still groaning in the doorway.

Conlon ran up the stairs and quickly checked all of the bedrooms for people. They were empty and only one had beds that had been recently occupied.

Conlon went back down the stairs and approached the man in the doorway. Conlon crouched down beside him, grabbed a handful of his hair, and pulled his head up. The man looked gray. His features were slack and his eyes struggled to focus. Blood ran down his face over his mouth and chin in a single thick red river and dribbled onto his chest.

"Hey," Conlon said. He slapped the man on the cheek. Once, twice. The eyes snapped into focus and found him. "Where's the money?"

The man blinked and then blinked again.

"Where's the money?"

He shook his head.

"Talk. Where's the money?"

"No money."

"What?"

"No money. It's not here."

Conlon nodded and then he threw a short punch at the man's nose, eliciting a scream. The blood flow increased. He coughed and blood flew from his mouth.

"It's not here; it's not here. We move it around in case somebody tries to lift it. I swear, I swear."

"Where is it?"

"He'll kill me."

"He won't kill anyone. Where is it."

"He'll kill me..."

"Do you know who I am?"

The man nodded.

"Don't worry about McPhail. I'll deal with him. Where is it?"

THE MONEY WAS IN A WAREHOUSE, about half a mile away, near the Sloblands on the edge of Fairview. From outside, the place looked closed up and sleeping but the man cautioned Conlon that there would be several guards, armed with rifles, inside the building.

Conlon took him seriously. He climbed the building next door—an abandoned shell that had once been a bakery—and watched the warehouse for almost an hour before making any attempt to enter. Reconnaissance had always been a strength of his; his attention to detail reflected in the plans he could formulate instantly. He remembered how impressed the Major had been in training by how rapidly he responded to observations.

Now, he crouched on the roof, pulling his coat tight to him against the cold and studied the warehouse. It was just over three stories tall. At one end, there were huge cantilevered doors to allow access to vehicles and carts for loading. That was all closed up from what he could see. The other end was where the offices were—staff rooms, toilets. There were windows there and a double door with frosted glass. He assumed at least one guard would be there. More windows ran along the walls, high up, all the way down the side of the building, which extended at least the length of a football pitch. There were skylights in the roof, which appeared to be composed of metal, perhaps copper. An access ladder led to that roof and he had identified it as the best point of entry.

He entered by a skylight and came out on a high thin walkway above the expanse of the warehouse space. Below, he saw that most of the warehouse was empty. The space was huge and echoed with darkness and the steady, determined drip of water from somewhere high up. The rest of the space was piled with wooden pallets in stacks and lines, filling about a third of the warehouse along one side. There was a mezzanine level near the offices on some sort of platform built above a cluster of machines and furniture, held up by pillars of wood or stone—Conlon could not tell from his position.

He moved patiently and quietly, letting the guards reveal themselves to him before they were even aware of his presence. He stuck to darkness and moved so slowly it was as if he was not moving until he could see all around him. Then he would determine how far he could go and what was the best path.

He discovered that there were three guards but he found one of them sleeping, one reading a paper, and the third daydreaming even as he walked around the warehouse floor. None of them took him more than five seconds to dispose of. Only the last one even saw his face, but what he saw was a shape move out of the darkness which sharpened into a face only at the very last moment, before he was unconscious like the others.

He found the money in the office at the back of the building, in a duffel bag under the desk. Conlon opened it briefly to have a look then he closed it up and started to leave. Then, through the window of the upstairs office where he had found the money, he glimpsed movement outside. He stood and watched. It was McPhail. He was carrying a rifle. There was a group of perhaps just over a dozen men with him, all similarly armed. McPhail spoke and pointed and they split off into groups.

They knew he was here. They had come for him.

11

McPhail had been interrupted in the middle of a game, which put him in a bad mood. All of his boys knew that, too, so if they were still willing to do it, any of them, then he was aware that it must be important. A year before, a young pup he had taken on from out near Swords had interrupted him over an injury suffered by one of his girls. McPhail had acted as if he were upset, as though the incident justified approaching him as he played. And then, later, he had beaten the boy into unconsciousness in one of his safehouses.

He was in a house in Stillorgan, enjoying a nice run at cards, when Stanno appeared at his side. Stanno had been with him for a while and had proven himself to be efficient and trustworthy. He looked terrible. McPhail winced. This house attracted wealthy men, and he was doing well here, up almost a hundred pounds. Stanno was waiting and McPhail could feel his anxiety, even without looking at him.

He leaned toward Stanno and cocked an ear. "Keep it simple," he said.

Stanno said, "Somebody hit the Crumlin house and the Dock house. Gene says he gave him the warehouse, too."

McPhail said to the table, "Sorry gents, an urgent matter needs to be dealt with. My apologies." He bowed, gathered his winnings, and nodded Stanno toward the door. After donning his jacket, they met there.

"Who hit us? The police?"

"No, no."

"A gang, the Fenians?"

"No. According to Harry and Gene, it was one man."

"Get to fuck."

They were walking now, down toward the center of town to get a cab, McPhail's long strides causing Stanno to have to hop into something like a run just to keep up.

"I swear boss, I swear. Harry recognized him."

"Who is he?"

"Tommy Conlon."

McPhail looked at him. They had killed one of Conlon's boys only the day before. They had been looking for Conlon for months but had been consistently told he was gone. And then he had returned and all he had done since then was cause McPhail trouble. He needed to be dead. "He had friends with him, no?"

"Not according to them, no. He's the boxer."

"I know who he is. I've fought boxers and won; it doesn't mean anything. Did he have a gun, at least?"

He had lied about fighting boxers but he wasn't sure why. Did Stanno care? Stanno was already afraid of him. Why did he bother? Because he needed his men to believe they could kill Conlon even though Conlon was already developing an aura of invincibility that would only grow the longer he remained alive.

Stanno remained silent and McPhail stared at him. "He was unarmed!?"

"Harry said he just tore through them. He'd never seen anything like it, he said."

"Harry better be at North Wall station when we get there. I need to talk to him."

"I'll have to stop and make a call."

"Do it. And get as many of the boys as you can. They'll need their guns. Get them to meet us at the warehouse as soon as possible. See how he tears through a dozen rifles."

Stanno peeled off at a certain pub and McPhail went on alone. He hailed a cab in the village center and sat brooding in the back as it made its way into town. He hated cabs; the rocking motion always got to his stomach.

That boy yesterday—they had taken him mainly to ask questions. Where was his share of the money? What was Conlon up to? Did Conlon still have his share? And the boy had been so meek and so willing to help in order to survive that it had enraged McPhail. All the boy had wanted was to get back to his wife, and he had begged, and answered their questions, and cried, and then McPhail had lost his temper and hit him. And then he put on his brass knuckles and hit him again and again and again until the punches met little resistance. All that and they got no money from it. The boy's share was all gone. Conlon was trying to find out what had happened to the other two. Conlon's money seemed to be gone; he had bought a house for his ma. These were the boy's answers.

Conlon had crossed Xavier somehow—the talk had always been over a girl. And they had run him out of town because of it. If he was back, that showed he was either tremendously brave or utterly stupid.

McPhail thought: there had been five men at the Crumlin house. How could he have beaten five men? At least two of them had been armed. If made no sense. Unless this Conlon actually was this good.

The thought sent a chill through him like a spear and he responded to his own fear as he always did, by transmuting it into rage. He was going to kill Conlon. Tonight.

———

WHEN CONLON SAW the band of men approaching the building, he crouched down and studied the group. They fanned out on approach, some headed toward the front door, and some, he assumed, moving around the warehouse to enter via the cantilevered doors. Perhaps a couple on or through the roof, too. He was trapped.

He was already realizing his mistake: he had taken too long to enter the warehouse. It had given one of the men from the houses enough time to recover and alert his mates and enough time for them to arm themselves and show up with some semblance of a working plan.

But they didn't even know for sure that he was here. If they found no trace of him they would assume that they had missed him. He would have to be sneaky, deliberate.

He put the duffle onto his back, a strap over each shoulder. He would have to be quick. He made for the door to this office.

The bullet took his leg at the same instant that he heard it break the window, its crack flat against the night sky. He went down and rolled for the door. Another shot came through the window, which shattered. With a burn in his leg, he rolled again. There was a sniper on the rooftop across the street. That was where Conlon would have put him, too. McPhail was thorough; Conlon would not underestimate him again. But now they also knew he was here so sneaking out of the building was no longer a realistic option.

He kept moving. If the sniper was any good, he would be moving, too, looking to finish Conlon off. He heard shouting from outside, from the front door downstairs. He pulled himself through the doorway and into the hall then ducked inside another room. He slid to sit against the wall and quickly inspected his leg. The bullet had entered his outer thigh about halfway between hip and knee and exited just above his knee bone. It didn't seem to have clipped any bone.

The adrenaline surging in him meant that it didn't hurt yet, registering only as a burning sensation and a sense that the upper half of his leg was locking up. But he knew that it would hurt eventually. He pulled out his handkerchief, ripped it in half, and tied it in a tight loop around his thigh, a loop so tight it made him grunt. Leaning his head back against the wall, eyes closed, he pulled the Bulldog he had taken from Harry out of his belt. It would only be useful in close quarters here. He wished he had brought out the Colt in his room at his ma's house. Better yet, he wished he had the Winchester that had served him so well in France.

From what he had seen, they had been carrying Lee Enfields and Browning shotguns and Mausers, and what had looked like one Chauchat. They were going to make a hell of a lot of noise, which meant they were confident they could take him quickly, before the DMP arrived.

He knew he had to get out of this part of the warehouse before they had him cornered here. They could go room to room and, with their firepower, he didn't stand a chance. He had to move now.

He was up and running with a limp, keeping low. Shots from the sniper strafed the wall behind him as he reacted to Conlon's movement. He could hear them downstairs, boots on the floor, voices raised, bolts in guns snapping. The sounds of imminent violence. He went up a short set of stairs and turned out onto the mezzanine. They could not see him up here—not yet. He ran across it, his limp worsening a little, and surveyed the darkness of the warehouse. The rows of pallets stretched away from him all the way to the wide doors at the far end, the other half just open floor, a field of concrete.

He took a few backward steps then ran at the railing which edged the mezzanine. Using it like a step, he jumped perhaps four feet through the air and landed on his hands and knees on a stack of pallets. His leg screamed in pain and he uttered a soft cry. He flipped over to lay on his back, the duffel making even that difficult, and edged himself into the middle of the stack, which had swayed a bit upon his landing.

The handkerchief had come loose around his leg. He wrapped it tight around his thigh to stop the bleeding and made sure the knot was secure this time. He lay there a few seconds more, listening.

Once they reached the mezzanine floor, they would see him and he was dead. He had to keep moving. He crouched, a little light-headed, then he stood and jumped across to the next stack. He walked across the top—again, the whole thing shaking and swaying faintly—and jumped to the next. Here, he climbed down, the pallets swinging precariously outward as he did so, forcing him to lower himself to the warehouse floor from perhaps twelve feet.

The drop made his leg crumple under him. He lay there, panting for a moment, gathering strength and his wits. Then he was up and moving again, away from the office end.

Before he had reached the folding doors, he heard men enter though them and suddenly there were two of them, perhaps twenty meters away. He ducked into the space between two stacks and then he knelt, waiting. He could hear them coming, the tired creak of shoe upon concrete.

When they were close enough, he edged out of the gap. The men were ten feet away. He fired twice. Head-shots. Both of them went down. There were shouts from all over the warehouse.

He took a few steps and helped himself to one of the men's rifles. It was a Carcano. Men appeared at the far end of the passage between the stacks and the wall. Conlon was ready and fired two shots from the rifle. A man fell. He retreated, aware that he was trapped between two groups of them and, that if they coordinated what they were doing, he wouldn't last beyond the next minute or so.

He slipped in a wet patch on the floor. He could smell it—a puddle of petrol. His leg was burning hotter now, the slip having pulled it more violently than he would have liked.

He was quiet, tucked into another gap between

stacks. He could hear footsteps from men running but could not tell from where they came. He crept to the end facing the expanse of the warehouse and peeked out. There was a man crawling on his belly along by the far wall, and one creeping along beside the stacks, patiently working his way down the line, disappearing into each gap, then reappearing. Searching him out.

There were shouts from the mezzanine now. This was too easy for them. He had to use this place, make it his friend.

He waited for the one who was trying to stalk him and, when he turned into Conlon's passage, Conlon smashed him in the head with the butt of the rifle then grasped the back of his neck and bounced his face into the ground twice.

He was armed with a Mauser. Conlon left it but went on searching the man's pockets. He found cigarettes and a book of matches. He tore at the cigarette packet then wedged it into a pallet. He pulled a few pages from Sean's notebook still in his pocket, and stuffed them around it, then he tore a strip from his shirt and dabbed it into the petrol pooled on the concrete nearby. This he arranged around the paper, hanging it off the pallet.

Ejecting cartridges from the Mauser, he smashed at one on the floor until it snapped on his third go. He heard them yelling at one another to be quiet. He tapped the bullet and its powder onto the paper. Then he set it alight. It went up with a quick little howl and, within seconds, the pallet caught, too. The fire climbed like a spider, all legs moving at once, and suddenly the whole stack was gripped by orange flame.

A man appeared around the corner, pistol already

raised, and got a shot off before Conlon could. It whined off the concrete and Conlon, rolling onto a shoulder, shot him in the gut. He fell back, firing again, the bullet lost in the darkness beyond them. Conlon aimed and his next bullet took out the man's eye.

He moved now, into the passage from which the man had come. Bullets cracked off the walls as he ran and fire leapt among the pallet stacks. He was in that place he reached when death was so close, perfectly calm, making decisions coolly, all other considerations cancelled out by the efficiency of the survival mechanism.

Now, he headed back toward the mezzanine. Shots were coming from the walkway under the skylight and from behind him, but Conlon was certain they couldn't really see him—not consistently—only the flash of him as he raced between pallets, movement as he went for the mezzanine. For a good sniper, that would be enough. They anticipated and shot based on their understanding of where he would be next. But these men didn't have that level of skill or training. They were more or less amateurs. They were firing at where they hoped he was but, with so much lead moving in the air, the chances of him catching another bullet were worrying. And, as Dalton had always said, all it would take was one bullet.

Conlon surged into the space under the mezzanine. The machines he had seen from above were printing presses, at least three of them—huge, complex metal networks of racks and chains, wheels, and ink racks. Desks and high chairs sat in clusters around them as if abandoned suddenly during a meeting.

The men were shooting at him from at least four

directions now and he jumped, sliding with little control, as though on ice, onto the floor and rolled behind one of the huge metal machines, panting. They kept on shooting, the bullets pinging and spitting off the metal, the rattle of gunfire deafening, echoing off the mezzanine ceiling above and off the walls.

Then they stopped. Silence.

He listened, looked around, evaluating, thinking. The silence stretched. He knew this meant danger. He was low, but on his toes, ready.

One of them came around the machine. Conlon, seeing him first, was up before the man could get off a shot. He hit him with a straight punch in the gut and the man crumpled, ribs gone, an internal organ ruptured, probably, and Conlon hit him again, taking out about half of his remaining teeth. The man went down, consciousness lost.

The firing started again, even more concentrated than before—a constant rain of bullets around him, pulverizing everything until even the air felt bruised and tender.

He had to hold his breath. He got his bearings and peeked through a gap between chairs. He could see six of them approaching, firing as they moved, cocky and complacent together. One of them put his hand up and they all stopped. He did not see McPhail among them.

"We've got him lads."

"Quiet!"

"He's fucking dead."

"Shhh."

"We got him."

He lowered his hand and they started firing again. Conlon ducked down and waited.

The machine deflected it all and he breathed. Some of them were terrible shots. The pillar behind him had been hit perhaps a dozen times. He saw lumps of plaster soar off in clouds. Beneath that, wood splintered and flipped away. The wall a few feet further back was pitted with bullet holes. They were closing in. The sounds of the firing were louder. They were confident of the advantage their superior firepower granted them.

A lump of the pillar the size of his fist dropped off. They were perhaps twenty feet away now, firing steadily.

They stopped again and it went quiet. Conlon knew this meant they were trying something different and tensed, alert. Another one had chanced it and he came over the top of the machine, half-falling toward Conlon, who met him with a straight kick to the chest. He fell back against the machine and Conlon shot him in the forehead. He fell with a messy clatter of his gun and meaty farmer's body to the concrete. They heard it on the other side of the machines.

"Did you get him, Wood?"

At the silence, they fired again and then stopped. In the silence, Conlon waited, tensed up at what might be next. He heard it before he saw it; a grenade hit the floor with a metallic ring and spun there like a top for an instant. He was already scrambling away, over one of the desks that had been felled by the gunfire, keeping as tight to the ground as possible.

The explosion was a wave of air passing over him, like someone body-charging you. It scattered chairs and smashed one or two into matchsticks. The gunfire started up almost as soon as the noise of the grenade was gone. The ceiling was on fire, he noticed.

He looked at the pillar. It had taken a battering and looked like a tree bent by wind. It had borne the brunt of the grenade, he realized. He knew what to do. How he might actually get out of this alive. He stood, still bent over slightly. The gunfire seemed to have intensified. They were making sure he was dead. The pillar took a few more rounds. He took a breath, put his head down like a bull, and ran. He charged at the pillar and hit it with his shoulder, all his weight behind it. It gave straight away, breaking like a chicken bone. He fell through it and rolled. A bullet seared his arm. He rolled again, starting to scramble away, his hands slipping and slapping against the hardness of the floor.

The mezzanine level above made a yawning noise and then the ceiling began to fall. He was running furiously for the doors, head still down. He could hear the wood and plaster around him start to shift, as if the fall of the mezzanine was going to pull this whole section of the warehouse down with it.

One of McPhail's men was standing at the doors already, rifle up, and he shot at Conlon. Conlon, picking up speed as he went, was almost on him already, and they flew through the doors together, in a ball. Conlon rolled away and then pushed himself up and fell onto the man. Three punches, then he was up again, worrying that the sniper could see him, crouching toward the fence, away from the warehouse building.

The noise from inside the warehouse was terrible. The fire had caught hold and the walls had gone up. The mezzanine had collapsed, taking some of the offices with it. The shooting had stopped.

He put the rifle down beside the man he had just punched, adjusted the duffle, which he had forgotten was on his back, and then, sticking close to the wall of the building from which he assumed the sniper was gaping as the warehouse began to collapse in on itself, he walked out and into the streets of Dublin, and he didn't look back.

12

Before he left for America with Orla, he had gone to visit Podge at the shop. He had seen Sean and George and a few other friends, too, but he told none of them that this was probably the last time they would ever see him. He kept it casual and just tried to be his best self. He listened and laughed and told himself to pay attention to his own enjoyment, to make sure he lived these moments with people who had always meant something to him.

He knew he would see his ma again. He would pay for her to come see him. But he doubted he would be back in Dublin. Doing this; leaving with the girl of perhaps the most feared man in the city, would mean that he could never come back, he thought. But that was ok. She was worth it. The way she made him feel was worth it, and though he loved this town, it could be claustrophobic, and there were days when the crowded stinking streets and the familiar faces and the posh people and the British and the Fenians and the Socialists and the prostitutes and the crooks just made him feel like he had to get out to be able to breathe.

There were also days when he would walk off a street onto the quays when the sun was high in the sky and a breeze would sweep down the Liffey and he would remember that he loved life, and remember how much his da had loved Dublin, and doubt that he would ever be strong enough to leave. But then all he had to do to know his own strength was to think of Orla. He would get to be beside her each day, even if it was somewhere else. He had never dreamed he would get to be with somebody as amazing as she was. Seeing her face every day, getting to hear her thoughts on any and every subject: That was enough. He would leave this city and his friends behind for that, in a heartbeat.

But Podge had been his best friend for as long as he could remember. Podge deserved more. Podge was something he would miss, more than he understood now, he suspected. So he showed up at the shop around closing time, hung around outside, where Podge could see him, and when his friend finally starting packing up to close, he approached.

"Do you want to go for a drink?" he asked from the doorway.

"That is a bit of a stupid question, isn't it. Who are you talkin' to, wha?"

"I was wondering if you were getting more responsible and moderate in your old age, see."

Podge laughed. "I am, sure. I keep my periods without alcohol to a minimum. Where we going? Will we get some tea, too?"

They went to Devlin's. Podge insisted on ordering,

and paying, almost as if he sensed that there was something important afoot. Conlon sat at a table, watching him joke with the barman and an old lad nursing a whisky at the bar. Podge returned with two pints and two beef sandwiches, their spongy white bread and the dark brown of the meat vivid and mouthwatering against the blue plates they sat upon.

Conlon told him about Orla for the first time as they ate. "I've been seeing a girl."

"About fuckin' time. Who is she?"

"You don't know her."

Podge made a face at that. "I don't know a lot of girls, Tommy. Who is she?"

"Her name's Orla."

"Tell me about her."

"What d'ye mean?"

"Jaysus. Tommy. What's she look like? What's she do? Where's she from?"

"She's...beautiful."

Podge made a noise; a sudden exhalation of air.

"She doesn't really do anything. She was a barmaid when we met. She's from Cork."

"And you love her, from the sounds of it. You finally in love, yeah?"

"I love her."

"Right." Podge smiled. "I'm happy for you."

"Thanks man."

"So what're you not telling me? Why've you got a face on you like a baby with a dirty bum?"

"I have to leave."

"What're you talking about?"

"I'm going away, with her."

"When? For how long?"

"We leave in a few days."

"For how long?"

"I don't know. We might not be back."

"What're you talking about, Tommy. Why would you not be back? For fucks sake."

Conlon lowered his voice and leaned into the table. "Podge, she's Francis Xavier's girl."

"She isn't."

"She is."

Podge looked at him for a moment, mouth hanging open. "Jaysis Tommy. How'd you—never mind. Fuck…"

Conlon watched him.

"So you're leaving why? So you can be together?"

"Without being murdered, yeah."

Podge heaved a big, theatrical sigh. Took a bite of his sandwich. Thought, chewing, which only served to give the impression that he was thinking ever more furiously. Then: "So this is you saying goodbye, is it? I won't be seeing you again?"

"Not for a long time, anyway."

"Where are you going?"

"America."

"America!"

"We need to get far away from him."

"Well you couldn't really get any farther, could ye?"

"I'm sorry, Podge. I wanted to tell you about her before…"

"No, I would've just told you you were a fucking eejit. I knew there was a girl. You haven't been around, and you've been off in your head when you have been. How are you going? Catching a ship?"

"Yeah. We're going to Donegal first, for a few days. Then from Derry to New York."

"New York." Podge shook his head in quiet wonder. "And you love her?"

"I love her. She's lovely."

"That's good. That's good."

He seemed stunned. Conlon didn't know what to say.

Eventually they returned to more typical subjects—safer ground for both of them. But there was an undertone to the conversation now, an edge of unhappiness. And though they lingered together in the pub for hours, slowly sinking into drunkenness, almost as one, that darkness never lifted from them on that evening. Conlon would think back to when he was in Turkey and France, and wonder why they had let it stay that way, when they both knew they might never see one another again. Because they were young, and stupid, and proud, and they barely understood themselves, let alone one another.

So they drank and talked, and later that evening they fairly staggered out into the streets of Dublin. They walked a few ragged streets together, before parting on a corner.

"Well," Podge said.

"Well?"

"You take care of yerself, ye gobdaw."

Conlon laughed at that. "I will. You, too, ye bowsie."

They were not going to embrace, but Conlon offered his hand, and his friend shook it with an almost comic vigor.

"I have a feeling we'll meet again," Conlon said.

Podge shrugged. "Well if we don't, it's been good, hasn't it? Never boring."

"Never boring," Conlon said, agreeing.

"Well. See you around Podge."

"See ye, Tommy."

And they walked in opposite directions.

———

HE DIDN'T HAVE many things he wanted to take with him: his da's old sketchbook, a few shirts and a suit, socks and underpants and a couple of books all fit into the haversack he slung over his right shoulder as he left for the station that morning.

He walked. He felt that if he was to never see Dublin again then he wanted to see it properly today, wanted his feet to touch its pavements and cobblestones, wanted to hear the salty speech of its characters, duck under its awnings and look into its shop windows. So he detoured through town, walking up Henry Street and turning up Sackville Street to then follow the Liffey to Kingsbridge Station, all the while listening and watching and taking in the people and the sounds of his city, trying his best to enjoy them in a way he never usually thought of.

It was one of those gray Dublin days when the sky feels like a lid someone has snapped over the top of the city; vaguely claustrophobic and stifling, a dull humidity softening the edges of the day. It began to rain softly at around the same time Kingsbridge came into view.

His timing was good. He bought a ticket, and his train was already on the platform. Orla was to meet him onboard, and indeed, after passing a half-dozen carriages in the corridor, there she was, facing the front, wearing a velour hat he had admired weeks before and a dress in a matching turquoise. When he opened the door, he saw her small case on the luggage rack and he pushed his bag into the space beside it. Her smile at his appearance made his stomach jump with excitement. They were really doing this.

He sat beside her and she immediately took his hand. "I was worried you mightn't be here," he said, barely managing to control the quiver in his voice.

"Ah don't be so silly. I was worried you weren't going to show up, too. And leave me sat on a train to Donegal on my own."

"No. I could barely sleep last night; I was so excited."

He saw something in her eye that meant that had made her especially happy and she said, "I didn't sleep at all, not a wink. If I fall asleep on you, you must forgive me."

"I don't know. That would be unforgivable."

She laughed and squeezed his hand and they waited for the train to stir. He knew that, like him, she was thinking that they would not be safe until they were beyond the walls of Dublin, and that they could not relax until the train was in motion.

After a few long seconds of silence, he said, "How'd you get out? What did you tell them?"

"Nothing. It doesn't work that way. They don't monitor my comings and goings every day, like I'm a prisoner, but I couldn't just go out with my case. They try to keep me happy with my own continued freedom. They don't watch me. I don't think so anyway. But I left the case at Alfie's place, and every day or two I'd drop off something to go inside it. That way, even if I was seen, I had the excuse of going to see my friend."

"You trust him enough?"

"Alfie?"

Conlon nodded.

Alfie was her only Dublin friend beyond the world she knew, which was utterly centered around Xavier—a slice of normality in her life, she would say. He was a waiter in a hotel near Stephens Green, and he had abandoned his studies for the Priesthood after six months or so, choosing instead to live like a monk in his flat on the edge of the Liberties, working and reading books on philosophy and theology, writing on—his only extravagance—a clattering, shining typewriter.

He and Conlon had met once, and discussed Dublin food and Rousseau, who the Major would later make Conlon and all of the unit read as part of a lengthy reading list of his personal favorites, designed to make them better, more rounded human beings, which would in turn ensure that they were better, more efficient warriors. Conlon had questioned how reading Jane Austen would make him a better soldier, but then he began to enjoy some of the books he was asked to read, so he kept his mouth shut. But when he had picked up the Rousseau book from the Major's library, kept in a huge, old trunk he had transported everywhere he went, he had been transported right back to that conversation, where Alfie had talked to him about this French writer and his theories—but never in a patronizing way, always as if he wanted to help Conlon understand life and the world better. He had liked Alfie, and appreciated that he cared about Orla and wanted the best for her.

"Yeah," she said. "He lives in a different world than the one we do. He wouldn't believe any of it if I told him, anyway."

"So do we, now."

"What?"

"We live in that different world, now."

"Oh I love when you say things like that."

His turn to laugh.

"Did you say goodbye?" he asked her.

"No. I'll write to him when we're settled."

"That might not be for a while."

"I know. Isn't it exciting?"

People scurried past their carriage in the corridor. And then, with a slight drift, backwards at first, like a boat rocked atop the gentlest of waves, the train began to move. Their eyes met. He kissed her.

————

SOON, they were heading out across the expanse of Kildare. It began to rain, a fine mist at first, but then a pulverizing deluge. They watched it together out of the train's window until it was impossible to make it out through the glass, smeared slick as it was by streams of rain pouring off the roof. The countryside then became a child's painting: colors softened by the downpour, greens and browns and grays daubed by clumsy fingers across the horizon.

A conductor came and checked their tickets, and they whispered together that the man had assumed that they were a married couple. Not long after, she did fall asleep with her head on his shoulder and her hand in his.

He did not suspect it then, but this was a moment he would remember often over the next few years; huddled in a foxhole, stalking a German sniper though woodland, lying in a hospital bed. The pure contentment of being with her, of having her safe and sleeping beside him, in the vivid reality of the world on that day, their future ahead of them and pure potential, but filled, he had been sure then, with love and simple joys.

————

THEY HAD to change trains a couple of times, waiting for an hour or so at Letterkenny station for a train to Burtonport. They had tea and crumpets in the tiny station café and watched the people coming and going. The train was late and there were only a dozen passengers, most of whom seemed acquainted of one another.

By the time they arrived in Burtonport, the Donegal sky was darkening. The tiny fishing village was a short walk down the dirt road from the station, and they headed for O'Donnell's Hotel, easily the largest and most impressive structure in the town. There was a boy from the hotel waiting around the station for the train, on the off-chance that any customers might be onboard, and he took their bags and led the short walk, rabbiting away about the village as he went.

Orla had her arm in Conlon's, and he felt nervous now; about the social niceties, about lying in order to get a hotel room. But it was effortless. He believed that it was her; the naturalness of her beauty swept people away with her. Nobody questioned her, they just smiled and tried to make her smile, too. She understood something of her effect on people, and she was graceful and unfailingly pleasant with it. The concierge assumed they were man and wife, Conlon signed a fake name in the register, and before he knew it, they were in the best suite in the hotel, on the third floor with a harbor view and its own water closet.

This was the first night they would spend together, and a peculiar shyness overcame them as soon as they were alone in the room, which was only broken when she emerged naked from the bathroom and climbed into bed. She patted the space beside her and watched him calmly as he undressed.

He slipped in beside her and she came into his arms and whispered into his ear: "I am so happy, my love."

He answered with a kiss.

———

THEY STAYED in bed the next morning, skipping breakfast and emerging for lunch instead. Sitting in the small hotel restaurant, they agreed that they would pretend it was their honeymoon, in case anybody asked. That would explain and excuse so much. After that, they explored the area, going on long walks together along the coast, chatting to fishermen unloading catch at the dock. Gnarled old nets lay piled by the sea wall, gulls pirouetting overhead. Boats came and went, the men silent and intense in their work. When they asked one of the older men for a recommendation of a good local place to eat fish, he made them wait, then led them out of town to his own house, where his wife cooked them some fish and potatoes, and the two of them told Conlon and Orla stories of great Atlantic storms, tales of ghosts and hauntings, and remembrances of all of their loved ones who had left for America.

The young couple held hands under the table, and every time their eyes met Conlon could feel her joy, see it in the glow she gave off. He felt lucky—perhaps for the first time in his life—that he got to be the one sitting beside her, that he was the one she had chosen to love. It barely seemed feasible.

Later, they walked back together in the darkness, toward the dull glow of the town and the sound of the sea. In bed they were tender, and after, fell asleep entwined.

In the morning the sun was unseasonably high and bright, and they took a blanket, towels, some water and sandwiches in a sack and walked far along the coast until they reached a long beach, deserted except for a couple of riders galloping in rainbows of spray through the waves. The sand looked pale gold under the sunlight. Conlon, raised on Dublin's beaches, which became crowded at even the merest hint of a warm day, was stunned by the beauty and peace of it, and they unfolded their blanket near the dunes. The sea smelled raw and exotic here, and they undressed and waded and swam together, laughing at the shock of the cold, splashing one another, finally emerging to make love in the dunes under the sun, then stand and watch the tide creep in, wrapped together in the blanket.

As they hungrily ate their food, she whispered to him that she thought this might be the best day of her life. He agreed with her, and they held hands all along the walk home, arriving at the hotel as the sun set out over the vastness of the ocean.

They had a late dinner in the restaurant, and then in

bed, they compared this day to their last day at the beach, in Cork, when they had been falling in love.

Conlon slept, that night, deeply, soundly, and woke with his hand wound in her hair like a clasp. Extricating it he woke her, and she kissed him, and climbed on top of him in the darkness, telling him that she loved him again and again.

———

XAVIER'S MEN found them the next day.

It was to be their last day here before they left to board the ship to America. They were up early and had breakfast in their room: smoked kipper and crumpets with jam and butter, tea and toast. Then they went for a walk, heading inland. It was sunny again, but dark clouds moved over the Atlantic and they asked the porter about routes and spots to stop before setting off.

Moving away from the sea, the land became hilly, with huge rocks jutting up from the ground and patches of woodland scattered on hillsides and split by the odd path or trail. The barren hillsides were flanked by bushes twisted and bowed by the savage winds carried from the Americas, and occasionally they would pass an isolated house, half-hidden in a dip or hollow between hills.

They stopped for lunch on a high riverbank, sitting protected from the sea breeze by a crop of rock which cascaded down into the water, perhaps thirty or forty feet below. The porter had recommended this spot, and they were hidden from the world here, tossing pebbles and twigs into the air to watch them spin and whistle down into the river, laughing and kissing, the last of the afternoon sun still on them in their alcove.

Conlon stood to find somewhere to relieve himself, and climbed back up the bank toward the heavy undergrowth off the trail they had followed. When he emerged through a curtain of green, three men were approaching, and instantly he registered that they were not right. They didn't fit here. Something of the city about them—their clothes, their walks, their faces, even. Almost in the same instant, he saw that one of them was carrying a pistol.

He turned, tensed, ready to do something although he had had no time to form a coherent thought, and then the gun was firing, and he had been shot somewhere low down between his ribs and his groin. He felt the shock of the impact, a sudden inferno of pain, and then a heaviness. His legs suddenly weak, he staggered toward the bushes. The man shot again and this one smacked him in the shoulder and turned him around, sending him sprawling into the foliage. He hit the ground and tumbled, a whirl of green and brown; bouncing once, twice before he collided with a tree, its thin trunk snapping hard into his breastbone, his nose smashing onto its bark. Later he would remember this moment chiefly for the cry he uttered when he hit the tree.

Conlon lay there for a moment, pain and shock turning his head into a fog of sensations and confused perceptions. He could hear the river.

Orla.

He pushed himself away from the tree and slowly stood. He prodded at himself, trying to determine the extent of his injuries before he took on three armed men. His shoulder was bloody and tender but appeared relatively undamaged. His gut was bleeding heavily, but he could not even find the location of the bullet wound because the pain was widespread, the washes of blood cascading down him only confusing it all further. Dizziness washed over him and he supported himself against the tree.

He heard his name. Somewhere. Focus. He listened. Orla, screaming his name. Close by. He began to move uphill through the bushes, staying low, one hand protectively cradling his stomach. She was crying. He could hear it between the screams for him.

One of the men said something, and she replied, an angry growl of a sentence, then called for him with renewed urgency. They were very close now.

Conlon stopped and crouched and another cloud of dizziness engulfed him. He very much wanted to sag against the nearest tree and sleep for hours, but he forced his eyes open, and listened. Their scrambling feet on the earth, Orla yelling his name once again. They were on the path back up toward the trail. A few feet away. He listened. There.

He ran forward and sprung out of the leaves. He put his head down and charged him, smashing into his torso with a combination of his head and his shoulder, sending both of them sprawling into the bushes on the other side of the trail.

A shot rang out.

He landed on the man, who was already bucking and kicking in an effort to shake him off, shouting in rage. Conlon felt the impact of his shoulder-charge and the landing as a burning pain in his side, and then the man was trying to hit him, in his panicky way, his legs and arms all moving at once, like a baby throwing a tantrum, and Conlon was slow to respond, the blood loss already affecting him. Swinging and missing with a clumsy punch as the man was already slipping out from under him, Conlon stumbled away and to his feet. The man was behind him, and he staggered in a semi-circle.

The man was looking around the undergrowth, his eyes sharp and anxious. He's lost his gun, Conlon realized. Their eyes met, and Conlon saw the man see something there; realize that he was vulnerable. His eyes swept down Conlon, and he must have noted the wounds in the stomach and shoulder, the blood stains growing. Because something very much like a smile came over his face as he raised his fists and came forward.

Conlon could feel his strength ebbing. He bent to support his hands above his knees. His vision felt dim now. He wondered if he was dying. He thought of Orla. Orla. Her face in his head. He had to help Orla. His eyes found a thick branch on the ground, and in one movement he picked it up and swung it in a sharp, rapid upward arc. It caught the oncoming man in the cheekbone with a meaty bang, and he fell instantly and heavily into a bush, senseless.

Conlon listened again. She called his name, from above. Hopeless. Her voice sounded hopeless, he felt hopeless. Everything had gone wrong so quickly.

He hurried out and was quickly onto the trail, climbing, using the branch to help him, feeling as if the last of his strength could desert him at any moment.

At the top of the trail, they were only twenty feet away, along the path back into town. Each of the men had one of her arms and she was struggling and writhing to get away. As he emerged from the bushes she shouted his name again—hoarse and desperate now.

None of them had seen him yet, and he tried to steady himself as he approached, but then one of the men glanced over his shoulder, and shouted, "He's fuckin' comin!" and, letting go of her arm, he turned and shot at Conlon again.

He saw the flash and heard the bang and felt it hit hard somewhere in his thigh but he could not stop. Three steps and he was close enough and he swung the branch like it was a lump hammer and the man—who was quick—blocked it with his arm, but Conlon heard the damage the impact made. The man cried out and half fell, half scrambled away. Conlon stumbled after him and swung the branch again. A crack as it struck. The man's gun spun away into the undergrowth. The other man was backing away, holding each of Orla's arms in his fists while she struggled and cursed at him.

She saw Conlon glance at them and she said, "I love you Thomas I love you," as he advanced on the man, who had drawn a knife from somewhere and was brandishing it at him. She was being pulled back toward the trail down toward the river now.

As Conlon looked at them disappearing back into the bushes, this one lunged at him. The knife made a vengeful little rip in the air inches from his side, and he stepped groggily away. He was slowing down more and more, by the second, his life leaking away. He had to put this one down quickly, if he was able.

He lifted the branch like a sword, over his head, and instead of swinging it, he kicked his foot up and hard to the man's gut. The man doubled over, uttering an *oof* of pain and shock and, as he was bent, Conlon smashed the branch down hard. It hit somewhere between the back of his skull and the higher reaches of his spine. He screamed, and shot upright, as if he had been penetrated, and Conlon, holding the branch in two hands like a staff, smacked him in the face with the it. His nose went, easily, like paper, and he reeled backwards.

Conlon stayed on him. Three blows became ten; a blur of swift, powerful strikes to his ribs and back until he wasn't even twitching or struggling, just lying still and ruined on the forest floor.

Conlon switched focus from the now still man and turned to pursue Orla and the last one back down the trail toward the river. He tried to hurry but his legs felt pitifully weak. I just need a bit more strength, he thought. Just for a few minutes. Standing there he could feel himself sway, the ground seeming to move in long undulating waves. He took a step, then another.

Orla called his name again.

Hurrying, he stumbled and fell onto the trail, tumbling a few feet, each turn and jolt searing agony into various parts of his body. He heard himself cry out, then sob, lying there. Orla in the distance. He struggled to his feet.

I'm going to die, he though coldly. Not yet, though. Not yet. He would not allow it yet.

He continued downward, and as he came out onto the ledge where only a few minutes before they had been sitting together, as happy as he could ever remember having been, he saw the last man there, holding Orla before him with an arm tight around her neck.

As Conlon emerged from the bush, the man shot at

him. He had been waiting, had realized that this spot was perfect for this kind of ambush. Only one way in. Nowhere to hide.

This bullet struck him in the chest, and he was thrown onto his back. He heard Orla cry out, and then she was sobbing. He couldn't move. He felt so weary, wearier than he had ever felt before. How many times had they shot him? Three? Four?

He tried to get up, and could only prop himself on one elbow.

The gunman had loosened his grip on Orla, who was holding herself and weeping. They both saw him move and she rushed over and bent beside him.

"I'm sorry, I'm so sorry Thomas, I love you, I love you."

He put an arm feebly around her neck, whispered, "I love you."

The gunman had a birthmark, large and purple over his chin and mouth, where a beard might have been. He smirked through it at Conlon, and raised the gun. Orla stood and faced him, putting herself between the two men.

"Get out of the way, now, before I have to shoot you, too," Birthmark said.

"You've done enough. You've done enough. He's hurt, please just leave him alone. I'll come without a fight. Just let him be, please."

"It's too late. He's to die, that was the word. You come back with us; he dies."

"No, please, please, have mercy, nobody needs to know, I won't tell. Please."

"Move. Out of the way."

The man was trying to draw a bead on Conlon past

Orla, but she kept moving, stepping from side to side, dropping and raising her palms, as if involved in some odd little tribal dance.

"Move! For Fucks sake, move!"

Conlon's hand scrabbled in the dirt for anything he could use. Birthmark stepped forward and grappled with Orla for a minute, before finally backhanding her viciously. She cried out and fell sideways and he raised the gun and aimed at Conlon. Orla sprang at him again as Conlon flung a fist-sized stone, which caught him smack in the cheek. He fired the gun, the bullet lost in the forest, and aimed again, but Orla was clinging to him, and she jerked his arm sideways so that this shot whined off into the trees.

Birthmark was shouting now, but Orla was like an animal, scratching and clinging to him, until he smashed her to the ground. He aimed once more at Conlon, who lay there, waiting. Orla leapt to her feet, screaming in rage and terror, just as birthmark fired. Conlon saw her body jerk with the impact of the bullet. Birthmark's face registered the disaster instantly. He stepped away, as if to disassociate himself from what had happened.

Orla took a couple of faltering, small steps, trying to keep her balance, the strength already draining from her. She looked around at Conlon. Her eyes were full of pain and confusion and fear. Her mouth opened and he saw tears in her eyes. She wobbled, and took a tiny step sideways in an effort to stay upright. Then another.

He only saw what was happening at the last instant. She took one more step and disappeared over the side of the bank and down toward the river.

He was up somehow—strength he didn't even feel

moving him. He heard the gunshot and realized that Birthmark had fired again and he felt no more pain. He went after Orla, wanting only to be with her now—death so close and waiting for them both—and he wanted to face that with her. He took two steps and then he was falling toward the water. He closed his eyes for the last time.

13

He took a morning train from the Broadstone. It reminded him inescapably, inevitably, of back then, with her. That train through the rain, her hand, eventually, in his. Looking at her incessantly. Conlon daydreamed of this, enjoying the memory, for much of the first hour after the train had left Dublin behind, smoke filling the cabin, the rattling and bouncing like the train was having a fit.

He was uncomfortable. The bandage around his thigh was forbiddingly tight. Theresa had cleaned his wounds and dressed them the night before, when he had returned to her door limping and bloody and carrying a duffel full of cash on his back. He remembered her face when she had answered the door: a mixture of horror and relief and something else he had been unable to identify. He had been sparing in details of what he had done, of what had been done against him, but she saw the bullet wounds in his thigh, and the stripe of raw across his arm where another round had nicked him, and she was intelligent. She knew, alright.

She had done a good job tending to his injuries, but she tied her dressings tight, jerking them around limbs as though angry with him. He assumed that she was just angry with life, with the world. When he had winced, she apologized quietly.

She had fed him, too, and replaced the bloody clothes with things from George's wardrobe. The moment when he realized that she was presenting him with her late husband's clothing something had shaken loose inside him, and he felt tears in his eyes. She took his head in her arms and cradled it to her chest and let him cry, her fingers in his hair, her own tears falling onto his shoulder.

They had talked after that. He would not be staying the night, he told her. He had already exposed her to enough danger, and he knew how dangerous these men were now.

Will I see you again, she had asked him.

Of course you will, he had said. George would want me to take care of you.

He would have wanted me to take care of you, she had said.

He had nodded, and indicated the bloody clothes on the kitchen table. And that's just what you've done. We'll have to look after each other from now on.

He told her he had to stash the money somewhere safe, first. And then he was going for reinforcements. But that when it was all over, he would come and see her, to make sure she was alright. To show her that he was alright.

What if you're not alright, she had asked.

And he had tried to look devil-may-care and swash-buckling as he said, Trust me.

But he had been afraid. He had just survived the warehouse. He had been stupid and cocky, and he had underestimated McPhail and his resources. He had been lucky to get out alive. He would hang onto the fear he had felt as he fought his way out, hang onto the sheer blind luck of the disintegration of the pillar supporting the mezzanine—it was the only reason they had not killed him. He had to remember that and take them seriously now. From now on, he would plan everything, he would account for everything, he would be prepared for anything.

And so here he was, alone and on a train headed West, going for reinforcements. If McPhail wanted a war, then Conlon would show him what war was. But to do that, he felt he might need some help from an old friend.

After a while, tiring of the dreary smeared green scenery beyond the fogged windows, he nodded off, only to wake in patches, dazed and dopey every few minutes, wondering exactly where he was. This was a sense of dislocation he had endured since the days in Turkey, an absence of the sense of the world's geography and his place in it. Instead, each day he woke and wondered where he might be, and why?

His quest to find out what had happened to his friends had given him a sense of purpose, some sort of anchor, something to focus on every morning when he got up, something to think about instead of dwelling on all of the many horrible things he had seen and done. Even now, with the sense that it was almost over, a part of him was wondering what was next...and another part dreading the inevitable emptiness he knew would come.

HE WAS the sole passenger to disembark at the station—
a peculiarly lonely feeling. As the train shook and
coughed its way westward, he stood on the short platform, watching it disappear into the distance.

There were no cabs outside; indeed, the village felt
half-asleep. In the first shop he came across, he found a
middle-aged lady with a severe facial expression and
eyeglasses behind the counter. The shop sold groceries
and she was directing a boy who stood atop a stool,
adjusting the positions of several jars on the highest
shelves on the back wall. The shop was underlit and felt
gloomy and small. They both turned to regard him
when he entered. She bent her head to look at him over
the rim of her glasses.

"How may we help you?" she said, before he had
even spoken—the kind of posh country accent that
sounded almost British to his ears.

He wanted to laugh, but he played it respectful and
humble: "Sorry, Missus. I'm looking for the Hurley
farm. You wouldn't happen to know which way that is,
by any chance?"

"What on earth would you want on the Hurley
farm? There won't be any work for you there."

"I'm not looking for work."

"Dublin lad, is it? Then what are you looking for?"

The boy had climbed down from the ladder and was
openly staring at him now. Didn't they ever get visitors
here? he wondered.

"Maurice is a friend of mine. Maurice Hurley."

The woman's face wrinkled with distaste at the

mention of the name. Conlon could see a smile around the edges of the boy's mouth.

"I can't help you, I'm afraid. Goodbye to you," she said.

Conlon just looked at her. He could not believe what she had said. Rudeness masked by extreme good manners had always enraged him. But he tried to stay sympathetic.

"All I need is directions. Just point the way and I'll find it. Please, Missus."

"Goodbye to you, I said," she repeated.

"Why would you—I don't get it."

"Goodbye. If you don't wish to buy something, I would prefer it if you would leave my establishment."

Conlon felt his temper go, and had to control himself. He glared at her for a full ten seconds. She lost her nerve three or four seconds in and began to retreat toward the door leading to the back of the shop. And then he felt guilty; since when did he intimidate women? Even ones crippled by snobbery and whatever local conflicts were animating her opinion on Mossy and his family?

Conlon said, "I'm leaving. Don't worry."

His eyes went to the boy as he moved to the door, and the boy seemed to shrug without moving his shoulders. Conlon returned the gesture.

In the street outside, he stood, uncertain of what to do or where to go. Mossy had just told him the farm was a little way outside the village, which still gave him a massive area to search. He looked around. There was nowhere else. The pub and post office both seemed closed. It was early enough, he supposed. The street was deserted.

He began to walk, heading what he thought was east out of the town. Perhaps half a minute later, he heard a clatter of footsteps behind him. He turned and the boy from the shop slowed as he approached.

"Mister," he said, "You're goin' the wrong way. The Hurley place is west, about a half an hour. Take the second lane on your right and it's about five minute walk beyond that."

Conlon nodded. "Thank you. I appreciate it. What was all that about?"

"Mossy..." the boy shook his head. "He's had a few adventures in town since he came back. He had a few scoops and beat the head off a lad two weeks ago. Threw him through a window, too." The boy laughed at the memory. "Lotta people want to see the back of him."

"That sounds like Mossy, alright. The police not been involved?"

"Ah no. They're all afraid of him, too. Who'd go to arrest Mossy? He'd kill them. He's got enough guns out at the farm to shoot the whole county."

At this Conlon laughed and the boy beamed. "I'd say you were in the War with him, were you?"

"I was. He's a friend. Just here to pay my respects."

"Well so. Be careful. He's always shooting out there. Has targets set up all over the place. You'll be walking across a field and a bullet just misses you."

"I'll be careful. Thanks for your help."

The boy nodded, and Conlon walked back with him, then on and out of the town.

———

HE COULD HEAR the shooting a long time before he could see the farm. The road from town meandered through some wooded sections of countryside before opening out into rolling fields, and about the time he took the turn the boy had indicated, he heard the shots. Mossy was using different rifles, based on the varying sounds Conlon could make out. It was a chilly afternoon, the air clear and damp, and the noises seemed to hang there for an instant.

These shots were machinelike in their regularity—every fifteen seconds or so, another clap of gunfire. He could picture it, based on memories of Mossy on the firing range at the Chateau. Rifles laid out before him; picking one up, loading with bewildering speed, firing, putting it down, picking up another, and so on. And his accuracy was astounding.

Mossy was the best shot Conlon had ever seen. He had made seemingly impossible shots look easy. He put it down to a childhood of hunting in this countryside with his father, but that could not explain his casual consistency and brutally lethal effectiveness with any firearm. He was a natural. They had met on the day Conlon had arrived at the Chateau, having been chosen by the Major a few days before. Sergeant Reynolds—the Major's favored pit bull, and their drill sergeant—sent Mossy out to test the new boy while the others watched from on high.

He did it in the courtyard, smiling while he advanced on Conlon, all six foot four of him, finally swinging a kick at Conlon's legs while he was only a foot or so away. Conlon went over, crying out, but once he knew he was in a fight, everything was different. He stayed away from the big man and tore his face to pieces with jabs from a distance, wearing him out with rapid combinations of body blows while Mossy huffed and puffed, and said, "All I need is one punch ye little fucker!" until he finally admitted defeat and sat down suddenly, his face a streaming red mess.

Conlon stood over and said, "Irish?"

"I am. You must be, to beat me that bad."

From that point on, they were friends, though Conlon had to get used to the big man's volatility and many quirks. In response, he became more laconic and quieter, forcing Mossy to do much of the conversational lifting, letting him get tired of constantly prattling. It was just like the scenario between them in their fight: Conlon was cagey and controlled; Mossy emotional and scattergun. But it worked.

After that they had been on over twenty-five missions together. Mossy had saved his life at least a half dozen times, and he had saved Mossy's just as much. They understood and complimented one another, and the Major had recognized that by pairing them up as often as he did. Conlon had seen Mossy do terrible things, heroic things, and hilarious things. He knew the man. He was a warrior, never happier than when he was in a fight, and Conlon could not imagine him even existing in the real world, away from death and violence. Which was a good explanation for the regular gunshots he was now walking toward.

He came through a gate and up a track toward the house and other buildings. A barn was half hidden behind sheds and low-slung stables. There were horses off in a field to his left. He could see no people, but it felt like there were people around, somewhere, the suggestion of activity somehow in the air. The yard around the house and outhouses was messy. Ducks and chickens circled, a bicycle lay on its side in the mud, a metal pail was filled with tools, and the door to one of the sheds hung wide open as he passed. Conlon followed the sounds, which led him around the cluster of structures and out onto a field.

Here stood Mossy. A table sat before him, covered with an array of rifles of varying size and age. He was shooting at the line of tiny targets balancing on a fence at the far edge of the field. He was wearing a shirt, untucked so that it hung low down over his hips, and a pair of high boots, unlaced, the laces dragging around on the ground when he stepped back and forth between the table and the spot from which he was firing, a few feet away.

Conlon watched him aim quickly and fire a shot. This close, the sound of this rifle was shockingly loud. Then he briskly moved back to the table, put down the rifle and selected another. He began to load it.

"Your shooting's getting worse," Conlon said.

Mossy turned, and tried to hide the smile that came at the sight of his friend. "Yeah well, I've had a fair few drinks."

"For breakfast?"

"O' course. Takes the edge off the day, isn't that what Robbins used to say?"

"Something like that."

He was walking slowly toward his friend, who looked him over. "I can't believe you snuck up on me."

"Hardly. Surprised you can hear a word I'm saying over that noise."

"I was always good at reading lips."

Conlon laughed. "How are you?"

"Bored out of my mind."

"I told you you would be."

"You did. What about you?"

"Bored sounds pretty good to me."

"Dublin still a horrible little kip, then?"

"The way I like it."

Now Mossy laughed. They shook hands, both smiling.

"It's genuinely good to see you, you big bastard," Conlon said.

"Good to see you, too, ye little fucker. Civilian life suits you."

"Ah I'm not sure about that now."

"I 'spose I should be showin' you around or something."

"Is there anything worth seeing?"

"To a Jackeen like you? You won't appreciate it."

"Is it just a load of fields full of shell casings from your target practice?"

"There are a few of them, yeah. Some dumb animals, loads of animal shit, and the house."

"You're not the only person here, are you?"

"No, unfortunately. Me family are around somewhere. They don't like the sound of the shooting, so they stay away."

"I can't imagine why."

"Cheeky get. Have you come from Dublin today? You must be hungry. Me ma is making gammon, I think. She'll be delighted to meet you. You're the only one I've told her about."

"I'm honored."

"Don't be. I didn't say I told her good things, did I?"

"You must have told her that I'm charming, like all

Dubs are with country women. Which remind me—is that pretty sister you were always talking about around?"

Mossy gave him a false look of anger then. "She's in Galway now. Got a job there."

"That's a shame. How about you—you found a job yet?"

"Not at all. I think I'm unemployable around here now."

"Would that be because you threw some poor fella through a window?"

Mossy laughed at the memory. "That gobshite. He deserved it. Here, help me with these."

He pulled out a big hold all and they placed the rifles carefully inside, one at a time. They were mainly older weapons, a Winchester, Manlichers and a Springfield and a couple of Remingtons. Mossy handled them with uncommon tenderness. He swung the bag over one shoulder and indicated that Conlon should follow him back toward the house.

"Anyhow—have you got a job yet?"

Conlon said. "No. Wouldn't know what I should be doing. I never really had a proper job."

"Apart from killing people."

"Apart from that."

"Do you miss it?"

"No. I'm glad it's over. You do, don't you?"

"I really fucking do. I miss the buzz of waiting to start, too. Remember, beforehand? When the nerves would hit, and you'd feel sick and then you'd be fine? I really miss that."

"I might be able to help."

"Don't tell me you're here for a reason."

"Apart from looking at your pretty face? I am, yeah."

"You've a job?"

They had stopped walking in the yard. Mossy looked at him.

"It's more that I need help," Conlon said.

Mossy nodded. "Is this...the kind of help that means I get to kill some fuckers?"

"It probl'y is, yeah."

"Sounds good. It'd have to be good to make up for being in Dublin. Right: tell me about it after. Time to meet the ma. On your best behavior now, Tom."

———

MOSSY'S FAMILY had adopted Conlon on sight, feeding him, clothing him, showing him the local country. For his part, he could not work out how two such normal, well-adjusted people could have possibly produced a young man like Mossy. They treated him like a big baby, laughing at his eccentricities, smothering him with affection and steering him away from ideas they saw might be dangerous to his wellbeing. Their five other children were scattered around the area, and dropped in to have a look at their little brothers Dublin comrade, meaning that Conlon had a series of cryptic conversations over the two days with a succession of curious siblings.

After dinner that first night, he and Mossy had walked out to a huge oak tree on the southern end of their land. Mossy had said it was his favorite place on the farm throughout his childhood. They climbed its thick, wide boughs and sat in the branches as the sun fell below the western horizon, Mossy smoking the cigarettes his mother forbade him to smoke around the house while Conlon explained the situation with McPhail in Dublin.

"Jaysis. You talk about me being bored easily and you go back to Dublin and you've started a gang war in a week."

"Does that mean you'll help?"

"It sounds like a nice way to spend a few days, sure."

Conlon was wondering if Mossy was regretting it within a few minutes of arriving at the Kingsbridge Station in Dublin, two days later.

It felt like what he imagined it would be like to lead a bear around the city—this huge, lumbering form beside and behind him, uttering responses to things Conlon no longer even noticed, continually offering himself as an obstacle to people on corners and at crossings, his size and personality making him as much a landmark as any of the city's monuments.

Sackville Street made Mossy groan. He muttered to himself as they passed through the Monto. Conlon didn't respond, but occasionally he would look around to see the big man's eyes widen in transfixed horror by the way somebody was dressed or the offerings in a shop window. Conlon stopped off at Wynn's to leave a message for BOD, and Mossy stood in the lobby with a look on his face that communicated an odd mixture of contempt and nausea. When finally they had settled in a pub off Church Street and were sitting at a table, pints before them, and he had gotten his bearings, Mossy said, "I don't understand how anybody can live here at all."

"Jesus Mossy, you've been in Paris and London. This place is tiny by comparison."

"Ah you're right I know. But my head was all bet to fuck back then, by the War. You couldn't trust anything I'd say or do. I wasn't in me right mind."

"When are you ever?"

Mossy chuckled and drank most of his pint in one.

"This just—it doesn't feel like Ireland."

"Your Ireland, maybe. This is Ireland, to me. I feel more like I come from Dublin than I do from Ireland."

"I can understand that. But to me it feels like I've gone back to Europe or England, only I never got on a boat. It's fucking disconcerting, so it is." He went to get another drink, and when he came back, he was all business. "So. What happens now, Tom?"

"Well. I have the money, which McPhail's probably worked hard for, or at least broken a lot of laws for. So I left a message at that hotel for somebody who can contact him. We're gonna meet him, tomorrow morning."

"Me and you?"

"Yeah."

"Where?"

"A park out in the suburbs."

"Right."

"And he'll bring his little army along."

"And we'll kill them all?"

"That's the idea, yeah."

"I like that idea. Are you gonna bring the money?"

"Is that a serious question?"

"I don't fucking know, do I? Never been on a deal with so much cash rolling around."

"No money. All we'll have is guns. That—" he pointed at Mossy's P14 rifle, wrapped in a large canvas and strapped up so that it looked more like fishing equipment than a weapon "—and a couple of pistols. One each."

"You're out in the open in front of them, I'm in cover."

"See? You don't even really need me to tell you."

"You're too exposed. I can only take out so many before one of them shoots you, for fucks sake. You're not bulletproof, Tom. You've got enough scars to prove it."

"Yeah, I've thought about that. You remember all those Jam Tin Grenades the major had us make…?"

————

AFTER PICKING up some supplies and provisions, they took a room in a hotel in Drumcondra and made their preparations. They worked happily, sometimes chatting, sat on their twin beds, intent on the task. Mossy had a habit of humming tunelessly under his breath, which Conlon had forgotten about until he heard it again.

In the afternoon they took a walk out to the location of the meet the next morning, twenty minutes or so away in the grounds of an Agricultural College. Mossy approved of the terrain, but he was certain McPhail would be thinking similar thoughts. Conlon told him that identifying and neutralizing any enemy snipers had always been his job, and that he trusted him.

As night fell, they walked the other way and had tea at Conlon's mother's house. She was delighted to meet one of her son's friends from the War, and embarrassed to be caught without some better food to serve him—a fact of which she reminded Conlon regularly through the ensuing meal of stew and brown bread.

Mossy did his best to distract her, telling her cleaned up stories of Conlon's exploits in France and beyond while Conlon squirmed and winced, then shifting tack to ask her a series of questions about her life and childhood and Dublin, so that she lost herself in her own storytelling. She told him things she had never even told Conlon. He saw Mossy in an utterly different light here, appreciating his gentleness and sensitivity, so often hidden beneath so many layers of machismo that it might as well not exist.

When they left, they agreed to stop for a pint on their way back, and ended up in a pub in Phibsboro. On their way in, they bickered about how much they could drink and how long they could stay. They would be up in the middle of the night, setting up the meet, and Conlon was far too nervous about something going wrong to take any chances.

Mossy knew that he had a safety net: Conlon. He would get there on time, because Conlon would make sure of it. Even if he was still half-pissed. Conlon would make sure he was there. That was the way Conlon was. When he wanted something to happen, he made it happen. Mossy had seen that on battlefields, in the face of an angry Major, in bars and brothels. He loved his old brother in arms, but more than that, he respected the way he forced the world to conform to his will. So he was the one who went to the bar and returned with four pints. Only one of them was for Conlon.

An hour later he was drunk. The four pints had become seven. He was getting loud and dramatic in his gestures and his sentiments. Conlon watched and kept him happy with replies and encouragements, quietly working up to the idea of them leaving. But Mossy was enjoying himself. Conlon persisted. Gently. Mossy started to sulk, like a big baby, his head hanging, mouth puckered. Until all of a sudden, his focus shifted to a group of three men sat near the bar. He stood.

"You!" he shouted. "You! The fella in the green tweed."

The man in question, middle-aged, craggy-faced, a pint in his fist, turned his head.

Mossy said, "What the fuck are you laughing at, ha?"

Conlon rolled his eyes. The man was already taking deliberate steps off his stool.

Conlon said, "No fighting now lads."

"He's startin' it son," the man said.

"And I'll fuckin' finish, too, ye ol' fucker," Mossy said.

Conlon stood between them and put a hand firmly in the center of Mossy's chest. "Mossy. Come on. Not now."

Mossy's eyes were a bit glassy, clouded by drink and fury.

"Mossy!" Conlon roared at him.

"Let's go." And he repeated it, as an order, in a tone Mossy recognized from the army. Mossy looked at him, focused, and a sullen cast rolled over his features.

"Let's go," Conlon said again, softer.

Mossy nodded, threw a last glance at the man behind Conlon, and turned.

Conlon followed him outside, and in the street, Mossy began a long, monotonous rant about people laughing at him, people in his hometown, people in the army, all his life, people, his family, girls, people in school. People.

He threw a punch at a sapling as they walked, and

Conlon heard the wood give a sharp, high crack. He was quiet, letting Mossy calm down. He knew how close they had come to Armageddon in the pub. He had seen Mossy lose control before, and his timing could be unfortunate. Only his knowledge of his friend's character had prevented a riot. Even now, walking along and grumbling to himself, Mossy kept on turning his head as if to go back toward the pub. Seeing Conlon would stop him each time, and he would bow his head and grumble away.

"You want to hurt somebody, Mossy?" Conlon asked him.

"Yeah, yeah I fuckin' do, yeah."

"Well just hold onto that feeling for a few hours. Coz then there'll be plenty of people to hurt. And they'll be trying to hurt you right back."

They walked on in silence, broken only by the odd furious whisper from Mossy.

14

THE MEET WAS SET FOR 6:30 IN THE MORNING. CONLON had chosen a remote bit of scrub set in the grounds of an agricultural college on the edge of Glasnevin, where the countryside began. He and Mossy rose in the dark, ate no breakfast, but had an apple each walking through the chill, black streets, their weapons on their backs, still concealed. They had been forced to creep around the boarding house, careful of creaking doors and moaning floorboards. Mossy showed no ill effects from the drinking of only a few hours before. In fact, he seemed energized and focused, the way Conlon remembered him from countless days and nights in the war.

They arrived close to five, and began to scout the terrain. Mossy set about moving around in a dense copse of bushes atop a small hill. Conlon would be meeting McPhail and his men on the scrub field before it. He would have a solid field of fire on more or else the entire area, and the density of the bushes gave him the chance to move around between shots.

He unpacked his rifle and, leaning it against the central branch of a bush, he prepared a bed for himself upon the dirt. He looked at Conlon, crouched down nearby. "I'll leave McPhail to you. The rest are for me. Right?"

Conlon shrugged. "Maybe leave one or two alive so they can tell the story. Gangsters love a good story."

Mossy laughed. "Alright, Tommy. Good luck out there. I'll see you after."

"Thank you, Mossy."

"No, pal. Thank you."

Conlon rose and went to wait elsewhere.

———

IT WAS misty when the men arrived, which Conlon knew might present a problem for Mossy. He saw movement in the dimness, barely discernable but there. He rose from his position, sitting cross-legged behind a large pine tree, but remained close to it, staring at the spot where he had seen something. It looked almost like movement in smoke, a natural twisting of the air. But he watched and after a few seconds dark shapes were in the mist, and perhaps a minute after that they were identifiable as figures.

A group of men. He knew Mossy would have seen them, too.

He took a step out from behind the tree, assuming that they would see him, too. They were fanning out. Four of them, their hats faintly silhouetted now in the dawn gloom. The mist was thinning, he thought, morning smells beginning to rise on the air to him as he took a few steps toward the scrub. The earthiness of the ground, the sweet sap of the trees here. He breathed. The pistol was in his coat pocket, and he removed it, slipping it into the back of his waistband. He picked up the duffel bag and carried it in one hand.

He walked down then, down the incline onto the scrub. They were approaching from the other side, perhaps ten meter spaces separating them as they walked in a line toward him. Two of them wore long coats. They were young men; around his age, he guessed. They walked slowly. McPhail's pace. He was desperate to show Conlon he was in charge here, to set a tone, establish himself as the one in control.

Conlon knew there were more men. There had to be. McPhail would have his own gunman concealed somewhere. He probably had Conlon in his sights at this very instant. If they were lucky, that was it, and there wasn't another group circling around behind him and Mossy to ambush them from the rear.

The line of men came on slowly. Conlon studied them carefully, taking in details. The silence was broken for him by the brushing of their feet through the grass and scrub and his own steady pulse, roaring in his ears. They stopped perhaps twenty feet from him. McPhail was one of the ones in the middle. Conlon watched his eyes for the last twenty feet or so, not blinking, keeping his face blank.

"It's you," McPhail said, laughing. "From BOD's. I'll have to have words with him."

"He's loyal to his friends. He mustn't like you very much."

McPhail shrugged. "He's loyal to certain friends, yeah. So: is that my money?"

"I'm not sure. Is it your money, or did you murder

people and steal it?"

McPhail looked at him, eyes blazing for a good ten seconds, and Conlon realized that the other man was enjoying this.

McPhail said, "You seem like a clever lad. You got outta that warehouse somehow. You fucked up some of my lads. Tell me this: if you had been here, and your mate came to you with his little plan to help the Fenians buy guns, would you have went along with it? Or would you have given him a slap and told him to keep on?"

"You know the answer to that."

The other three were twitchy, Conlon saw. The one on the end couldn't help himself from looking around, his eyes darting, fingers opening and closing. McPhail, for his part, was stalling. Waiting for others to be in position.

"So your pals—they were fuckin' stupid, you know. They were asking to be robbed."

"And murdered?"

McPhail shrugged. "Maybe not. But literally asking to be robbed." His eyes held something Conlon didn't understand—a private joke there.

Conlon said. "Your money."

He crouched to the bag and two of them raised guns instantly. He smiled at them, hands up, still crouching, and looked with a query in his eyes at McPhail, who said, "Why don't you toss the bag over here?"

Conlon nodded and picked it up. He had the string attached to the firing pin in one hand, and when he threw the bag to one of McPhail's men, he held that tight, and felt the pin spring free. That gave him five seconds.

McPhail's man caught the bag awkwardly, turned

and had taken two steps when the grenade inside blew. Conlon was on the ground instantly.

He and Mossy had built two jam jar grenades and tied them together, rigging a firing pin to activate one, which would in turn detonate the second. The effect was devastating, but it also created a great deal of smoke and confusion.

The blast tore the man in half and threw McPhail a few feet sideways. The sound was deafening, like a hole torn in the air itself. The silence in the immediate aftermath was impeccable but broken when Conlon heard the loud report of Mossy's rifle and the man farthest from him smashed to the ground backward, his hat spinning in the air like a falling leaf. Another rifle shot, from another direction, and the earth beside Conlon jumped as a bullet buried itself there. He rolled away, into the swelling cloud of smoke, and focused on the last of McPhail's men, who was groggily climbing upright nearby. Conlon aimed quickly and shot him twice.

He peered around through the smoke. A figure was rapidly moving away. McPhail; running.

His sniper tried again and Conlon heard the electric whisper of the round pass within inches of his head. Then Mossy's rifle replied. Two shots in quick succession. And then he heard more gunfire—the sharper pop of pistols from Mossy's position, a bright crescendo of them. McPhail had sent another group around. He paused for a second, and then thought: Mossy can handle it. McPhail had to be his priority. Mossy's rifle barked again.

He saw McPhail, running for the tree line at the far end of the scrub, and he took off after him.

———

McPHAIL WAS NOT the type to run. He had planned this meeting out. He had installed Sliney in a tree with a rifle, with orders to take out Conlon the minute anything had looked funny or dodgy. Sliney was a fine shot, by all accounts. He had sent three others around in a wide arc to come upon Conlon and whoever was with him from behind. But he had underestimated this boxer. Twice now, he had been confident he had him.

In the warehouse, he was cornered like a rat, desperate, yet he had gotten out, somehow. He had killed ten of McPhail's men there. He had destroyed the warehouse. He had taken the money. A handful of others walked in the aftermath, and McPhail realized they were afraid of this man. McPhail had brought down most of the force at his disposal, and Conlon had survived, almost crippling him. His lads had gone into the warehouse confident and aggressive, certain that they had the number of this little fucker who had been messing with their business. And he had killed more than half of them.

But when he reflected on it, McPhail realized he had been hasty, had rushed in, literally with all guns blazing, and assumed that the firepower and numbers would be enough. He hadn't planned it or thought about what might happen if Conlon turned the tables on them. That wasn't like him, really. He was good at thinking things through and making sure they went the way he had thought. But he had been annoyed by Conlon and his brass neck in going after what was McPhail's, and he had acted in a fit of temper. He should have waited, calmed down, made a plan. But he hadn't.

Today though—today he had. Sliney was insurance. The other three were insurance.

He hadn't counted on that bomb or whatever it was. Conlon was talented at wrecking plans by fucking destroying things, he thought as he ran. And Conlon had his own sniper, which McPhail had expected. But Conlon's sniper was better than his. Perhaps he should have expected that, too.

Conlon hadn't brought the money. Conlon had never intended to give it to him, he realized with an odd feeling. So why had he come then? What was in it for him? McPhail wondered.

Then it came to him: Conlon wanted to kill him. That was all. He wanted him dead.

And now Conlon was coming for him. And McPhail was running.

He slowed down and then stopped altogether, looking around. He was in the middle of a muddy field. It had been ploughed recently, the lines of earth in little uniform trenches and hillocks. He didn't run from anybody. He would fight. He was proud—of his reputation, of his fighting ability. He would kill this fucking boxer who had crossed him and cost him so much.

He bent over and pulled the knife from his boot and fit the brass knuckles over his fist. He saw Conlon emerge from the tree line, and he nodded, smiling. He felt no fear whatsoever.

———

CONLON SLOWED DOWN. As he emerged from the trees the sun seemed to bleed into the sky above. They were still shadowed and the grass was painted in dew, but the sky was lit by peach and pink.

McPhail was standing in the center of the field, waiting for him. He heard more gunshots from behind. All pistols now. McPhail had lost his gun when the grenade exploded, he assumed, which would explain why he was standing there, nodding and grinning, a knife in his hand.

Conlon stopped and stood watching him.

McPhail said, "You gonna shoot me? Or do you want to settle this like men?"

Conlon tossed the pistol at his feet, knowing he should not, but unable to resist the chance to hurt this man who had hurt so many he cared about.

McPhail's grin widened, and he nodded vigorously.

Conlon made his way toward him, suddenly aware of how much that run had taken out of him, how much the wound in his thigh was slowing him down, how tight his arm was where the bullet had creased it.

McPhail adopted a pose as Conlon moved for him and Conlon saw the flash of light on the brass knuckles as McPhail threw a quick left cross at him. He dodged it, but McPhail was like liquid, following up with the other hand and the knife. Conlon saw it late, and got his arm down to bat away McPhail's forearm. They spun away from each other and McPhail said, "You should've shot me."

He came forward again, always the aggressor. Conlon let him come, and this time he led with the knife. It sliced through the air toward Conlon's head but at the last instant McPhail dropped to a knee and drove it at his gut. Conlon twisted but it bit into his hip and only turning away allowed him to avoid the second stab. McPhail guffawed.

Conlon put a hand to his hip. It came away with a smear of blood across the palm, but there was no pain yet, just that feeling of tightness. He had to be smarter. He was fighting with emotion. Use your head, he told himself, hearing the major.

A single pistol shot echoed from elsewhere in the park, and he knew that Mossy had finished off the men who had come for him.

He nodded at McPhail again. "Come on, then."

McPhail advanced. He threw a rapid series of strikes; the knife high, the knuckles following, the knife low. He was incredibly quick, and he knew what he was doing. Conlon had been cocky before this fight, but that had melted away now. He needed to concentrate.

McPhail came again, watching Conlon for a gap, a hesitation he could exploit. He attacked in little triple combinations every time: a high strike with the knife, then low with the brass knuckles, then again with the knife, and this time was no different: a direct attempt at a stab, a swinging cross, and when Conlon was off-balance, a short, hard upwards cut with the knife toward his Adam's apple from chest height. Conlon blocked the knife arm both times at the wrist, but it was too close and too risky. He needed to disable that weapon. He circled, and McPhail's eyes narrowed. Then McPhail darted in again.

Conlon stepped outside his attack, and punched down, throwing McPhail off balance. He reeled, swiping blindly with the knife. Conlon allowed the knife slash to cut beside his head and then he gripped McPhail's forearm and snapped it violently, with a great wrenching swing behind the other man.

McPhail cried out as the knife spun into the mud they had already kicked up. His arm was at his side, twisted and useless. He looked at Conlon and for the first time there was panic in his eyes.

Conlon could have enjoyed that, but he knew this needed to be ended. He took a step forward and swung a punch. Just one. It was from his side but upwards, and it carried much of his weight in it. McPhail's nose crunched and he fell backwards heavily onto the earth. A noise came out of him. It sounded more like surprise than pain.

Conlon turned and went to retrieve his gun. As he bent to pick it up, he heard shuffling and turned quickly to see McPhail charging at him, the knife in his good hand, his face stretched and contorted by pain and thoughts of murder. Conlon let him come, then at the last instant he sank onto one knee and caught McPhail's charge with a tackle that allowed him to grasp McPhail's wrist, his knee forcing one of McPhail's legs upwards, the two of them locked together like dancers.

McPhail's eyes met his as Conlon forced the knife to turn backwards. He saw the awareness of the position open inside McPhail. Any movement to escape would force them to fall together, and the knife would be driven into his chest.

"No," McPhail said. "No."

Conlon said nothing, just swept his leg across McPhail's so that they fell together, his arm locking McPhail's hand in place. A second later, he kicked

McPhail away and stood, slapping the muck from his trousers.

McPhail was still alive, the knife lodged tight, perhaps an inch to the left of his sternum. His eyes were unfocused and huge and blood bubbled to his lips.

Conlon stood and watched him die. Then he picked up his pistol once again and walked back toward Mossy, somewhere off beyond the trees.

———

THREE OF THEM had come for Mossy. He had killed two, but the third was still alive. Mossy had shot him in the knee, and he lay, groaning and grasping at the ruined joint, a boot of blood casing his calf and foot. Conlon approached and he and Mossy nodded.

"You alright?" Mossy asked, nodding at his hip.

"Yeah. I got sloppy."

"We done here, hah?"

"I think so, yeah."

"Good, I can't wait to get out of this shithole." He looked at the man on the ground. "See ya now. Be good."

———

HE SAW Mossy onto his train with a handshake. They hadn't spoken about the morning—the violence or the death, what it meant or what happened next. Instead, they had spoken with reverence about the milk they had enjoyed from a particular cow from a specific farm outside a fondly remembered village in France.

When Mossy was gone, Conlon returned to his

mother's house. He changed clothes, cleaned and dressed the slash in his hip, and replaced his older dressing, too. Then he called on Theresa.

Her face when she saw that he was alive was something he would keep in his memory for a long time, calling it up when he needed to feel better about things.

"I told you everything would be alright," he said as she took his hand in the doorway of the house. He could tell she wanted to embrace him, and he desperately wanted that, too, but George's mother was lingering behind her.

Instead, she said, "I've learned never to believe anything a man tells me."

"That's probably sensible, alright."

He had retrieved the money and now he split it, leaving half for her and George's mother, despite their protests. They fed him, and asked what had happened and who had helped him. He told them to pay attention to the newspapers over the next few days, and that he couldn't tell them anything except that it was done. As he left, she came to the door with him. He turned and looked at her.

"Will we see you again, Thomas?"

"Well, I have to look after you, don't I, now?"

She smiled then, a warm and girlish smile. "I thought I was to be looking after you, so I was?"

"I 'spose we'll have to see how it goes, Theresa. See you soon."

From there he walked straight to the house of Sean's landlady. It took her a minute to recognize him, and then she was suspicious. That was until he gave her most of the remaining cash.

"Sean told me to give it to you," he said. "To buy coal."

The old lady was so stunned she neither protested nor thanked him, merely watched him with her mouth half open in silence. He left her feeling better about himself than he had done for a long time.

———

IT WAS dark as Conlon approached his mother's house once again. He felt lightened somehow. What would he do now, here? He had no idea.

A man appeared in his path from the shadow under a tree a street or so away from home. He looked just as he had done the night he had approached Conlon after a fight with the offer to come and meet Xavier.

Jordan Devereux. His suit just as sharp, hat angled just so, mustache oiled to two little tips, his eyes still lit with that smug amusement.

"Young Mr. Conlon," he said.

"Jordan," Conlon said. He stopped and waited. "What do you want?"

"He wants to see you."

Conlon felt his stomach flip at that. He had not expected it.

He stayed calm. "Tell him I wasn't arsed-tramping over to Merrion Square tonight."

"Oh, Mr. Conlon. He's come to you."

Conlon felt a stab of rawest panic: his mother. Again, he controlled it. "Where?"

Devereux indicated the pub on the corner, a low-slung bunker with one room and a decent number of regulars.

Conlon said, "There?" He was unable to visualize Xavier mixing with the Stoneybatter working men who patronized that establishment.

"Indeed so." Devereux was already stepping into the road and waving for Conlon to follow him.

Conlon put his head down and made his way after the other man with a degree of reluctance that would have been obvious to anyone observing him. As he crossed the street, he saw a man in the doorway of a house two doors away from the pub and, looking around, another one up on the corner. Xavier had a fear of assassination, and he took at least three bodyguards with him everywhere he went. There would be one more in the pub, at his side, Conlon thought.

Devereux opened the door for him, but did not come inside. The place was absolutely deserted. Only Mick, the loquacious middle-aged barman, was there, and his eyes were a miniscule wider, his breath short, manners nervy. A young man leant on the bar wearing the smart suit and hat which Xavier's men wore like some sort of uniform.

"You want a drink, Mr. Conlon?" he asked Conlon as he entered.

"No, I'm alright thanks," Conlon replied.

The man nodded to the barman and Mick hurried off without even looking Conlon's way.

Conlon looked at the bodyguard and he gestured to his right, and walked past Conlon and out the door of the pub, back into the street.

Conlon looked to his right. There at the far end of the room, utterly alone, Xavier sat on one of the benches by the wall.

Conlon walked to him and sat down across the table without waiting for an invitation. Only then did Xavier look up. He had been engrossed in eating a sandwich. Even now, as he and Conlon studied one another, he was still chewing, his mouth shut, jaw clenching mechanically, a slight wet chopping emitted from his lips. He placed the remainder of the sandwich daintily on its plate.

He was in his fifties but well-preserved. A stocky man with physical solidity, a thick barrel from his hips to his shoulders. His hair was coal-black, and he wore a finely trimmed beard upon his chin and upper lip. Above that, his eyes, too, seemed black, or at least such a dark shade that any color was impossible to discern. He wore a dark gray suit with a navy bow-tie. On many men, that might seem whimsical, unserious. On him it seemed a streak of humor in the darkness.

His fingers were long and thick, giving the impression of strength. And yet Conlon knew that such a physical description of Xavier was not enough. This man who sat before him was just a man, like any other. Conlon could probably kill him in seconds if he wished to. He ate and drank and slept and pissed like any other man. And yet. He ordered the deaths of people casually. Men would kill for him and die for him. Men *did* kill for him and die for him. He had so much blood on his hands it was inconceivable. Women and children. He was one of the most powerful men in the country, but most people had never heard of him and would never hear of him.

At the slightest angle of an eyebrow, he could order the murder of a family, the burning of a town. He was wealthy beyond most people's dreams, yet it was never enough. Xavier had taken the first woman Conlon had ever loved in a manner that had left him broken, and he believed that it was only years of training and killing, of bonding with new brothers and discovering something new within himself that had helped him to recover.

He had taken the first woman he had ever loved from Conlon.

So they looked at one another in silence for a moment, and Conlon remembered that from Xavier's position, Conlon had taken Orla from him, Conlon had betrayed him. Looking at it that way, what choice had a man such as Xavier had when faced with such absolute betrayal? It was a wonder Conlon was alive at all.

He waited for Xavier to speak.

Xavier did his mirthless little laugh after ten seconds or so. "Are you waiting for me to talk, Tommy? Always the hard chaw, aren't we?"

Conlon had never forgotten his voice—a strong Dublin accent evident in every syllable, and yet such precision in that deep timbre, a vocabulary and sense of the theatrical in his way with words that did not suggest Dublin's inner city.

Conlon shrugged. "You wanted to see me."

"That's right, I did."

"Any reason?"

"I thought we should catch up, really. You've been busy. Finch said you were looking well."

Conlon did not know what to say to this. That was often his response to Xavier; he had no idea how he should respond. And Xavier spoke slowly. It was as if time itself was altered in his presence.

He just looked at the man and nodded.

Xavier said, "Mr. McPhail and many of his associates murdered last night, I hear. Something akin to a pitched battle in Glasnevin, it seems. The police are baffled, but they are inclined to blame the Fenians, since McPhail was a known gun smuggler. That is impressive. Are you finished, do you think?"

"Finished?"

"That was...revenge? For the killing of your friends, yes?"

"It was."

"So are you finished? Is that sufficient?"

"What are you saying?"

Xavier allowed a smile to play across his features without surrendering fully to it. "You may believe—wrongly, I have to tell you—that you are finished. There is an envelope on the bar, with your name written on it. Inside there is a piece of paper with an address on it. You should go to this address. What you find there may change your perspective on this entire matter."

Conlon tried to control his features as he sought the right words. "What—why would you tell me this?"

"You once knew me, Tommy. This is purely because it is good business."

"I don't understand."

"You will, after you have taken the envelope and done what I say."

"Why should I trust you?"

"Do you seriously think that because you survived one clumsy attempt to end your life, you are invulnerable? Do you think that because you slapped around some louts I sent to talk to you, you are untouchable? If I wanted to kill you, I could kill you at any moment of any day. You are alive because I allow it. You walk the streets of my city because I deem it acceptable that you should. Remember that, please." They were silent then, for a good twenty seconds. Again, Xavier broke the silence. "I am not a man who regrets things. But I have a few regrets over how our relationship resolved itself."

Conlon looked at him. "You killed her. You tried to kill me."

"Understand: what you did was an insult that could not be borne, not by a man in my position. But I might have handled it differently."

"She's dead."

"Yes. I was fond of her. I was fond of you. I ordered your death. But I never intended for her to die. That was an accident."

Conlon struggled for words. He had never expected to discuss this with Xavier. Years of bitterness stubbornly refused to alchemize into language upon his tongue.

"We will never be friends now. But I will do you no harm, as long as you refrain from involving yourself in my business."

Conlon nodded.

Xavier said, "What will you do? You have returned to this city, but what can you give to this city?"

"I'm not sure yet," he said, and stood. Xavier watched him.

Conlon said, "I understood what you said about killing me whenever you wanted. But you should know: if I want to, I'll disappear in minutes. And then you'd never see me coming. And if I get into a room with you, nothing could stop me. You're alive because I've decided not to kill you."

Xavier smirked at that, and nodded. Conlon turned to leave.

Xavier said, "Don't forget the envelope."

Conlon stopped, picked it up off the bar, and slipped inside a jacket pocket. He and Xavier exchanged tips of their hats. He left. Behind him, Xavier returned to his sandwich.

15

THE ADDRESS WAS OUTSIDE THE CITY, A TOWN SOME WAY up the Northern coast. A fishing village, as far as he knew. He asked some of the ould lads in the pub when he stopped in on his way to the station, and they muttered and cracked jokes about inbreeding.

The train took an hour. It was a slow but attractive passage along the coast, meandering through some of the prettiest villages North of the Liffey—villages that felt more like rural Galway than the city he had grown up in. That sense only increased as the distance between the train and Dublin widened. The towns grew less frequent and less obviously affluent. The line ran close to the sea on a few occasions, snaking along the seaboard as it did, and he watched the great heaving gray expanse of it as he thought about what he could be walking into.

He had been racking his brain all night for some inner knowledge that would explain all this, but none came—except for what McPhail had said to him, in the scrub, before the shooting had begun: "Literally asking to be robbed." What could that mean?

Conlon asked for directions at the station where seagulls dived and swung over the tiny station house, raising a racket. The house was on the main Dublin road out of town, no more than a ten-minute walk, he was told by a man waiting on a train, who identified himself as a salesman, but said he knew the village well from years selling to its population. It was a chilly afternoon, but the sun was still in the sky, and he felt the energy put some spring into his muscles. So he walked it. His leg still ached, and there were fresh bruises sparking to life in various parts of his body, but all things considered, he felt well.

As he left the town, he watched dark clouds cluster over the sea and make for land with a head-down obstinacy that almost made him laugh. Within minutes, the horizon had disappeared and the light had slid sideways from the sky. An odd dimness filled the heavens and the air was suddenly charged. That and the blackness above suggested that it would rain any moment.

Virtually running, he spied the house ahead, and entered the front yard. The gate was lying in the grass there, but aside from that it was a fine old house in a commanding position on a bend in the road, double-fronted with a pair of large, curtained bay windows. The door knocker was bronze and heavy, and he let it boom against the dark blue of the door just as the first drops of rain fell with a spatter of contact against the road and garden path. He was glad to be sheltered on the porch, as, within seconds, the air was utterly filled with rainfall.

There was no answer. He slammed the knocker once

more, and this time heard movement within. The big door swung open, leaving him face to face with BOD. The older man visibly started.

Conlon just looked at him, hiding the shock he himself was feeling.

"Thomas..." BOD stammered in a small voice. The blood had drained from his face, and Conlon was pleased to see that now, as he wrestled with his own feelings.

"BOD. I think we need to talk."

BOD faltered then. He did not know what to do, and Conlon knew with sudden certainty that there was something inside BOD did not want him to see. He stepped inside the door, brushed past the old man, and walked through the hall and into one of the reception rooms. Podge sat at a table, a bowl of stew before him. His mouth opened just a fraction at the sight of Conlon.

And now it started to stick in his mind; what McPhail had meant, why Xavier had told him, even why the fat man, Farrell, had taken over Podge's shop.

They just stared at one another for a moment, silent.

Podge spoke first. "Tommy."

"Did you kill Sean?"

BOD had edged into the room behind him now.

"No, no, of course not—no."

"Then why is he dead, Podge?"

"Things were...he wasn't—" He shook his head.

Conlon looked at BOD and put some stone in his eyes so that he knew not to try anything, although he knew that this could only go one way. They all knew it, probably. Conlon was wishing he had brought his pistol.

"Ok," he said. "Let me try this on: you needed the money?"

Podge nodded, his eyes shut. He looked ashamed now, having a conversation he had never expected to have.

"How, Podge? You had the shop, you were set up. How did that happen?"

"Gambling," he said. "That's how I met McPhail, too. I owed a lot of money, Tommy. I've owed money on and off for years. I usually get by, somehow, by the skin of me teeth."

"You never told me."

"No, I didn't. Once Orla came on the scene you had no time for me."

There was a startling bitterness in the way he said that that caught Conlon by surprise. He ignored it, and prompted: "Sean?"

"I told McPhail about the money—our money—but you were gone, and nobody knew where you had put yours. So that left Sean, and George. There was a plan. McPhail had done things like that before; he knew what he was doing.

And then...then...it just got a bit out of hand."

"A bit out of hand. Look at me."

Podge looked at him, and Conlon could see the boy he remembered from tenement steps and swimming in the canal in that face, but deep down, like a coin flashing at the bottom of a pond.

"Sean's dead, Podge. George is dead."

"I know, I know. McPhail said nobody had to die, but Sean didn't—"

"You can't make excuses for this."

"I know. I know."

"You were going to steal from them, anyway. You did steal from Sean."

Podge nodded, and then he began to weep. Conlon watched him in silence for a minute or so as he cried. He felt nothing for this man anymore except disgust and contempt.

"So what was the plan? Why are you all the way out here?"

"I gave up the shop as a way to pay a debt. I was gonna leave and then you showed up and started poking around."

"And you thought McPhail'd take care of me?"

Podge shrugged. "Eventually. Then I could go back."

"Start gambling again?"

"I had a streak of bad luck. They never last."

They were silent again. Podge would not meet his eyes. Conlon decided to give voice to a suspicion he had been nursing for a long time.

"Did you tell Xavier? About Orla? About where we were?"

Podge looked at him, silently, for a moment. Then he nodded, and closed his eyes.

Conlon could not even process this feeling. Betrayal, rage, sorrow, loss, the need for revenge, all swirling around inside him. He focused.

"Why? Why would you do that? How would that benefit you?"

Podge shrugged. "I wanted that money. I needed it. And you weren't you anymore, since you met her. I'd lost you anyway, you were going to America, what difference did it make?" He threw up his hands. "I just didn't think about it. I haven't thought about you much, these last few years, Tommy. And when I did, it was of you when we were lads. That was Tommy Conlon, my best friend."

"You were still my best friend," Conlon said.

"Yeah, but then I grew up, Tommy," Podge said with a sudden grin.

Conlon heard the click as BOD aimed a pistol at his head from behind.

Conlon laughed and saw Podge jump slightly. Podge drew a pistol himself and pointed it at him.

"Are you a gangster now, too, Podge?"

"We can't let you walk out of here, knowing all this, Tommy."

"So who's gonna kill me? You? BOD, you ever killed anyone?"

BOD's voice was steady, sure. "I have not, Thomas. But this is self-preservation."

Conlon nodded. Podge was standing now, the gun leveled at Conlon's waist.

Conlon said, "Well if I'm gonna die, I want to say a couple of things. You were still my best friend, Podge. You could've just asked for the money. I would've given it to you, If I knew you needed it. You should've asked."

Podge was expressionless.

Conlon said, "And I'm gonna give ye some advice about how to do this kind of thing. BOD, you should have just drawn that and shot me. I'm a dangerous man, and you've given me the time to figure out how I'm going to kill the both of you."

Podge tried to chuckle but it came out strangled and painful.

Conlon went on, "I came here unarmed. But in about five seconds I'm taking that gun off you, BOD, and I'm going to shoot Podge with it."

BOD said, "How're you—"

Conlon took a half-step and slammed his heel into the edge of the table. It drove into Podge's gut and he scissored onto it, then rolled off and was dragging himself to his feet as Conlon moved backwards. The bowl of stew rung like a bell on the table edge, liquid splattering the wall. Conlon was already stepping backward toward BOD, then whirling so that BOD's gun hand was behind him. Grasping BOD's wrist in his left hand, he hit him once, hard in the nose, as Podge recovered and took a shot. The bullet lodged in the wall about two feet above Conlon's head.

BOD went loose, stunned. Conlon stepped around him as Podge shot again. The bullet took BOD somewhere in the midriff. He shook and made a gurgling bark of pain, and Conlon wrested the pistol from his fingers, steadied it as BOD began to slide down him, and shot Podge twice in the chest. Podge disappeared behind the table as BOD fell into a rug of limbs and blood. Conlon shot him once in the head, then stepped around the body and around the table.

Podge was still alive, on his back, arm twisted beneath him, the gun a few feet away on the floor. His eyes found Conlon's; desperate, frightened. Don't kill me, they said.

"Sean and George are dead, Podge. Orla's dead. That's all because of you." He trained the pistol on Podge's temple. He pulled the trigger, then watched in silence for a moment.

He walked back through the house. The rain was stopping as he opened the front door. He walked back to the train station as the light dimmed in the sky. Along the way, he tossed the pistol into the sea. He looked up at the sky as he walked. He felt tired but also better in a way he had not expected. Lighter, easier. On the train back to Dublin, he fell asleep and dreamt of Orla.

———

THREE WEEKS LATER, Conlon organized a party for his mother's birthday. He made sure all of her friends were there, and he invited Theresa and Sean's mother. They ate cake and drank sherry and brandy and ended up playing charades, hooting loudly and shouting guesses at the performer on each occasion. Theresa and he shared numerous quiet glances as they ferried food and drink on plates and saucers around the room, and once, when they passed in the kitchen, she said, "This'll be the last time you get a load of oul' ones drunk then, I think?"

He laughed. She was wearing what looked like a new dress, and she had had her hair done, and he had to fight the need to just stare at her whenever she was in the room. And yet he felt like it might be too early—for him, for her—and so he would do nothing but smile and make her laugh when he could. And wait, wait for the day when it felt like the right day.

He watched his mother. She was happy, a loud and sparky presence at the center of the noise and giggling, a glass of sherry in her hand as she roared laughter at a friend of hers, pantomiming an animal for them from the space in front of the stairs. He knew he would have to find his own place soon, but for now it was nice to be here with her, and he liked how it made her happy to have him back.

There was a knock on the door, and he answered it with mild relief to escape the rising hysteria.

Detective Barry was waiting, his eyebrow already cocked. "What in the name of God is going on in there?"

"Birthday party for my ma."

"Ah. Is there cake?"

Conlon chuckled at that. "There is. You can have some if I don't hate this conversation too much."

Barry nodded. "Well hello to you, too, Tommy."

"Hello. How can I help you?"

"I came to help you, in point of fact. Or to give you some news."

"Go on."

"There were quite a few bodies discovered in Glasnevin a few weeks back. Sure you might have seen it in the papers?"

"I did. Fenians, or something."

Barry smiled at that, telling Conlon that he was in on this act. "Well, one of those killed was your old friend McPhail."

"It was?"

"It was. Somebody had beaten him a bit, too. Stabbed him in the chest. A few of his men dead with him. The whole thing looked almost like a military attack. Soldiers or people with combat experience. The coroner reckoned some of them were killed with a rifle, from distance, imagine. All that after another massive gun battle in a warehouse near the docks a few days earlier. We only found out about that because the whole place burned down and the Fire Brigade found a loud of bodies in the ashes."

"That Fenians, too?"

Barry couldn't hold back the laugh at that. "That's

the official line. Some big turf war between factions or something. What do you think?"

"Sounds good to me."

Barry nodded slowly, studying him. "Now, your name has been mentioned around the station. Some of the lads know enough people that it got back to them that you and McPhail were circling each other, but no more than that, really."

Conlon said, "What are you saying to me?"

"Because I know you, I put in a word—nothing to do with you, and all that—so you won't be picked up, or questioned. This should just pass by you."

"I appreciate that."

"And well you should." He leaned in. "The next time you want to start a war on the streets, Tommy, you need to let me know about it first."

"I kind of did."

"You did, my bollocks! I thought you might have a fist fight or two, not blow up a fuckin' warehouse and stage a battle in Glasnevin."

Conlon nodded.

Barry said, "Are you done, then? Is it done?"

"Yeah. It's done."

Barry nodded. "Get me some of that feckin cake then, ya bowsie."

When Conlon returned, Barry ate it there in the doorway, Conlon grinning at his enthusiasm.

"That was lovely, that," he said, wiping at his lips with a napkin. He sized up Conlon. "So what now. What will you do now?"

"I haven't a clue. I'll see what shows up, I suppose."

"A man needs a purpose, Tommy. You need to find one."

"We'll see."

"Alright. Be good now. I'll see ye."

"Bye, Barry."

"Tommy."

Conlon watched the policeman walk away.

AFTER THE PARTY, Theresa and George's mother remained behind to help clean up. The house was quiet except for the splash of water on crockery from the kitchen, quiet voices. In the living room, they were all working together in companionable silence when there came a knock on the door. Theresa was nearest and she volunteered to answer it.

A few moments later, she was back. "It's for you, Tommy."

"Who is it?"

An odd, preoccupied expression came over her face, and she retreated into the hall. Confused, he stepped in beside her.

"What is it?"

"I told her to come. Her name is Mary Delaney. I used to work with her."

"Alright. What is she doing here?"

"She needs help."

"What kind of help?"

"Her daughter's after going missing."

And at that, he felt it: the hum in his ears as it started up, a buzz of excitement.

"Will you help her?" Theresa said.

He smiled at her. "I'll go and have a chat with her."

They were standing very close together and her face

was looking up at him and in that instant, he was desperate to kiss her. Instead, he made a safe, non-threatening face and made to step around her. She squeezed his hand, retreated back into the dining room, and he moved toward the front door.

When he got there, a woman was standing on the pavement—middle-aged, her eyes wet, pale face long with grief. Well-groomed in a smart dress and hat, wearing incredible shoes that shone like glass, she looked like she could barely stay upright, like loss had pulled the flesh from her bones.

"Thomas Conlon?" she asked before he was even fully at the door.

He nodded. "Yes. How can I help you?"

"I hear you find people."

16

He had awoken in a tiny bedroom, barely able to breathe for the pain in his chest and stomach, bandages tight on him, and croaked her name into the darkness. A woman had come then, drawn by the sound of his suffering. She was middle-aged, her face lined by pain and nature. She shushed him and gave him water, and he slept again.

She was there over the next four or five days each time he woke. Sometimes she was joined by a man—a big man with a kind face and rough hands, who murmured to her quietly by the door.

She fed him soup when she believed he was ready. She showed him the bullets they had cut from his flesh, explained the poultices she had used. Her husband had found him clinging to rocks on the shore, half-dead. They were miles up the coast from the town of Burtonport, he was told. How he had survived was a miracle.

His strength returned quickly after that. But he stayed in bed a few days longer than he needed to. Because re-entering the world meant acknowledging what had happened. Orla was dead. And trying to decide on a future. What to do. Where to go. How to live, without her.

———

HIS LAST MORNING THERE, he lay in bed, and remembered their last peaceful moments together, before the guns and the blood and screaming. They had held hands, sitting there on that high ledge. The blue sky was held at a distance by the trees, but a patch of sunlight warmed them, and even the gray of the rocks held its heat, pleasant and live beneath his hand.

She swung her legs slowly, and hummed an air. They kissed every few minutes, something they seemed unable to go any length of time without doing, and she smiled, and they talked of where they might live, and how they would spend their days and their nights.

And she had said, "Do you know what I often think of? I can't help it, and I know it's silly. What if I hadn't met you? What if you'd come into McClean's a minute later, or I'd been working in the back that day? Or one of us had been sick. Imagine that."

"We would've met anyway. It was meant to be."

"I think so, too. But you never know, do you? Just imagine. What would you be doing now?"

"I'd be miserable. Training, probl'y."

"I'd be dreaming of you. I dreamt of you for years, before I saw your face. I knew you were out there, waiting for me. I could feel it."

He stared at her, lost for words. He shook his head faintly.

"What...?" she said, laughing.

"Nothing. You—you're lovely."

She laughed. "I am."

"I love you."

"I love you."

And he had kissed her. For the last time.

A LOOK AT BOOK TWO:
FIGHTING STOCK

Dublin, Ireland 1918

In the years between the bloody 1916 Rising and the start of the War of Independence against the occupying British forces, WWI veteran Tommy Conlon is making a living tracking down missing children and trying to avoid trouble.

But when he accepts a case from two nuns who believe somebody is abducting street kids from the inner city, he finds himself digging into the darkness of the second city of the British Empire—its poverty, the corruption of the Church and the warring gangs who control its vice.

Eventually, Conlon's investigation uncovers an organization seemingly intent on dominating the criminal landscape of the entire country—an organization manned by American veterans who ship young girls across the Atlantic Ocean like cattle—and he reacts the only way he knows how. He goes to war.

Suddenly, Conlon's life and the lives of everyone he loves are in danger as he finds himself in the crosshairs of an opponent more dangerous than any he has ever faced. And even with formidable training and the help of his friends, Conlon seems to be outnumbered and outgunned by a ruthless and supremely organized foe.

Set against the backdrop of a Dublin ravaged by the Spanish flu and simmering with the tension of the brewing War of Independence, Fighting Stock is a crime thriller filled with action, intrigue and atmosphere.

AVAILABLE APRIL 2023

ABOUT THE AUTHOR

David Michael Nolan was born and brought up in Dublin, Ireland.

He studied English Literature and Film Studies at University College Dublin and is obsessed with movies, comics, books, rock music, soccer and boxing—many of which find their way into his writing.

Currently, he lives in Manchester with his family.

www.ingramcontent.com/pod-product-compliance
Lightning Source LLC
Chambersburg PA
CBHW010801250626
47155CB00016B/3600